Chapter One

In the bunkhouse that morning the gray eyes of Kelly Boyle, great shaper of Texas dreams, seemed washed of color as he contemplated the turn his luck had suddenly taken. Just yesterday he'd argued again with Luanne about the pact he had with Carl Tripp. Just one more year till they got Diamond Deuce on solid footing. 'Carl won't take a wife and neither will I till we get two decent houses built at the ranch,' he had reminded.

Luanne had studied him while taking exciting nibbles at her lower lip. 'I don't want to wait,' she had said. 'But I guess I can stand it. After all, we do have my fur coat.'

It was a private joke. They both had laughed. But that was yesterday, and the dream was solid. When thinking of Luanne's reaction to the new situation, the cheek muscles of his long, brown face drew his mouth into a sour smile.

Boyle rolled out of his bunk and hastily dressed, avoiding his three ranch hands who had the good sense not to ask questions about the business of Carl Tripp last midnight. Wearing his old sheepskin coat against the bite of lingering winter, he stepped to the yard and stomped up a path on long legs. A breeze carried the odor of ripe droppings from the corral, the chatter of birds in cottonwoods. Everything he could see or touch or smell here was a piece of his dream. A persistent dream, as much a part of him as breath in the lungs, first taking root when escaping tragedy in Mexico some years before, a dream that had not diminished through many cattle drives to Kansas and beyond, the last five made as trail boss. And now just past his twenty-fourth birthday, the fulfillment of that dream of being his own man, of making something for Carl and himself out of the memories of blood and terror.

From a rise of ground he looked back down the slant at bunkhouse and barn and near it the adobe house, little more than a shack. Kelly Boyle found his thoughts drawn to possibilities of what might be transpiring behind flour-sack window curtains on this chilly dawn. Conjecture that caused a warm pull at his groin.

Damn Carl!

Boyle had halted beside the rusted windmill, its blades locked in place. For pure cussedness he threw a lever. A damp breeze off the river caught the blades. Gears that somebody had neglected to grease began to screech at the morning. Boyle was not surprised when the house door was flung open. A rumpled Carl Tripp, wearing only faded red long johns, filled the doorway.

'Who the hell...?' Then he saw Boyle stepping down the path from the windmill. 'I was tryin' to sleep,' Tripp complained, still fire-eyed from last night. 'Flo said the noise is givin' her a headache...'

'It's past sunup,' Boyle interrupted, 'and we've got cattle to move. We're two days late as it is.' He didn't mention that it was the length of time Carl Tripp had been away. Tripp had gone to Bluewater for supplies and a couple of drinks. Then maybe up to Lucero for a little fun, he had said with a broad wink.

One of these days, Boyle had cautioned his partner as before, *you'll bring home more than dust on your boot heels ... and be yelling at Doc Starrett for the cure.* Good-natured joshing on the surface, but Boyle had meant it. Carl had the selectivity of a tomcat. And now Carl Tripp had brought home more than the possibility of dust on his boot heels. He had brought home the whole package.

Few men had ever seen Kelly Boyle really angry. He would usually shrug off trouble or meet it with a hard smile. He was a hair under six feet tall, narrow-waisted so that breadth of shoulders was accentuated, an impression of latent power that reached women deeply and gave notice to men that he was ready to be friend or otherwise. It was up to them. About the only way a man could tell if Boyle was stirred up were his eyes, normally

9

a soft gray but under certain conditions the color seemed to wash out. A signal for a man to back off if he didn't want real trouble was the word passed on cattle drives and at cow camps.

Boyle had started in the cattle business after their escape from Mexico, and at fourteen, big for his age, he was already with a herd going north. In those early years he accepted hoorawing to a point because of his inexperience. He spoke Spanish like a native and wherever possible seemed to enjoy the company of *vaqueros*, which upset some people. Boyle was a quick learner and made few mistakes at roundup or on drives. There had been added pressure because of Carl Tripp, taller than Boyle, three years older, and cursed with oversize ears and protruding front teeth that invited jibes and trouble. By the time Boyle was seventeen he had stopped most of it.

Carl Tripp's homely face became a subject to ease tensions. One of the earlier examples: 'Hey, Carl, tell us about that purty whore in Abilene who fell in love with you. Too bad the poor gal was blind.' Then, just as Tripp started to steam at howls of laughter, Kelly Boyle stepped in, saying: 'Carl's my partner. The same as my brother.' Spoken softly and those washed-out gray eyes freezing a man's backbone were usually enough. Most men soon learned when to leave him alone. They were the smart ones. The few who pressed too hard never saw Kansas again or the home place back in Texas.

'Why'd you go an' turn loose the windmill!' Carl Tripp shouted from the house.

'Why'd you go and bring the woman home with you?' Boyle mimicked his partner's deep-well voice.

'Done told you last night.'

'When you were too drunk to spit straight, let alone talk. Maybe I didn't hear you right.'

'I married Flo ... up at Empire.'

Boyle remembered, all right. 'Seems you forgot our agreement, Carl. No wives till we got this damn' place on its feet. *Remember?*'

Beyond Tripp's heavy shoulder was a pale and frightened-looking female face. Kelly Boyle had been walking down toward the house, close enough so that Tripp could see the change in his eyes. Tripp muttered – 'Jeezus.' – and hastily closed the door.

Windmill gears still screeched. Boyle walked back up the path and locked the blades. Waking Carl up that way had been childish, he supposed. In the abrupt silence, blackbirds fluttering about the trunk of a fallen cottonwood, set up a minor racket of their own. Boyle returned to the bunkhouse where he had spent the night because of Carl Tripp and female companion.

Pete Lambourne, frying up breakfast in a pair of cast-iron skillets, took some of the sputtering grease on his gray whiskers. 'Was lookin' through the window an' seen the filly out back that Carl brung home last night,' Lambourne said with a chuckle. 'A fancy bundle of pale hair an' lots of soft flesh. Wonder what cat house she's from?'

Boyle threw a long leg over the bench and sat down at the table. 'Carl claims he married her.'

'Son-of-a-bitch!' Lambourne exclaimed. 'Reckon I shouldn't've said nothin' about a cat house. Don't let on to Carl, huh?'

Don't put cat house clear out of your mind, Pete, Boyle almost said, then was ashamed for even thinking it. He knew nothing about the woman, had only seen her in the dark when Carl came bumping along the rutted road at midnight, wagon team at a fast trot. 'This here's Flo...,' Carl had announced when Boyle came out of the house with a rifle.

'Florence, please,' she had corrected, huddled in the wagon, hair loose, eyes large and searching in the moonlight.

Tripp had held her left hand high so that Boyle could make out some kind of a ring on the second finger. 'Preacher up at Empire done tied us up,' was about all Tripp could get out. So stupefied he could hardly talk, and, with the woman trying to hold him up, they lurched off to the house. A faint scent of expensive perfume lingered on the night air, the kind that built erotic dreams, a jolting reminder of Luanne.

Boyle had gotten his blankets, put up the team. By then the lamp was out in the house, the curtains drawn. *Honeymoon!*

Now in the dim morning Boyle poured molasses over corn cakes and bacon. 'I feel like kicking Carl's ass,' he remarked. With roundup looming and Carl saddled with a bride.

As he ate, he began to wonder if Carl Tripp had had time enough to drive the big wagon all the way up to Empire and back. Sure he had, Boyle answered himself. Two men whose partnership had been spawned in blood when both were boys wouldn't lie to each other. Not about something so important.

For the seven months they'd owned Diamond Deuce; everything had been going so well. Carl Tripp seemed reasonably content to settle down on a ranch, and Kelly Boyle had found a good slice of his dream in Luanne. Without a woman, a dream was cold ashes. Just thinking again of Luanne's remark yesterday about her fur coat and them laughing now so excited him that he was embarrassed to get up from the table and get the coffee pot. He passed his cup to Pete Lambourne who sat near the stove. Lambourne had been up the trail each time Boyle bossed a drive. He was known as one of the best branders in the business, despite his age. The

13

other two Diamond Deuce hands were lean, wind-burned men. They might be new-comers but knew when to keep silent.

Boyle drank his coffee, thinking of their return to Texas last year, of taking his fee as trail boss partly in cattle, which he did at times. By then he and Tripp had over a thousand head on leased grass up north. Their good luck was still holding because a letter from a Tom Stubblefield was waiting. Stubblefield, an old man, had heard that Kelly Boyle was looking for a good ranch cheap. Stubblefield had four hundred head of beef that he hadn't sold off and some Texas acres. He wanted to live out his days with an old maid sister in Joplin, and this was his excuse for a quick sale. After checking boundaries with Stubblefield and a rough tally on the cattle, an agreement was reached. At Empire, the county seat, Boyle had paid off the old man out of gold from the money sack, his and Tripp's. They signed papers and filed the deed. Then, after a hasty handshake, Stubblefield had hopped aboard a stagecoach that would take him to the railhead, miles north, as if anxious to get a train and clear out of Texas.

The county clerk, a thin-faced man with a wise smile, had said: 'Major Ransom's big ranch borders what you fellas just bought. He won't take kindly to old man Stubble-field sellin' out. He always had an eye on the place for himself.'

'Reckon that's why the ol' bastard lit out so fast,' Carl Tripp had ventured.

But Kelly Boyle had only smiled. In his short but turbulent lifetime he'd faced worse threats than Major Terrence Ransom's vast holdings.

Pete Lambourne slid another cup of coffee along the bunkhouse table to Boyle, saying: 'Sure looks like Carl beat you gettin' married.'

Boyle gave a short laugh. 'Now that Carl has broken the ice, it's no problem for me to marry. Carl and his bride can have the one-bedroom house, so I'll buy a tent for you boys and move you into the cottonwoods, and I'll have the bunkhouse.'

'You joshin', Kelly?'

'Luanne Ransom won't mind that the bunkhouse roof leaks in a few places. And when the wind blows just right through cracks in the walls, you can smell the hotel privy all the way from Bluewater.' Boyle made a face. 'I could double kick Carl's ass.'

After breakfast, Carl Tripp, looking fairly presentable, came to the yard with his bride. He had combed his thick, light-brown hair and shaved. 'This here's Flo, the missus,' he said, pointing at the slender young woman in pale blue. Pure silk, from the looks of it, and expensive. And the wedding band on her finger wasn't brass, for sure.

15

'I'd rather be called Florence.' Lips that were ripe and red curved in a tentative smile.

'Yeah, I kinda forgot,' Tripp apologized awkwardly.

Boyle nodded to her and said – 'Ma'am.' – when he was introduced, as did Lambourne and the other two men, Tinkey and Smoot. She had done up her yellow hair. Ringlets hugged her high forehead.

'I'm very pleased to meet you gentlemen,' she said softly.

Probably in her early twenties, younger than her new husband by a few years, Boyle reflected. Seeing her there with wind rustling her silken hair, obviously cold because she wore no coat, Boyle was reminded of the *ricas* in their fine gowns that he used to see at some of the grand hotels of Mexico when he was a boy. It was the cultured voice, the way she held her head.

Her dark blue eyes looked directly at Boyle. 'I'll try not to be a bother here.' Then she excused herself and walked to the house, her back straight, a faint movement of hips. Lambourne and the two cowhands followed her with their speculative eyes – how could a homely cuss like Carl Tripp end up with a fine-looking blonde lady for a wife? There was a shaking of heads as they went to get their horses.

Tripp nudged his partner. 'Kelly, you still mad?'

16

'No.' There were cows that had strayed down to the river and must be moved. 'I suppose Missus Tripp realizes she'll be alone a lot?' he ventured.

'I done told her. I'll leave her that pea-shooter pistol I got off that gal up to Ellsworth that time.'

'Having a gun and knowing how to use one isn't the same thing,' Boyle pointed out. 'You better make sure. With all the trouble across the river ... oh, hell, you stay home this time, Carl. We'll manage. Get acquainted with your ... wife.'

'Naw, she'll be all right.'

'Looks like a solid gold wedding ring. You must've dug deep in your money sack, Carl.'

Tripp scratched himself, looking down. 'Yeah, reckon.'

When Tripp went to get his horse, Boyle rode up to the house where the woman was in the doorway, a raggedy-assed broom in her slender hands. 'We're pretty isolated here, Missus Tripp...'

'It's what I love about the place ... the isolation.'

This caused Boyle to look at her closely. 'Have you ever fired a gun?'

'Yes,' she said after a moment, and went back into the house.

Boyle rode away, puzzled over her strange reaction to mention of firearms. She had looked startled, then saddened. Some deeper emotion produced a sag in her fine shoulders. Kelly Boyle wondered about it.

The five-man Diamond Deuce crew rode toward the river to start their work.

Chapter Two

It took them the better part of four days to locate the scattered bunches of cattle and drive them back from the river. Boyle wanted no Diamond Deuce beef to be a temptation to *insurrectos*. With the river low as it was this time of year, rustlers would only have to drive cattle to Mexico instead of swimming them.

Two nights they were close enough for Tripp to ride home. He'd catch up to them, usually by mid-morning. He seemed content and that counted for something. At first, when Boyle had been enthusiastic over acquiring Diamond Deuce, Tripp had grumbled about settling down and the fun he'd miss in hell holes along cattle trails where he found pleasure and often trouble.

When the job was finished, they were running low on supplies. Supplies had been what Tripp was supposed to pick up during his absence from Diamond Deuce. Instead, he had brought home a bride.

Kelly Boyle put on a pair of pants, the pockets stiff with newness, a fairly new shirt, and his sheeplined coat. He managed to sneak some blankets into the wagon and cover them with a tarp. Then, with heartbeat quickening even before catching sight of Luanne's lively eyes, her scent in his nostrils, he started off.

After an hour he came in sight of the two-story Box R headquarters. Chinaberries and leafless cottonwoods contrasted to the startling white of the mansion with its Grecian columns and leaded glass windows. Major Ransom had tried to duplicate an *ante-bellum* home on the frontier for his late wife, so the story went, to remind her of a girlhood in Virginia.

Boyle tied his team to the iron boy, then climbed to the wide verandah. His knuckles rapped on a varnished door. He knocked a second time. Sarah, the lean-faced cook, finally looked out and, before Boyle could open his mouth, ducked from sight behind white lace curtains. She didn't open the door.

Damned strange. He knocked again. He was starting to get mad when Jack Quester came from the ranch office built under the verandah on the north side of the house.

'Hi, Kelly,' he called, recognizing Boyle by the front door. Quester and his brother, Al, owned a small spread north of Diamond Deuce. Jack earned extra money as the major's bookkeeper. A slender, affable man of thirty, Jack Quester came up the verandah steps to shake hands with Boyle. 'Afraid there's nobody home here but me,' he said, not meeting Boyle's eyes, 'and a couple of servants.'

'Where's Luanne?'

'Well ... she's not home.' Quester rubbed at a smudge of ink on his white shirt.

'How about Missus Blankenship?' She was the housekeeper. 'Could I have a word with her?'

Jack Quester shook his head. He was small-boned, a contrast to his rough-house younger brother, Al. 'I don't think she's here.'

Boyle tried not to show his exasperation. 'Where'd Luanne and Missus Blankenship go?'

'Kelly, I put columns of figures in ledgers for the major. Nothing else.'

'Hey, Jack, this is Kelly Boyle, not some stranger.'

A pained expression spread across Quester's face. 'I'm sorry, but I work for the major. And that's the way it is.' Which meant that the major's hand was mixed into whatever was going on.

Boyle decided to fish. 'You hear about my partner getting married?'

'There's about ten column of figures to add up before noon. Sorry, but I've got to get back to my desk. I'll be going home to work roundup with Al. See you then, Kelly, in two weeks.'

Jack Quester was gone.

For some reason today Boyle had worn his

gun but had had the good sense to remove it before seeing Luanne. Usually he just brought a rifle. Maybe with talk of trouble on the other side of the river he had, without thinking, decided to strap on a gun. Or was it just plain hunch? Early in their delightful association, Luanne had let him know of her dislike of firearms, especially a holstered weapon, considering it to be an invitation to disaster. When out of sight of the house, he buckled on the gun, looked back at the mound of blankets under the tarp in the wagon, and sighed deeply. At least, Carl and his bride had a bedroom. Not a wagon and Luanne's fur coat.

On the outskirts of Bluewater he passed the remains of a mill that had been hit by mis-directed cannon fire a decade before when there had been another batch of trouble across the river. It had never been rebuilt. Then he came to Doc Starrett's adobe office where an adjoining pen held a sick-looking goat and a mule. The talents of the doctor were not always exclusively for the human animal. There were a few blocks of modest homes, the usual shacks, and several com-mercial buildings that paralleled the river.

Boyle had a crazy hope that he might find Luanne in the Miller Store but found only Miller himself, chewing a licorice that stained his meager mouth. Boyle left an order to be filled and loaded into the wagon, then crossed to the Great River Saloon.

Only two men were at the bar in the large, high-ceilinged place. A deal table at the far end was occupied by four men. Boyle recognized Major Ransom, back turned, military bearing evident even when seated and studying his cards. To Ransom's right was Rex Uland, Box R foreman, who would make two of his employer. No one at the table looked up as usually happened when someone entered a saloon on a quiet afternoon. The other two men in the card game Boyle didn't recognize. They were probably Box R riders. There were so many of them a timekeeper would have trouble keeping track.

Boyle got a bottle and glass from Pinky, the balding barkeep, thought of going over and speaking to the major, but their last meeting, two weeks ago, had been unpleasant. From the first, the major had tried to show his power, appearing one day when Boyle had first taken over at Diamond Deuce. With him was Uland and a dozen men.

'So you're my new neighbor,' the major had said gruffly to Boyle, not bothering to offer his hand or step down. 'Know anything about cattle?'

'I know which end of the cow not to kiss,' had been Boyle's reply, deciding to accept the insult and turn it back.

The Box R riders had stiffened, the major's lips under a trimmed cavalry mustache pinched at the corners. Uland's shaggy reddish brows lifted as he had awaited orders from his employer. But then they all had noticed Carl Tripp in the doorway of the house with a rifle and Smoot and Tinkey similarly armed in front of the barn. And Pete Lambourne by the corral. He was maybe gray-whiskered, but in the capable hands of the old brander was a double-barreled shotgun, sawed off.

Major Ransom's laughter had eased the tension. He had dismounted, removed a gauntlet, and introduced himself. He and Boyle had shaken hands. The major's hazel eyes had been slightly mocking but at the same time evaluating the neighbor. 'I thought I had an agreement with Tom Stubblefield to sell to me whenever he felt like quitting,' the major had begun. 'Oh, well ... just happened by today, Boyle, but maybe next time we can talk about Mexico. I understand you're an expert.'

'I spent some years there, but am hardly an expert. Those days I don't even want to think about.'

'We'll see.'

Another time in town the major had braced Boyle on the subject of Mexico, hinting at some grand plans. Again Boyle had explained his views. This time the major had been angered.

When Luanne had shown a surprising interest in the young rancher, Ransom was openly displeased at first, later, saying to Boyle, that it was something he hadn't counted on, but a situation he seemed to accept.

Two weeks ago Boyle was invited for Sunday dinner – not the first time. After cigars and brandy, the major had taken him to the smaller of three barns, set by itself in a screen of cottonwoods. A storage barn. Under a mound of loose hay was a locked trap door, beneath it a natural rock-lined depression in the earth. In it were crated rifles, ten thousand of them, and ammunition, rifles originally intended to blunt the driving ambition of the Indian, Benito Juárez, some years before. 'Some of us felt that Mexico would be better off with an emperor,' the major had said that day. 'Great riches almost within our grasp. But, alas, Maximilian was doomed before we could rally sufficient support.' He had gripped Boyle's arm. 'But this time, Kelly, I won't be denied. I need a man who knows the Mexicans, who speaks their language, who knows how they think. You are that man.'

'It means dead *peones*, and I've already seen enough of that. No thank you. Major.'

Major Ransom had argued, threatened, but finally accepted the inevitable, or appeared to.

And Luanne that day, her violet eyes

25

wicked under jet black brows, had tried to pry from Boyle the reason for the quarrel. Her father had returned to the house, white-faced, and gone upstairs due to a sudden attack of gout.

'You thwarted my father in some way. It showed. I know him so well. How did you do it, my love?'

Major Ransom had asked him to give his word not to mention the rifles, which Boyle had done. He told Luanne it was just something that her father had wanted him to do, and he had refused.

'I love you for defying him,' she had whispered, hugging him fiercely. Then, raising her voice in case her father might be listening from upstairs, she had said: 'A chilly day, but no rain. I'd like a Sunday drive to town. Wait, and I'll get my fur coat.'

At mention of the coat, they had almost broken into hysterical laughter. *Paradise!*

In the Great River Saloon, Pinky came strolling down the bar with glass and bottle, his barkeep's smile in place. The sparsely manicured lawn of his hair was parted precisely across the top of a rosy skull. He nodded toward the major far across the room, rigid in his chair. 'Hear his daughter's gone to Saint Louis to visit friends,' Pinky confided.

Boyle nearly choked on his whiskey. 'Who told you that?'

'The major did hisself.'

'How long's she going to be gone?'

'Might be a year. Hear you're sweet on her.'

'A year...?' St. Louis! That he had never expected. Kelly Boyle felt his stomach drop coldly. Suddenly he didn't want to be under the same roof with the major. Spinning a coin across the bar top, he walked out without finishing his whiskey.

Wind off the river had stiffened and now cut through his sheepskin coat. He started down a path to the river, wanting to walk, to think. Luanne. A whole year?

In the saloon, Uland said under his breath: 'Boyle's gone, Major. Walkin' along the river.'

'Those two men we talked about,' Major Ransom said quietly. 'They dependable?'

'When I hire 'em, they're dependable.'

'Good with their fists?'

'Saxton was a bare knuckle champ up at Denver.'

A spare smile quirked a corner of the major's mouth under the mustache. 'A little raw meat this day for Doc Starrett to patch up. I rather think we'll find that Mister Kelly Boyle is human after all, not a Greek god, as some people seem to think' – he meant Luanne – 'but who can bleed just like the rest of us.'

'Saxton and Chollmar are waitin' at the

27

livery barn,' Uland said, getting up, raw power evident in the man. He straightened his hat on thick, rust-colored hair.

The other two men in the poker game, wearing work clothes, studied their cards as if unaware of the exchange between employer and foreman, not wanting to know. Some things a Box R man soon learned were best not overheard or seen. Uland had ordered them to town as escort for the major. These days the major did not ride alone near the river, due to the trouble on the other side.

'Let one of them say that Boyle insulted his sister,' the major said to Uland. 'That'll do for openers.'

Hank Wendover, the ferryman, with thinning gray hair and liver spots on the backs of his hands, that day had at long last decided to grease the winch and check his cables, because before a man could even start thinking about roundup on the ranches strung along the border, spring would arrive and with it the high water. One day there would be a railroad trestle and a bridge for wagons, according to talk, which would send the ferry into oblivion along with the musket and percussion pistol. Wendover happened to look up and see Kelly Boyle walking from the direction of the Great River Saloon. It was a day when the sun barely penetrated a deepening cloud cover. Up the river the rock dam spilled a little water into the *acequia madre* that was used to irrigate fields adjacent to town.

Boyle kicked at damp sand until reaching the beached ferry. There he stood looking at the river, hands thrust into his pockets. Under the heavy coat was his .44 with polished cedar grips. Absently he watched blackbirds skimming the cattails and reeds, looking for prey in the stinking ooze of river mud. Dogs barked in Los Maligros, the village on the Mexican side that had recently been hit by raiders. Many residents had fled after *Federales* had brought up cannon, driven out the invaders, then departed for another trouble spot far to the south. Today Luanne crowded his mind more than ever, missing her already a terminal ache. Remembering their last meeting and her saying mischievously: 'Damn if I'll wear a corset next time. For one thing they're a nuisance, and you're absolutely no good stringing me up in one afterward.' The ache in him was deepening along with the clouds.

At this time of year the river was little more than a sluggish brown stream. Hank Wendover was grumbling about rust on his cables. It was the first time Boyle knew that anyone was near.

'Work on this scow's never finished,' Wendover complained. 'Hear your partner got hisself married.'

Boyle looked at the sinewy old ferryman in surprise. 'How'd you know?'

'Was over eatin' my supper when he come rollin' into town. He went to the store, purty drunk. But his wife ... a real fine-lookin' woman, what I could see.' Boyle waited for the usual caustic reference to Carl Tripp's homeliness. But Wendover only said: 'Yep, a real nice-lookin' lady.'

Boyle had to agree. Carl Tripp had won his prize. Kelly Boyle's had turned to vapor. All the years he and Carl had put saddle shine on their pants from first light to last, the many deals with ranch owners to trail herds to market and lately to new range beyond Kansas, taking some of their pay in cattle, selling for a profit when the market was on the rise, banking their money toward a day when they could have their own place, sometimes drawing less pay than the hired hands. And now Luanne had to go and spoil it. No, he corrected, it was Carl's fault, sure as hell.

'Company comin', looks like,' Wendover said from where he was crouched at the winch with a grease swab.

Boyle looked around at two men strolling toward him, hands in pockets. The tall wide-shouldered one kicked a stone that went plunking into the river. Boyle dismissed them as strangers who were likely discussing nothing more serious than women or last night's poker game. He put his gaze on the far side of the river, his thoughts drifting to the days at the great *rancho* that his father had owned with Luis Leonardo Montez, now in other hands. His father and Montez had grown careless and lost their dream and their lives. Boyle had no intention of losing his in the tangle of Mexican politics. Hell no, never! Not for Major Ransom, for sure. His personal dream was Diamond Deuce, and no one was going to uproot him.

A gust of cold wind caught the back of his neck. He was just about to button his coat when he realized the two men had halted a few feet away and were staring. They didn't seem to notice Wendover on the ferry with his grease can. In those few seconds, Boyle endured the rake of eyes. On this of all days, he was in no mood for trouble, if that's what they wanted. And they did, the tall one saying: 'You insulted my friend's sister.'

'Just where did I insult her?'

'Tucson.'

Color seemed to wash out of Kelly Boyle's gray eyes. 'Last time I was in Tucson, I was six years old. What'd I do ... steal her licorice?'

The two men exchanged glances as if waiting for the other to give a cue for the next move. Shoulder width of the tall one made him appear top-heavy in contrast to long shanks. 'I'm Billy Saxton' he said gruffly with the look of someone who expects the name to impress. 'This here's Benny Chollmar. Says he thinks it was Mexico he remembers you from.'

The features of both men were windburned. Their clothing of wool and canvas showing wear, recently laundered. Chollmar's gun was black-butted, carried on the right side. Billy Saxton's ivory-handled weapon was in a cross-draw holster. But it was something in their eyes, not the guns, that rolled tension coldly down Boyle's spine, the smell of trouble more pronounced than stink from the river. Chollmar's heft had gone into width instead of height. A scar over the left eye gave him a squint.

'I was only a kid when I lived in Mexico' Boyle said, after looking Chollmar over.

Saxton said: 'Chollmar claims you did insult his sister. An' guess it was Mexico instead of Tucson'

'Let him tell me that,' Boyle snapped.

'I am tellin' you,' Chollmar cut in. 'You put your hands on her one day. She was a purty little thing.'

'You've got me mixed up with somebody else,' Boyle said, giving them a chance to call it off if they wanted.

'He's the one, all right, Billy,' Chollmar said to Saxton with theatrical toughness.

'You apologize to my friend for what you done to his sister,' Saxton ordered coldly.

'This is a tired game, *amigos,* and you're

32

not very good at it,'

Boyle said.

'Tough son-of-a-bitch, ain't you?' Saxton sneered.

'Call me that again and your teeth'll be in the river.'

Chollmar gave a nod of his head, as if in a signal, and came in swinging a pair of heavy fists, moving swiftly for one so chunky but solidly built. The blow, had it landed, would have knocked Boyle into the cattails. But he sidestepped, hit Chollmar just below the scarred eye, splitting the skin. Chollmar staggered back, his face bleeding.

It was Saxton's turn, and he aimed a round house. But the swinging arm fell like a shot bird when Boyle's powerful jab just above the belt buckle drained his face and doubled him up.

'All right, tough son-of-a-bitch!' Chollmar yelled through a film of blood.

He and Saxton drew at nearly the same split second, but not before Kelly Boyle's gun smashed sound along the riverbank, sending birds into panicky flight. Saxton uttered a strangled cry and did a ballet step before falling against the scow. Chollmar fired wildly, missed, his bullet ripping through the cattails. Before he could snap off a second shot, his right shoulder was suddenly jolted. Mouth hanging open, he collapsed.

Boyle stared, automatically reloading.

There was shouting now from the street. The only movement from either man was one of Saxton's booted toes that gracefully tapped the ground, as if he was trying to catch the beat from some unseen fiddler, on the verge of leaping up to fling himself into a wild polka. Always an aftermath to such an explosive moment was a weakness at the knees. Boyle saw the blood on the men, on the dark river sand, the sudden, punishing silence as echoes of the gunshots rattled away. He thought of Luanne Ransom and her fear – hatred almost – of firearms, Luanne at this minute taking her dimpled self to far-off, civilized St. Louis.

Reeling to the far side of the beached ferry, Boyle vomited into some reeds. He was just wiping his mouth on a bandanna when excited men began streaming down from the business block. In the lead was Rex Uland, thick legs braced as he came sliding down a sand bank to the river's edge, big hat far back on bushy hair, held in place by a strap under the heavy chin. His pale eyes swept the scene, settled on Boyle.

'Looks to me like it was plain murder.'

Behind him were other men, red-faced from the run, panting, with them the major, pushing his way through the ring to stare at the crumpled casualties on the damp sand. Uland repeated his charge of murder, waiting for Major Ransom's confirmation. But the major seemed almost in a state of shock, lips white under the cavalry mustache. Then he seemed to recover and reached for a linen handkerchief to blot beads of sweat from his forehead.

In all the yelling and the shoving of men trying to get a closer look at what one gun had done to a pair of men who only minutes before had been strolling along river sand, Boyle happened to glance up at the high bank. He saw a woman who stood with feet widespread as if the earth rocked under her. She was quite tall and wore a divided leather skirt and a wool shirt, the ends tied in a knot at her waist. She wore boots and spurs, but it was her eyes that held him. Under the wide brim of her hat some sunlight leached through overcast so that he could see that the eyes were of a startling green. She wore an expression he could not fathom. Shock, loathing? As he stared, she turned on her heel and vanished among the onlookers above.

Hank Wendover was yelling from his scow. It took a moment for Boyle and others to realize what he was saying over the babble of excited voices. 'I seen it!' More men came pounding down from River Street. 'They jumped Kelly Boyle. What you figure that pair was up to, Major?'

'Hank, I have no idea.' Color was returning to the major's face. Boyle's hand was clamped to the butt of the holstered .44, one eye on Uland. The major said: 'They were probably trying to steal the man's money.' He looked at Boyle with concern. 'You all right?'

'Seems so,' Boyle said, not taking his eyes from the Box R foreman.

Almost everyone stared at Boyle in awe. A gray-blue film of gunsmoke hovering near the scow was whisked away by a sudden gust of wind that shushed sand against boot tops and made the cattails dance. Major Ransom in his pressed whipcords peered down at Billy Saxton, crumpled beside the scow. Blood, still pumping from an exit wound at his back, stained the planks.

'He's dead, obviously,' the major said, and looked around at the crowd. 'How about the other man?'

'Bone stickin' outta his shoulder,' someone said.

'Better get him over to Doc Starrett' the major advised, 'although I personally feel he's better at doctoring horses than humans.'

'Never in my life have I seen such shootin',' said a shaky Hank Wendover. He still clutched his swab, and there was grease all over the front of his shirt. 'I thought Kelly Boyle was a goner, sure 'nough.'

Major Ransom laid a hand on Boyle's arm. 'Let's go have us a drink. I need one, and Lord knows you do.' He gave a shake of his head as they started away together. 'I saw enough blood and broken bones in the war, but all the same it still upsets me.' He gestured at his foreman. 'You take care of things here, Uland.'

They walked up the path together, every eye following them.

'We've both lost someone dear to us ... temporarily,' the major continued. 'Luanne. You've heard she's gone to Saint Louis?'

'Yeah. Heard about it in the saloon a few minutes ago.'

The major's thick brows arched. 'Oh? I was there. Why didn't you come over and speak?'

'I was pretty upset about Luanne ... and other things.'

'I assume you mean your partner getting married.'

'Seems it was no secret. I didn't know about it till he got to the ranch about midnight Monday.'

'He made a spectacle of himself here in town. I feel sorry for the woman, whoever she is. They say he's bad-tempered and a trouble-maker.'

'It's an old story. Carl can't help his looks. If people didn't pick on him, there'd be no trouble.'

'Maybe the woman he married is ... well, no great beauty. I didn't get a look at her. Anyway, let's hope she isn't as spoiled as Luanne, as stubborn. In that case, your partner may find some of the bliss we all hope for.'

'They'll get along.'

'Unfortunately, I didn't find it with Luanne's mother.'

In the Great River Saloon the major waved away some of his cronies who started to drift over, got his private bottle from Pinky, and poured.

'This abrupt move of Luanne's may be the best thing that ever happened to you,Kelly.'

'I don't see it that way.' The whiskey slid easily down his throat, removing the taste of bile and gunpowder. 'If there was any way I could sprout wings and catch up to her, I'd do it ... that's how I feel about Luanne.'

Eli Cord, tall, stoop-shouldered, came clumping over. A deputy badge pinned to an old brown vest shone dully. He spoke to Boyle about the shooting.

'Who you reckon them two fellas is?' Cord demanded, squinting suspiciously at Boyle. 'Ever seen 'em before?'

'Probably a pair of drifters, Eli,' the major said with an easy smile. 'Don't bother Mister Boyle with questions. He's still pretty upset. Hank Wendover saw the whole dirty business. I'll get word to Sheriff Temple up at Empire, and you won't have a thing to worry about. Pinky, set out a glass for Eli.'

The deputy grinned. 'Well, thanks, Major. I sure will have that drink.'

The major told him to have it at the other end of the bar. 'I have some personal business to discuss with Kelly Boyle.' As Cord clumped away in his old boots, the major said: 'I told the sheriff when he appointed a deputy for Bluewater that I preferred one who was taking a walk when the brains were passed out.' Major Ransom grinned. 'Seems I got my wish.'

'Doesn't take much talent for a thankless job,' Boyle pointed out, but the major was talking about trail drives now.

'Most of the trail bosses I ever met have women and hot pistols on their minds. Or maybe it's the other way around.' He chuckled. 'You're a different breed. You speak well, for one thing.'

'My father was a mining engineer, and I had tutors.'

'And I remember hearing that he gave up mining for the cattle business.'

'He had his dream.'

'As you have yours, I guess.'

'I'll hang onto mine.' Boyle finished his whiskey. 'He let his slip away. It killed my mother. I'll never put Luanne through such hell.'

'What if you've lost her, Kelly?'

'I've got a strong feeling I haven't.'

'Let's get out of here and ride out to Box R together,' the major suggested.

Boyle thought about it. Whatever else the major might be, he was, after all, Luanne's father, and, if he intended making Luanne his wife, he would have to do some light treading on eggs where the major was concerned.

'I've only got the wagon?' Boyle said tentatively.

'I've ridden in wagons many times. I'll bring a bottle and cigars. We'll have a long talk.'

Ten minutes later, when they were heading away from the Miller Store, Boyle could see a knot of men still at the scene of trouble by the ferry. He felt a chill.

A young Mexican boy, diminutive on the back of a big mule, came pounding up to grin at Kelly and shout: '*Un gran hombre*, Don Kelly!'

'Fighting with guns doesn't make a man great,' Boyle pointed out. 'My regards to your mother, Chico.'

Then the boy happened to recognize the austere man who shared the wagon seat. The boy hastily drubbed heels against the mule's flanks and went bouncing on up the river road.

'Felicita De Gama's son,' Boyle said. 'Nice people.'

'I don't know why they don't go back across the river and live with their own kind,' the major said.

'The De Gamas have lived in Texas for two generations.' Boyle's voice took on an edge. 'They're my friends.'

40

'You understand the Mexicans. One thing that makes you valuable to me, Kelly. You called the boy Chico. Isn't his real name Guillermo?'

Boyle nodded.

'He has an Uncle Jaime?'

'Felicita's brother,' Boyle said. 'Her husband was killed a couple of years ago when somebody tried to steal his horse.'

'Ah, yes, I remember. A mighty handsome widow, that Felicita De Gama. I can understand your friendships, Kelly.'

Boyle bristled at the major's sly smile. 'It's not like that at all. Luanne is the only woman for me.'

'We shall see.' The major uncorked a bottle of whiskey with his strong teeth, took a long pull, and passed the bottle to Boyle. It was going to be one hell of a long ride to Box R was the thought percolating through Boyle's mind along with the fumes of good whiskey. 'You're a young man,' the major went on, 'with the opportunity to enjoy great wealth longer than I will.'

Boyle groaned. Mexico again. 'My money will come from Diamond Deuce. Even though now it's only a pebble alongside Box R, it'll grow.'

'I'm talking about a mountain of minerals ... copper, silver, gold ... not to mention tons of wool and great herds of cattle. We'll build a smelter in Bluewater.'

'No Mexico. I've told you before.'

'As Luanne's father you owe me the right to be heard.'

Boyle barely listened. In the jolting wagon he smoked a cigar, taking one hand from the reins whenever the major passed the bottle. Most of the time he put his tongue over the mouth, only pretending to drink. He didn't want his reflexes numbed. Two strangers had jumped him today, and they might have friends, and there was Uland with the two ranch hands, one of them with the major's saddle horse a hundred yards behind the wagon. He could almost smell Uland's hatred.

The major began talking about the rifles hidden under the floor of one of his barns. At last, Boyle's nerves, after a bad day, became frayed. 'I listened to you again out of courtesy, Major. I've seen your rifles. A waste of time to show me them again.'

'But they represent raw power that could unlock a treasure chest in Mexico. I'm talking about a railroad...'

'It's no use, Major.'

'I've managed to use my political influence to have our Texas tracks swing toward Empire and then south where they will eventually reach Bluewater. A strange name for a town. No blue water to it. The river, most of the time, is the color of a privy pit in a flood.' The major's laughter was flawed.

'I'm a rancher, not a railroad man.'

'I've investigated your background, and it fits perfectly with my plans. I want us to have this railroad, Kelly. It will please me mightily, please the many stockholders. But in order to run our rail line deep into northern Mexico, we must have a stable political environment. Do you understand what I mean?'

'What you plan in Mexico is your own business. But I'd advise against it.'

'Just why, tell me why!' the major demanded, turning in the wagon seat. A redness crept across the cheeks and the bridge of the nose, the mouth tense under the mustache.

'I've lived through it down there. Anglos should keep out of their troubles.'

'I understand your father didn't keep out of it.'

'And it cost him his life and broke my mother's heart long before that.'

'So I've been told, so I've been told.' The major sighed. 'I can say with certainty that my daughter has never cast eyes on any other man but you, so look cheerful, my boy, not so glum. She'll get over her pique, this I promise.'

Or you'll hit her in the face as she claims you did her mother, Boyle wanted to say.

They were in front of the main house, Uland and the others disappearing through the trees, heading for corrals and bunkhouse.

'You sleep on it tonight, Kelly,' the major said jovially, 'and weigh everything carefully. And if all goes well, I'll write Luanne a strong letter. And she'll be on her way home. I haven't forgotten how to issue commands, when necessary.'

'I want her home because she wants to see me, not just because her father orders her.'

'Luanne needs a little nudging. All females do. Not quite a ring in the nose, maybe, but close to it. And one of these days I'd like you to meet my stockholders. Fine men, the best.'

They're not the ones who'll have to face those ten thousand rifles was on the tip of Boyle's tongue, but he held it in.

The major stepped from the wagon, looking up at Boyle. 'I'm glad you're alive and not dead like that poor fellow ... what was his name?'

'I don't even want to think about him. *Hasta pronto*, Major.'

Boyle's back muscles were tense until he was clear of the house and on the ranch road. After leaving the major, he sorted out his impressions of the day. He could hardly remember the faces of the two men who had tried to murder him. Vivid in his mind, however, was the green-eyed woman on the high bank above the river. Never would he forget her eyes.

Chapter Three

It was the first time in six months that the Shellys, father and daughter, had been in Bluewater with the big ranch wagon for supplies. Usually they went to the Forks, a trading post nearer their Broken Wheel Ranch.

'Guess the story about our new neighbor is true,' Rob Shelly muttered, as they were leaving town. 'Reckon he's been too busy to get at the killin' till today, eh?' He was tall and at one time filled out, but the years had whittled him down to leather and bone.

Roundup was coming, and his daughter worried. 'You stay clear of Kelly Boyle. You hear, Dad?'

'Been takin' care of myself a long time, Sammy.'

She winced at the name. She drove the team like an expert, lines wrapped around gloved hands.

Her father said: 'One of these days I'll just let the major have the damn' place. An' we'll go over east an' live with your Aunt Margaret. She'll make a lady outta you yet. I ain't had much chance since your ma died.'

'A little late to make a silk purse out of you know what.'

'Sow's ear, huh? Hell, don't run yourself down, Sammy. God knows, you're purty enough.'

'Purty enough for what?' she chided. Although it did hurt, living in such isolation. Their Broken Wheel adjoined the Quester Circle Q which, in turn, bordered Diamond Deuce. 'You go live with Aunt Margaret,' Samantha said lightly. 'I'll run the ranch.' *Which I'm doing now*, she almost added, but she didn't want to hurt her father.

She tipped back her hat on the dark red braids of hair. A few freckles were scattered across cheeks and strong nose. Her mouth was wide, the lips full. Her most arresting feature were the deep, green eyes.

'They claim Boyle just stood there, laughin', hands at his sides,' her father said, 'an' he let them two scalawags draw on him. He killed the two of 'em, by Jupiter.'

'He only killed one of them, Dad.' She wondered about Boyle who could kill a man and then calmly stand at the bar with Major Ransom and drink. She had seen him through the window, a tall, gray-eyed man who showed no visible signs of remorse for having taken human life, no matter the circumstances. 'Cold nerve,' she remarked. 'Boyle's from the same mold as Rex Uland, I expect.'

'Speakin' of Uland ... now there'd be a catch for you, Sammy.'

'I'd sooner hibernate with bears.'

Rob Shelly gave a hoot of laughter and slapped his knee. Then he grew serious. 'I should've hired a coupla younger fellas so's you could've had a pick, instead of them two stove-up old cowhands we got.'

'Dad, I'll do my own choosing in my own good time.' Her voice shook slightly.

He glanced at her tall figure in wool shirt and leather skirt. 'You oughta wear a dress once in a while.'

'Now I'd look pretty silly herding cattle in a dress.'

They both smiled, Samantha a little bitterly. That day, upon hearing the gunshots, she had run like everyone else from the Miller Store, excitement tearing at her because there was so little of it in her life. She got there in time to see Kelly Boyle down by the ferry, hands on hips, calmly looking at the man he had killed as if he might be something discarded in a gunnysack, cold-blooded, absolutely without feeling. She hoped she would never meet him but supposed she would, because whether her father knew it or not, or even liked it or not, she was going to be at roundup. And to hell with what anyone might say about it being undignified and no safe place for a female. She would be there not only to protect her father, but to keep an eye on their interests. She didn't trust Major Ransom's Box R bunch, and she certainly had no faith in the newcomer, Kelly Boyle – not after today she didn't, a killer, for sure, and possibly not above slapping his Diamond Deuce brand on somebody else's calves.

Had things gone differently along the river, never again would Kelly Boyle have known Luanne's love. In his bunk that evening, he ached for her. Through his mind spun a picture of that scene last fall when she had come into his arms for the first time, how incredible her softness and how amazed he had been at her passion because most of the time she seemed aloof. After their tumultuous adventure he had experienced only a momentary wrenching regret that things had not been quite as he had envisioned. She must have read his mind, for she had lifted her head, hugging herself and him deeper into her fur coat that had warmed them both. Her sweet breath against his face, she had spoken solemnly of the academy for young ladies in St. Louis: 'There we were taught to accept life as a challenge. Not very lady-like, I suppose some would say. I'm sure, had my father been aware of Miss Gramercy's philosophy, he would have stormed about and raised all manner of hell, especially if he suspected that his chaste daughter could have been attracted to one of her instructors, a much older man, but kind and thoughtful.

Do you understand, Kelly, my dear?'

'It doesn't matter.' They were in his wagon in the trees along the river.

'I didn't love him, but he was an experience.'

'I understand.'

'In one generation things have changed, Kelly. There was a time when a man would have been shocked to learn he had not been the first.'

'I tell you, it doesn't matter.'

'But he would have kept his pride and made the woman suffer for the rest of their married life. I often think that perhaps it was the case with my mother. My parents together were like a wolf and a mountain lion in the same cage.'

'There wasn't much love between my own parents.'

'I saw my father strike her once. It was when I was quite small. I sometimes have a strong feeling that quite possibly the major is not my father...'

'You must be joking,' Kelly Boyle had said, and kissed her mouth.

'I even believe I know who my father was ... not that I ever saw him ... but I know his name.'

Sounds of a team and wagon on the road had silenced them. Boyle had lifted his head cautiously above the sideboard. Not fifty yards away he had seen two couples in a

49

hack wagon through the trees, moving along the town road. Two men on the seat, the women in the bed of the small wagon, legs dangling over the lowered tailgate.

When the sounds had faded, suppressed laughter had begun to bubble out of Luanne. 'I wonder what they would have thought if they knew that the daughter of Major Ransom was wrapped in a fur coat with her lover, wearing only her skin.' The violet eyes had danced.

'Warm skin, very warm.' He had smiled.

She suddenly had seemed anxious. Her high forehead, crowned by blue-black hair, had worn a faint frown. 'Were you disappointed in me, Kelly?'

For an answer he had hugged her fiercely, then asked his own question. 'Were you with me?'

'With my instructor it was like ripples on a placid stream. With you, Kelly, it was a mountain crashing.'

'Part of my dream, Luanne … owning a ranch and having the right woman to go with it. You better get dressed, or you'll be wearing goosebumps till Christmas.'

He had rolled aside, made adjustments in his clothing.

'Help me with buttons, my love,' she had said lazily, sitting up in the wagon.

He had managed to fit small pearl buttons into the proper holes so that the gap in her yellow dress was closed.

That fall and winter and into the spring, the fur coat had become a ritual with them. Now memories of Luanne deepened his ache. Why had she gone away without giving him a chance to explain about Carl's taking a wife? He ground his teeth. No warm breath of Luanne upon his cheek, no whispered endearments. Instead, he had the midnight company of three cowhands, one old enough to be his father. In another bunk Pete Lambourne's cracked voice muttered nightmarish challenges to blue bellies at Fredericksburg, and Smoot was snorting like a winded horse. Only Tinkey was sleeping quietly. He heard a splatter of rain on the bunkhouse roof, and a drop struck his nose like a cold finger. He pulled up a blanket to cover his face.

It turned out to be a freak late winter storm that laced the rangeland with icy needles of rain. There was talk of bad floods to the north. The Diamond Deuce crew spent their time strengthening corral fences and fixing the windmill so it no longer made war with the eardrums. Harness was mended, and some of the remuda they'd use on roundup was shod. Two days later Boyle ate his first meal with the Tripps.

'You must make a needle fly, Missus Tripp,' Boyle complimented. 'All you've done in such a short time.'

There were new curtains to replace those

made of sacking, and she had taken some of the blue cloth and stitched together a cover for the narrow, old, cowhide-covered sofa in the parlor so it hid the tufts of stuffing that poked through. A steer had been butchered for supper but, not having hung long enough, it was tough and stringy. Yet the addition of dried onions which old man Stubblefield had willed them had helped make it palatable in a stew.

'Missus Tripp sounds so ... so formal,' she said. 'Couldn't you call me Florence?'

Boyle disliked being on such relaxed terms with her because he still smarted when thinking of the changes her arrival had made in their lives, but she seemed to be going out of her way to be pleasant. She had pushed up the sleeves of her gray dress to expose forearms, rounded and white with a woman's softness. When she got up to get the coffee pot and refill their cups, Boyle was aware of the swish of her skirts.

'A fine meal, Florence,' he said.

'Carl didn't think I'd like the house or my life at Diamond Deuce. But I do.'

When she lifted her coffee cup, there was a faint, sensual adjustment of her breasts. Boyle realized she wore no corset. 'I'm glad you like it here, Florence.' *How the hell could she like it?* 'You're lucky, Carl.'

Tripp forked into his mouth a mound of onions and beef, and stroked the back of her hand with hard brown fingers. She had been staring across the table at Boyle. Touch of her husband's fingers brought a faint, startled look to her eyes, as if she had stepped from bright sunlight to shadow and wasn't quite sure who was sitting next to her at the table.

Florence picked up her empty plate and Carl's and took them to the cramped kitchen. She seemed surprised when Boyle carried in his own plate and cup.

Wiping shapely hands nervously on her apron, she said: 'You'll spoil me.'

'You've worked like the very devil to get this house fixed up and cook us a feast.'

'Not exactly a feast.' But she seemed pleased.

'What you two jawin' about?' Tripp called from the parlor, sounding cross.

'He's terribly jealous,' she said softly. 'But I didn't think he'd be of you.'

He patted her arm. 'You're something to be jealous of.'

When Boyle returned to the parlor-dining room, Tripp was stretching long arms, yawning. 'I feel tuckered out. It's bed for me an' the wife.'

Florence Tripp seemed slightly embarrassed because of what her husband had implied. Boyle told them good night and stepped out into the darkness. A handful of stars had broken through the overcast, and a golden half-moon far to the east was on its back. It was supposed to mean no rain. He hoped it was true.

Boyle started for the bunkhouse, thinking of Carl's wife. Obviously she had some breeding. What had caused her to select Carl Tripp for a husband? He was big and homely and uncouth; even Boyle had to admit it. However, nobody else had better say it.

Tripp followed him outside, caught up with him. 'Never knowed it could be so nice just puttin' out your hand no matter what time of night, an' she's right there. Sure beats prowlin' trail-town cribs.'

'Yeah, I expect,' Boyle said coldly.

Tripp gave a big horse laugh. 'Hell, I was just joshin'. You'll know how it is when you an' Luanne get yourselves hitched.

The corners of Boyle's mouth tightened, for it brought back Luanne's flight – all because of Carl's getting married. He knew it as surely as he knew his feet were planted in Texas mud. 'Sure,' was all he said, because for one split second he almost slammed a fist in the center of that homely face. 'See you *mañana*, Carl.' And he hurried to the bunkhouse.

Long ago Florence had learned to close off her mind and accept, but that night it wasn't easy, for she kept thinking of Kelly Boyle. It was suddenly his strong shoulders she gripped, and it was his strength blended with hers. Her arms tightened across Carl's back as through her mind tore an irony of her life – why couldn't it have been Kelly Boyle who had saved her from oblivion instead of Carl?

Kelly, she murmured silently against Carl's eager mouth.

The only provision for most passengers at the railhead was a canvas lean-to adjoining the headquarters car that was office and sleeping quarters for superintendent and foreman bossing the laying of track toward Empire to the south. Because she was the daughter of an important man and a major stockholder in the line, Luanne and her traveling companion, Irma Blankenship, were allowed a sleeping car on a siding. It was some days since she had left home, two spent in Empire, then a trip north by stagecoach through driving rain. Arrival of the train from the north, that would take her to St. Louis, had been delayed. There was much flooding. It would be in by morning, she had been assured.

Mrs. Blankenship complained of wet and cold, but Luanne had borne up well, possibly sheltered from reality by her hurt and anger directed at Kelly Boyle. An hour before the train was finally due to chuff northward, she overheard a man relating exciting news – Kelly Boyle had killed three men at Bluewater, possibly four. He had barely escaped with his life.

'My darling,' she breathed and jumped to

her feet and pressed the bearded news carrier for details. There were few. That Kelly Boyle's life had been in the balance was frightening. Had he been killed, it might have been months before the news reached her in St. Louis.

Her heart pounded with excitement and she wanted to shout: *Darling, you're alive, and thank God for giving us the glorious years that lie ahead.* Once Kelly understood how she felt, he would agree that it was best for them to get out of Texas and move where it was reasonably civilized. Perhaps California. He had escaped a trap set by three or four vicious men and next time might not be so lucky. And not only that, but it would be impossible for her to live for any length of time at Box R with her father, not after their terrible row.

Soon she and Mrs. Blankenship were in a jolting, southbound coach. Irma Blankenship, a plump little woman with small eyes in a smooth round face, seemed relieved. 'Lordy, am I glad you changed your mind,' Mrs. Blankenship confided. 'It's such a ways to Saint Louis, and I'm always scared to death of Comanches. They'd likely rape us an' slit our throats.'

Luanne laughed.

'You seem in a fine mood, Miss Luanne.'

'For a change, you mean. Have you ever thought of living in California, Missus Blankenship?'

'California, lass? Why, to the ends of the earth, that place?'

'I understand the sun is warm all year 'round, and the Indians are friendly.'

'You thinkin' of *livin'* there, lass?'

'At Mission San Gabriel there is an orange grove.' Luanne sat with eyes closed, head rocking to the rhythm of the coach. 'Do you remember when I was a little girl ... the year Mama hung an orange on the Christmas tree? ... and we peeled it, and I divided the slices? Mama was horrified because I let the juice run down into my bosom.' Luanne started to laugh, then her eyes filled.

'Your poor mother,' Mrs. Blankenship said, clucking her tongue.

But her mother's illness was not what had caused the stinging at Luanne's eyes. Seldom did she mention her unless it just slipped out as today. One of Luanne's first memories was of a name. It sounded like Shawn. Luanne remembered her father's screaming the name at her weeping mother. And Luanne could still hear the flat of her father's hand against her mother's face, seeing the blood at the nostrils. Luanne did her own screaming then and with tiny fists pummeled her father about the stomach, which was as high as she could reach at the time.

Her mother had cried out: 'Terrence, your foul accusations have upset the child.'

And at night sometimes in a bedroom apart

from the major's, she'd hear her mother's muffled sobs and the name: 'Shawn ... Shawn.'

When Luanne was about five, the name came up again, and she was terrified when her father removed his belt and used it on her mother as he would whip a disobedient horse. Later, after her mother died, Luanne went through her trunk. She found a daguerreotype hidden under the lining. It was of a handsome young man dressed as a cowboy, taken by a photographer in San Antonio, and written on it was: Forever, Sean. She was old enough by then to realize the name was pronounced Shawn.

One summer, when she was home from the St. Louis academy and the major was in one of his despicable moods, Luanne reminded him of the quarrels she had witnessed as a child and of overhearing the name that kindled such jealousy and hatred. The major had taken it well enough. They were in his ranch office, the walls lined with books. The saber he had carried in the war was over the fireplace. He had sat erect in his leather chair and explained quite rationally, for him. 'I suspected your mother of an ... indiscretion. Mainly it was that she had dared destroy my pride in such a way.' His smile had wavered, making the ends of his mustache twitch. 'She was unresponsive to me ... I'm sure you're much too young to know what I mean, but...'

'I haven't been exactly raised in a glove box, Papa.' She had kept a straight face as his hazel eyes probed in that chilling and familiar way.

'I pay good money for you to receive a fine education. I certainly hope discussions there are not of a ... a worldly nature.'

'You and Mama quarreling. Things that go on between a man and a woman?' – she had paused a heartbeat – 'or what doesn't go on ... I learned from you ... not from the academy.'

'Empty your mind of it!' he had ordered. 'No decent female would even harbor such thoughts until she takes a husband.'

Luanne knew she had angered him. She had smiled prettily. 'Have you ever noticed Rex Uland's eyes when he's around me? They acquire a special glow, and I feel him looking right through me to my backbone.'

'He knows better, unless you encourage him!'

'Speaking of husbands, I think he'd marry me in a minute. Possibly less.'

The major had come up out of his chair. 'I'd rather see you in your grave next to your mother than have you marry Uland!'

She would remember that remark.

The major had said: 'You've chided me enough for one day, Luanne.' He had dropped back into the big chair, his body popping against the padded leather. 'Sometimes I feel you ... you almost hate me. Do you?'

She had met his stare and remained silent.

He had lifted his hands. 'Is it because of your mother?'

'I saw you beat her...'

'A terrible thing, I admit. I tried to make it up to her shortly before she died.' He stared at the wall.

Luanne had left the room before she blurted the truth – her mother's sobbing a name in her sleep and of the hidden daguerreotype under the trunk lining, reasonably certain that it was a likeness of her true father. Her mother, it seemed, had not been without passion, after all.

That same fall the Cattleman's Association had held their convention in St. Louis. That was when she had first heard the name Kelly Boyle. She had been allowed to be absent from her classes at the academy for young ladies in order to have a reunion with her father at his hotel suite. There important men gathered to sip whiskey, smoke cigars, and talk of the changing cattle business from trail drives to railroads. Abilene was long finished, and the move westward had used up Ellsworth and Newton, with Dodge City the last of the trail towns. Her father enjoyed showing her off. Tall and beautiful with shiny blue-black hair and violet eyes, there were many generous compliments, much kissing of her finger tips. She had three proposals of marriage which her father waved off with a cold smile. School would soon be finished, he had said, and she would be living at Box R for a few years. Plenty of time for him to find her a suitable husband, he had assured her in front of a roomful of chuckling men.

While she bit back her anger and humiliation at being treated like a child, she had overheard someone talking about Kelly Boyle who, some years before at nineteen, had saved a herd of Texas cattle when the trail boss died many miles south of Baxter Springs and the *segundo* was shot in a brawl. Kelly Boyle had pulled the crew together, rounded up the strays, and, losing only eight head out of three thousand, made a triumphant entry into Kansas. Another rancher in her father's hotel suite had looked into Boyle's background with the idea of hiring him. Boyle and Carl Tripp had been raised as brothers in Mexico. Boyle had the brains, the tough know-how. Carl Tripp followed his lead, often sullenly. Whenever Boyle took a job, Carl Tripp had to be included. It was no use trying to hire Boyle for a lifetime job as foreman or ranch superintendent because he intended to be his own man. In a few years he and Tripp would have a ranch of their own.

Her father, she remembered, that day had seemed particularly interested in Boyle's background in Mexico and asked for more details. Learning that Boyle's father had been mixed up in a plot to unseat Porfirio Díaz was of particular interest.

'They failed because of poor planning,' her father had said, brushing cigar ash from his fawnskin vest. She remembered how he had sat there that day, swinging a foot, a bemused smile showing below the cavalry mustache.

It was later that she again heard the name Kelly Boyle. School was finished at last, and she was living back home at Box R. The day Luanne learned old man Stubblefield had suddenly sold Diamond Deuce for less than it was worth, she had confronted her father. It had been a warm afternoon in the fall.

'Father, I thought you intended to let Stubblefield just wither away from old age, then move in.'

'What nonsense is this?' His hazel eyes had danced.

'You and your Machiavelian mind,' she had accused.

'I should never have sent you to that fancy school. Females are supposed to be subdued, not flippant.' He had been suffering from gout and was upstairs in his room, bandaged foot resting on a low stool. Through the window she had been able to see cottonwoods shedding leaves, and there were the great honking migrations of wild geese heading south. 'When the rail line finally reaches Empire,' her father had continued, 'I'll do considerable entertaining. You'll be an asset as my hostess.'

'Plans all made, I see.'

He had peered up at her from his big chair. 'My plans never fail. Sooner or later I have my own way.'

'You seem to ... most of the time.'

'I was determined to marry your mother. She had three suitors at the time. But you see who won.' He had smiled, expecting praise.

That was when Luanne had almost hurled a name at him ... Sean. Just to get his reaction. But her mother was dead and it no longer mattered. 'Yes, you won, Father, you *won* Ellamae Harkness ... as they say.'

'What a strange mood. I notice when you disapprove of me, it's Father, not Papa,' he had chided.

'You want me to be dignified when I act as hostess to the stockholders in your railroad, so I have to get used to addressing you as Father.'

Because Saturday was usually the day ranchers came to Bluewater for supplies, she had spent three of them there in a row. She had seen Kelly Boyle at a distance on the ranch road, but never close. She had intended to remedy that, if possible. Each of those Saturdays she had driven a buggy to town, always accompanied by two or three Box R men.

Rex Uland usually arranged to be part of the escort. At times, just to pacify the big, shaggy-haired foreman with the dangerous eyes, she would share a sarsaparilla at the Miller Store or let him buy her some rock candy.

On the second Saturday she had seen a Diamond Deuce partner arrive with a wagon, a man as big as Uland, scowling, with enormous ears and two widely gapped large front teeth. When he had departed with a few supplies, she overheard someone say: 'He asked about Lucero. An' I told him.' It had brought on subdued male laughter in the crowded store.

All that she knew about Lucero was that it was a tough place where there were any number of what her aunt in St. Louis referred to as 'fallen women.' She supposed there were also some here in Bluewater, although it never seemed to be mentioned as it was in connection with the river town some miles from Bluewater.

Uland was beginning to enjoy the Saturday town visits, having no idea of the purpose, smugly supposing it might be the major's daughter unbending a little to his charm. On the fourth Saturday she wore a new green dress, and she had her hair up. It must have been a hunch, she thought afterward. She had just allowed Uland to loosen the cork fastener on a bottle of lime water when she saw the wagon pull into the turn-around beside the store. Burned into the side of the wagon was the brand: a diamond and in its center the numeral 2. A tall man with thick, dark-brown hair jumped lightly onto the loading platform. She had waited so long and was so keyed up that just sight of him made her upper body strain against corset stays. 'Isn't that ... the other partner at Diamond Deuce?' she had heard herself ask no one in particular, although she had known it was.

'Him,' Uland had grunted.

Setting down the bottle Rex Uland had just handed her, she had hurried out to the platform. Removing her glove, putting on her best smile, she had walked right up to him and thrust out her hand. 'Welcome to Tyburn County, Mister Kelly Boyle. I'm Luanne Ransom.'

And right there it had happened, in the eyes, the press of her flesh against his callused palm. Not caring that nearly everyone had come to stare out at her still hanging onto his hand, *easy, Luanne*, she had cautioned herself, *you're no longer fourteen*. She had dropped his hand and, still smiling, had said: 'My father speaks well of you.' It was the damnedest lie she had ever told in her life, but it was all that came to mind in that moment of shallow breath and runaway pulse.

'That was nice of you to say, Miss Ransom. Mighty nice.'

In the stagecoach with Irma Blankenship, now rattling south out of Empire, heading for Bluewater, Luanne thought back on that day with a smile. She didn't care that everyone had stared, Rex Uland malevolently. Meeting Kelly Boyle had been a beginning. And to think she had almost spoiled everything by running away like a foolish child.

She spoke to Mrs. Blankenship about Kelly Boyle. 'He'll be my husband.'

'Your father might not like it.'

'What have I ever done in life that he *did* like?'

Mrs. Blankenship looked surprised, lowered her voice below the rumble of the stagecoach, careening across the Texas frontier. 'You owe him your respect, lass.'

There was a rustle of silk as Luanne angrily threw open her green cloak and crossed her legs. The two obviously shy male passengers in the facing seat tried to look elsewhere but failed. She barely noticed, not caring if they saw her ankles. She was thinking of her father, the major. Her respect he would never have.

Chapter Four

On a drizzly day Kelly Boyle met Rob Shelly of Broken Wheel and his two ranch hands for the first time. They were on the east road that was just a pair of wheel tracks through mesquite and *tornillo*. Shelly was about fifty, rode slouched in the saddle, and had the eyes and veined nose to declare him a lover of strong drink. The two hands, both older men, didn't join in the conversation when Boyle and their boss talked briefly about roundup.

'By the way,' Shelly said, when they were ready to ride their separate ways, 'you better watch out for my foreman. Mighty tough. Name of Sam.'

Boyle noticed that the two ranch hands were grinning. 'I've faced tough foremen before,' Boyle said, thinking it must be some kind of a joke, but having more on his mind than to wonder about it. With weather clearing, he had had a crazy hope that Luanne might have changed her mind and come home. But she hadn't. 'Tell your foreman, Sam, that I'll keep one eye open,' Boyle said in parting.

Shelly and his two cowhands laughed. Some kind of a joke, for sure.

Boyle rode through the mesquite down to the river and the De Gama place. There had been gunfire across the river, and he wanted to make sure that Felicita and her son and her brother, Jaime, were all right.

They were. Chico was in Bluewater where he boarded and attended school. Jaime was in his quarters, a lean-to built against the barn. Felicita was in the house that she shared with her son when he came home Saturdays. As usual, Felicita was neatly dressed, her black hair slicked back, hoops of silver at her delicate ears. She gave Boyle her fine-boned hand. Blood of Spanish grandees had left its mark on that classic face.

She heated coffee, and they talked. He spoke of the shooting that day in Bluewater and how Chico had seemed so impressed. 'Talk to him, Felicita. Make him see that there is no honor in killing a man.'

'But you are alive, and one of them is dead. So, you see, there is honor, after all. In this time in Texas that is all that counts. Perhaps someday...' Her voice trailed away, and he wondered if she thought of her husband, Teodero, who had not been able to shoot fast enough and who now lay buried beyond the barn.

The following day he drove the wagon to Bluewater for things they would need at roundup and also to pick up some extras for Felicita that he would drop off on his way home. In town, at the Miller Store, he over-heard someone say that the wounded Ben Chollmar had been shipped off to Laredo and Billy Saxton buried at boothill; both men had been hands at one of the Box R line camps at North Ranch, so the story went.

'The major in town?' Boyle asked casually.

The faces of some men at a counter, especially Miller's, who had been talking, drained white. Miller's tight, little mouth flapped open, and he looked as if death had just whispered in his ear. 'Major was over yonderly about an hour ago,' he faltered and gestured at the Great River Saloon up on the corner.

Just as Boyle, walking with purposeful stride, reached the saloon, the winter doors parted and Major Ransom stepped out, looking jaunty, cigar like a cannon under the bristly mustache, eyes shining.

'Ah, there you are, Kelly,' he said jovially. 'I knew I shouldn't have had Pinky put my bottle away. Come in and we'll drink.'

'Did you sic Chollmar and Saxton on me?'

A group of men stepped around them in order to enter the saloon. They nodded to the major, noticed the washed-out look of Boyle's eyes, the hard set of the mouth, and hurried inside. The major was wearing a freshly ironed gray suit, the ends of a string tie lying against the snowy bosom of a shirt.

'I did suggest they jump you, Kelly,' he ad-

69

mitted calmly, then made back off gestures when Boyle took a forward step. 'To test your mettle with their fists.'

'They tried.' Kelly Boyle halted and dampened his urge to smash that cheroot against the major's white teeth, which would have been no credit to him – not only an older man, but Luanne's father. He forced himself to watch blackbirds skimming the cattails, then soaring into the cloudy sky. It smelled of rain. 'Then why didn't you tell them to leave their guns, if you wanted fists?' Boyle calmly asked.

The major got Boyle by an arm. 'I assume it's safe to put a hand on you' he said, laughing carefully, 'seeing that you nearly became my son-in-law. Still might, far as that goes. Let's walk and get away from the big ears in the saloon.'

'To test my mettle ... sending those two against me ... why?'

They were now walking together along River Street. Men watched tensely from the Miller Store.

'Partly because you had upset my daughter and should be taught a lesson,' the major said. 'But mainly because of my dream that you refused to share. To pierce the heart of northern Mexico with rails...'

'You're not the first one who's dreamed it,' Boyle said, still fighting his anger.

'So you told me.' the major chuckled.

'When you struck a bargain with old man Stubblefield, moved in next door, and then had the temerity to come calling on my daughter under my very nose ... well, I had to conclude you were either a fool or possessed with the guts I had when I was your age.'

Some of the heat was leaving Boyle's face, the eyes returning to their normal gray. He spoke of the floods and the possibility – the hope – that Luanne might have decided to return home.

Major Ransom shook his head. 'Not that girl. I'm sure she beat the floods and is well on her way to Saint Louis. She'll never give in, so don't count on it.'

'But I am.'

'The only thing that will bring her home before the planned year is up will be a strong letter from me ... which I'm quite willing to write, as I told you before. And may I add to my earlier evaluation of your guts? It took plenty to turn me down on my own ranch where I could whistle up twenty men who at my orders would hang you to the nearest tree.'

'It would *take* twenty men.'

'I expect so, Kelly. I expect it would. You see, I need a tough man for my venture, one who is not afraid to take chances. You proved you're that man by the way you handled that pair earlier in the week.'

'By killing a man? Practically shooting the

arm off the other?' Boyle's mouth twisted. 'I didn't shoot to prove how tough I am. I did it to keep from getting blown out of my boots.'

'Self-preservation, of course.'

Their heels echoed hollowly to the end of the boardwalk then crunched in river sand. The river was up slightly following the rain. The major spoke of the recent troubles across the river.

'I happen to know the man behind it all. The one great power in northern Mexico.'

Boyle's laugh was dry. 'Every five years or so there comes a great power all blooms and shallow roots. Who's the savior of the *peon* this time?'

'Diego Esparza.'

'I see. His father was *norteamericano*. He took his mother's name.'

'A half-breed, then,' the major conceded, blowing a jet of cigar smoke from a corner of his mouth.

'You make it sound like a disgrace. It isn't.'

'But he looks Mexican.'

'On second thought, in his case it is a disgrace ... to his Mexican blood.' Boyle's thoughts tumbled to other years. 'He could have done something with the money his father left him, instead of throwing it away and hating Anglos because there wasn't more money.'

The major turned to look up into Boyle's tight face. 'There's a good chance this Mexi-

72

can friend of yours might succeed where others have failed.'

'He's hardly my friend.'

'So I've heard. But he needs guns. And I need a man to deliver them and handle other negotiations.'

'Deal with Esparza and he'll want more than guns. He'll want your head.'

Major Ransom laughed. 'You know him well, I see.'

'We were boys together.'

'Can't you see that this is destined?' The major's voice sharpened, shook. 'Come in with me. I'll buy your ranch. Let your partner go his own way.'

'I won't cut Carl loose. And I don't figure to give up our ranch.'

'Be your own man. Not his.'

'I promised to look after him. And I will.'

'You owe yourself first.' The major halted to relight his cigar. His hand trembled. The jacket of the finely tailored gray suit hung open to reveal the polished heel plates of a revolver. 'These are arguments my daughter would throw at you, Kelly, were she here. Believe me.'

'I gave you my answer the other day.'

They were standing on the high bank above the river. A faint sound of hammering came from the beached ferry up ahead. Hank Wendover was bent over his winch.

'Think how lucky you are, Kelly,' the major

said, drawing on his cigar. 'Had it not been for Wendover, witnessing the altercation the other day, you could very well soon be buckled up in hangman's straps and ready for the gallows.' His lips stretched into a grin under the mustache. 'I'm not serious, of course.'

'At times you try a man's patience, Major Ransom.'

'Pay no attention to me, Kelly. I'm just disappointed, but, of course, there's always hope. And I do need you. Luanne needs you.'

'I'm sure that girl has nothing to do with your grand plans for Mexico,' Boyle said, trying to make it light, to ease the taut feeling in his stomach.

'That was some shooting the other day, Kelly. Hank Wendover's had more free whiskey retelling it than he ever had in his life before. He claims he never saw anything so fast in his life. That the pair had you euchered was the way Wendover put it. But you drilled Billy Saxton dead center, and he's been up against some real tough ones, so they say.'

'I didn't enjoy killing him,' Boyle said in a dead voice as memory of those few seconds roared back at him, concussion bordering on pain in the eardrums and gunsmoke burning the nostrils like acid.

'It'll be a miracle if Chollmar ever uses that arm again,' the major said. 'Doc Starrett claims your slug mangled his shoulder and part of the collarbone.'

'Good God, and all I was doing was taking a walk and trying to get over my hurt because Luanne had run off to Saint Louis.'

'If anyone's to blame, it's Rex Uland.' Ransom looked up into his face. 'But he's the only foreman I have ... for now. There's room at the top for a superintendent who can either handle Uland or kick him off the ranch. Whichever.'

'One day I may talk to Uland about Saxton and Chollmar.'

'If you ever decide, Kelly, go all the way. Because he'll stomp your head and kill you if he can. He's been in love with Luanne ever since she was a kid.'

'I guessed it.'

Ransom removed a gold watch from his pocket, flipped the case open, and said slyly: 'I have what I hope is a momentous engagement up at Lucero.'

'Lucero?' Boyle had heard of the place, a haven for the unscrupulous from both sides of the river.

'Tie your horse to the back of my rented buggy and we'll ride together and talk. It's only a few miles upriver and not too much out of the way for you.'

'I have my wagon.'

'Your wagon again, eh? Seems I remember you always calling on Luanne with the wagon. Ever think of buying a buggy?'

'When we marry, she'll have the very best

75

of everything.'

'Come in with me and it's guaranteed. With Diamond Deuce, it's only a hope. Like one of those observation balloons in the war. Those lofty things riding on the wind. But one cannonball and it becomes only a puff of smoke.'

'Very poetic.'

'I want the best for my daughter.'

'And the best for yourself,' Boyle added with a hard smile.

'A man would be a fool to wish otherwise. We can do it, Kelly. The two of us!'

Boyle spoke carefully, still retaining part of the smile, not wanting to alienate but to press home a point. 'You'll be my father-in-law, and I'll always do the best I can for you. Because of Luanne. Everything but Mexico. And I won't walk on the heads of *peones* just to fill rail cars with ore.'

'We'll see. And don't count on my being your father-in-law unless I write a letter that will bring my daughter scampering home.'

It was Boyle's turn to say: 'We'll see.' But in his heart he wondered if the major might not be right.

Ransom gave him a friendly slap on the arm, and they walked back in silence. Uland and two hands Boyle didn't know were waiting in front of the saloon, Uland's hat tipped back on shaggy, rust-colored hair. One of the men was sitting in a fancy red-wheeled buggy. The man got out, holding the reins until the major was settled in the seat, then handing them over.

Ransom gave Boyle a jaunty wave of the hand and set the dappled gray in the buggy shafts into a smart trot. Uland looked long and hard at Boyle from under craggy brows, then mounted up. He and the others rode behind the major along the river road.

A man slicked up in a fancy suit and renting a red-wheeled buggy has female on his mind, Boyle thought as he crossed to the store.

The day had been interesting at that, Boyle thought on the way home. He had the major's admission of responsibility for Chollmar and Saxton, but to a point, blaming most of it on Uland. Boyle wondered how the day would have turned out had he been fool enough to accept the major's invitation to ride to Lucero with Uland and the others at his back? And a few miles out of Bluewater, with no Hank Wendover around as a witness, what then? A beating that would take Doc Starrett a month to mend? Or, if things got out of hand as before, a slit in Texas river sand with perhaps something a little green sprouting in the spring as sometimes happened from lonely makeshift graves. Boyle shivered. Luanne would never know what had happened to him.

Where was her father off to today, slicked up like a Frisco nabob? Female business at

Lucero? Boyle felt an itch, and his thoughts pinwheeled from far off Luanne, being rocked to sleep on steam cars, and to the female close as the short toss of a rock from his bed in the bunkhouse, living in a house filled for the most part with rough, home-made furniture; even though she'd brightened it up with her needle and thread it was no place for a refined lady. The whole thing reminded him so much of younger years in Mexico, after fleeing, then going back time and again to find the killers of his father, and failing. Not that Florence Tripp blended particularly with hazy memories of his own mother, except that at times he detected tragedy in her eyes. His mother had followed that adventurer Tim Boyle around Mexico, the bad years, then the good. Only one time had Kelly Boyle ever heard of his mother standing up for herself, insisting that Kelly be born in the United States. And he had been – in El Paso. Finally his father's persistence in a dangerous game won him the big pot, a vast ranch, *Ojo del Diablo*, Eye of the Devil, in partnership with a lawyer and friend, Luis Montez. The partners flourished, but it was too late for the mother of Kelly Boyle. Years of tension, of uncertainty had drained her beauty, finally her life. Just before she died, she had asked to see Kelly alone. His father had been in Ciudad Chihuahua on 'political business' as usual with a young and pretty woman. Even at eight, Kelly Boyle knew his father well.

'Take care of Carl,' his mother had said, clutching Kelly's hand in her thin one, hot with fever. 'Carl lacks your intelligence and your charm. Aim high, Kelly, and take poor Carl with you.'

Two years after Boyle's had mother died, Carl had displeased the father in some way. Tim Boyle had wanted to kick Carl off the *rancho*, but Kelly had stood up to his father.

'It's best for everybody if Carl gets out,' Tim Boyle had said sternly, not giving his reason.

'Momma made me swear to look after him and I will!'

This had caused Tim Boyle to look down into his son's strange, gray eyes. 'Integrity at your age? Or at any age in these times ... astounding.'

It was later that Tim Boyle and Montez chose the wrong side in a political upheaval and were murdered in their beds. Kelly Boyle and Carl Tripp were hunted. Somehow Kelly, three years younger, got them across the border. In the toughest years of the cattle drives they signed on. Boyle, by applying himself, learned the business. Tripp just rode along.

Boyle was still thinking about those years when he reached home. Florence came to the door, lamplight at her back. Sight of her always produced a tension lately. Either resentment that she and Carl had spoiled things, at least temporarily, with Luanne, or tension produced of a night when he thought of her in the bed he used to share with Carl, that rich yellow hair spread out and her wearing something soft and ... *Christ, stop it!*

'Would you like to join us for supper?' she asked as he stepped down from the wagon. 'I made a stew.'

'No thanks, Missus Tripp. I'll rustle something up in the bunkhouse.' Then he could have kicked himself because her face fell, and in the faint wash of lamplight her eyes looked hurt. 'I'm just tired is all. Got to unhitch the team and I better be getting at it.'

'Carl, why don't you give him a hand?' she suggested, turning to look back into the house. 'Kelly seems about done in.'

'Kelly likes to do everything for hisself.' Carl sounded sullen which made Boyle wonder if he and the bride had quarreled.

'Good night, Florence,' Boyle called, trying to make up for refusing her invitation and addressing her as Mrs. Tripp in the bargain. But she had closed the door.

A week prior to his daughter's having thrown a tantrum and announced her intention to visit friends in St. Louis, Major Ransom had gone upriver to the settlement of Lucero, a

80

collection of mud *casitas*, a hotel of dubious reputation, two brothels, a cantina, and the Big Store. The main function of the border village was as a source of information concerning conditions in turbulent Mexico.

That day the wind had been up, and Ransom had just been dismounting in front of Hagar's *cantina* when he had noticed a tall woman coming along the walk on the opposite side of the street. Something in her carriage, the way she held her head, denoted breeding. A traveling cloak of some heavy dark material was molded to her body by the wind so that he had an exciting impression of a voluptuous figure. Strands of rich golden hair were whipped from under a bonnet by a gust of the insane winds that swept the river country this time of year.

He had sensed handsome features although he couldn't be sure because of a black veil that covered her face. One gloved hand anchored the lower half of the veil against her throat so it couldn't be lifted by the wind and expose her face to public view. Not for some years had the mere sight of a woman intrigued him so.

'Wonder who she is,' he had said aloud.

Uland, just tying his horse, had laughed. 'In *this* town?'

Ransom had turned on his foreman. 'Obviously not one of *those*,' he had said coldly, and Uland had hastily backed off.

In the *cantina*, Major Ransom was still thinking about the woman when Hagar, owner of the place, had come crisply up on small feet to talk about Mexico and Diego Esparza whose uncle was said to have left him a million hectares of land. Uland and the others were at the north end of the bar. The major seldom drank with his men. Midway down the bar two Mexicans hung their boots over the rail. One wore a blood-stained bandage on his head.

'Railroads I want to talk about,' Joe Hagar had whispered to the major. He was a dapper little man known to deal in any commodity that yielded a profit.

'You mean our Texas railroad getting closer every month?' the major had asked innocently.

'A railroad that comes through Bluewater. Or why not here at Lucero?'

'Lay track in Mexico and you'd have to deal with *el presidente*. That could be bloody.' The major had been feeling his way.

'If Diego Esparaza keeps Porfirio Díaz out of it, there sure wouldn't be none of *our* blood.' Hagar had grinned at him.

'Getting rid of Díaz,' Ransom had said in a low voice, nodding at the pair of Mexicans drinking mescal, 'is dangerous talk ... even on this side of the line.'

'A little of our money spent here and there and we'd have a river of silver an' gold, not

82

to mention cows.'

Major Ransom had looked slightly shocked. 'You're talking about insurrection.'

'It's not firecrackers they're shootin' off across the river. We could help those who figure to help us later.'

'You'll never get rid of Díaz.' The major had known it was possible but wanted to milk Hagar for his ideas on the subject.

'Ship weapons to Esparza.'

Major Ransom had worn his poker face. 'That would mean raiding an armory.'

'You'd know how to manage it, if anybody would.'

You've had your pimp ear to the ground, Ransom had thought, then said: 'I've no idea how to get my hands on any guns. And as for the railroad coming through Lucero instead of Bluewater...' He had been leaning back against the bar, glass in hand, when through a front window he saw the veiled woman just emerging from the Big Store. She carried a small package in a gloved hand.

'Who is she, Hagar?' he had demanded, his voice thick.

The saloonman had looked around, seen who he meant, and said she'd been in town three days and that her name was Taylor. 'Dusty over at the ho-tel got a look at her face an' says it's swole up an' she's got a black eye.'

'Any man who'd beat a woman should be gelded,' the major had said angrily. Then

83

memories of his own marriage had put a strained look on his face.

'Might not be a beatin', Major. Mebby she just fell. Listen, I know how to reach Esparza. He'd listen to me, an' if that railroad come through Lucero ... an' we just happened to get our hands on some guns...'

But Ransom had set down his glass and walked out to stare at the woman. He had been thinking that with Luanne on her way to St. Louis and any one of those big upstairs bedrooms available ... his pulse had quickened as he had watched her walk toward the hotel, having a sudden adolescent hope that tumbleweeds would spook a team, that she would be endangered by a runaway, and he would rush to her rescue.

She had entered the Rio Vista Hotel down the block. It didn't bother him that unattached females, unless of low morals, rarely accepted lodging in a settlement such as Lucero, or stayed in a hotel like the Rio Vista. But with the new trouble across the line, anything was possible. He had felt a throbbing of excitement.

Hagar was tugging at his coat sleeve. 'Major, you never did answer me about Esparza.'

'Anybody who tries to deal with such an upstart,' Ransom had said coldly, 'has left his brains too long in the sun.' He had walked away.

84

Because he was known at the Rio Vista, he had no trouble getting her name and room number. She was registered as Mrs. S. J. Taylor, San Francisco, and was in an upstairs front room. He had knocked lightly on her door.

'Samuel ... is ... is that you?' the voice anxious, but cultured as expected.

When she had flung open the door, her had jaw dropped. She hadn't been wearing the veil. Soft white arms and good shoulders and a fine bosom, the waist nipped in. The dress of good silk. She had been holding a small piece of beefsteak over the swollen right eye. The left cheek had been slightly puffy.

'Oh, my God,' she had gasped. 'I ... I thought it was someone else at the door...'

'You've been hurt. I want to help.'

She had shaken her head violently from side to side. Light from a dirty side window touched the golden hair. He could almost feel his fingers curling in its softness. She had said: 'I ... I am quite all right. We were... I mean *I* was across the line and there was trouble and ... will you please get your foot out of the door?'

'One day soon, if you like,' he had said smoothly, 'when your face is better, I'd like to return...'

The unswollen eye was a deep blue, penetrating. 'Perhaps,' had been all she had said,

85

but he had read a promise in her manner.

'My dear young woman' – he had judged her to be twenty-two or three – 'I am Major Ransom, at your service. Should you ever need help, dear lady, anyone can tell you how to get in touch with me.'

'Thank you, Major, I will remember.'

'I'll be back. Say in three days?'

'Yes, fine, fine.

He had removed his foot, and she had closed the door.

Somehow he had felt it was ordained. He'd return, and she'd still be here. If her friend Samuel was across the line some place in such bloody times, he might be a captive. Or dead. When her face had healed, she would be more receptive to his advances, the major was sure. He had always prided himself on his ability to capture female hearts. And he had been certain that the enigmatic Mrs. Taylor, despite the ravaged face, had shown an interest in him.

On the way back to the ranch that day, he had jerked his head at Uland and let the other two men ride on ahead. 'Rex, Hagar hinted about those rifles under the barn floor. Have you talked?'

'Hell, no. Not a man on the place is left who knows about 'em.'

'I thought as much but wanted to make sure. One of these days, when I give the word, you might let Hagar know that I have my own plans. And if I should want to include him for any reason, I will. Otherwise, he's to keep his nose out.'

'I'll ride back now an' bounce his head on the floor a few times.' Uland had been turning his horse.

'Later ... later.'

That night Major Ransom's dreams were filled with the mystery woman of Lucero so vividly that he was in the throes of copulation when he awakened. More than ever he was determined to have her. Luanne and that nosy Irma Blankenship, being away, only heightened the excitement.

As it happened, however, he hadn't been able to get back to Lucero as soon as he had originally planned, having been delayed among other things by a meeting of railroad stockholders. So it was a good ten days later, following his unsuccessful meeting in Bluewater with Kelly Boyle, that he again entered Lucero. He was again driving the buggy with the red wheels. His hunch was that it would be a suitable vehicle for her entry to the Box R, although perhaps it might be better at first to rent the suite at the Bluewater Hotel, a get-acquainted night. In this mood, as he saw the Rio Vista Hotel ahead, he hoped Luanne stayed in St. Louis two years instead of one.

'Go over to Hagar's and get yourselves a drink,' he told Uland and the others.

Right then Hagar himself came skipping

from his *cantina* on short legs, grinning broadly. 'I knowed you'd be back, by Christ.' He fiddled with a row of gold nuggets attached to his watch chain – panned in the Mother Lode when he was a kid, he always claimed; others said they were stolen. Then he seemed to notice the buggy for the first time. 'Who you figure to go callin' on? Cleopatra?'

The major wasn't amused. 'How's Missus Taylor's face these days?'

'What still shows she covered with powder.'

'She at the hotel, I expect?'

'She's gone.'

Lips under the cavalry mustache whitened. 'I had a strong feeling she'd wait.'

'Dusty over to the ho-tel says this Samuel Taylor come back ... purty drunk he was. Him an' the gal ... they had a helluva row. Next thing Dusty knows, she's with that big fella I hear moved in at Diamond Deuce.'

'Kelly Boyle, you mean?' Ransom almost choked on it.

'The other one. Big with bat ears. Word is that Tucker Thiebault, the Bible Shouter who comes through here once in a blue moon, married 'em up nawth somewheres.'

'How in the holy hell could she marry a man when she already has a husband...?' Major Ransom broke off. Had Mrs. Taylor been the woman Carl Tripp had married

88

and brought to the Diamond Deuce? It was unthinkable. 'Are you trying to tell me that she'd go off with that ... that *monster?*' Then he shouted for Uland, who came running. 'Have Conover drive this damn' rig back to Bluewater!' Major Ransom was screaming. 'I want his horse!'

Hagar was trying to shout something about Mexico and Diego Esparza and riches to Ransom, but the major wasn't even listening. He swung a leg over the back of Conover's sorrel and went spurring back along the Bluewater road, Uland and Jake Roone trying to catch up, Bert Conover, cowlick blowing in the wind, driving hellbent in the red-wheeled buggy.

All the way back to Bluewater, Major Ransom ground his teeth until they ached. He had been in town Saturday night when Carl Tripp had rolled in, staggering drunk, and with him in the big wagon had been a woman, his wife, somebody said, a woman huddled under a blanket so no one could get a good look at her face. The major, drinking at the Great River Saloon that night, had heard about it. 'She must be second cousin to a mud fence to marry anyone as homely as Carl Tripp,' he remembered having said at the time.

Joe Hagar couldn't figure why Major Ransom, who knew all the important people in this isolated corner of Texas, would go flying apart just because of the blonde, acting like a greenhorn who thinks he'd found true love in a parlor house. Then he began to laugh. It was all kind of funny, at that, the stiff-backed major screaming at his foreman like a hysterical female. Two or three days before – he couldn't really remember exactly, it was so unimportant – Samuel Joseph Taylor, who insisted on the three names, had cornered him in his *cantina* office. Taylor's clothes were muddied from wading across the river and one arm was in a sling. He smelled of *sotol*, which could set the Anglo brain afire.

Taylor had a wild story about a big gambling game at an American-owned mine some miles beyond the river and a cache of silver bullion. Obviously Taylor needed a stake, but Hagar gave him only the courtesy of listening. He'd heard many variations of this story and waited for Taylor to get to the point.

Taylor had mentioned the pale-haired woman, then said: 'Hagar, we're both men of the world. I know I am. I take it you are. You being in business in a place like Lucero...'

'What's the woman got to do with it?'

'We've traveled about the West. I ... well, to put it bluntly, from time to time when I need a stake...'

'You mean for a price ... she's willing?'

'Don't make it sound so crude, sir.' Taylor

had been trying to sound tough, as if resenting someone for usurping a few lines from
his carefully prepared speech. He hadn't
quite known how to proceed from there, his
brain being awash with *sotol*.

Hagar had said: 'Friend, there's a room in
the back. Fixed up nice where she can...'

'No scum off the river, if you know what I
mean. Surely in such a place as this there are
men willing to pay dearly for their adventures.'

'How long you been doin' this?'

'Only when my fortunes are at a low ebb.'

'Her face healed up?'

Taylor had seemed almost embarrassed at
mention of her bruises. He had been sitting
next to Hagar at a rolltop desk, cracking his
knuckles nervously. He had center-parted,
brown hair, honest brown eyes, and a timid
smile. 'She cursed me, and I lost my temper.
But I believe she's learned her lesson. A week
should be enough. Then I'll cross the river,
recover my money, and we'll be off to new
horizons.'

Taylor had then slipped back across the
river on some loco business he was trying to
work over there. Whatever it was, if he sur-
vived, it would be a miracle in these times.
As was his custom, Hagar had kept his
mouth shut about his dealings with Taylor
until he had talked to the woman. Not even
mentioning it to his nephew, Hiram, who

had showed up last month on the dodge from some trouble in Missouri. It was kind of all mixed up, now that Hagar thought back on it, because that same evening Dusty over at the hotel said somebody had made off with his shotgun. About half an hour later the Taylor woman had come up from the river, leaning on Carl Tripp's arm as if her legs had given out and her face the color of caliche. Tripp had been carrying the shotgun, and the woman was soaking Tripp's coat sleeve with her noisy weeping.

Then Carl Tripp had given Dusty back the shotgun, glared around at those who had come to stare, and announced he and the woman were heading out to get married by the traveling preacher. Carl Tripp and the sobbing woman had left town in the Diamond Deuce wagon. And that was the last anyone had seen of them, the wagon lurching off down the Bluewater road. Almost everyone in Lucero was glad that Carl Tripp had notions of settling down, no matter with whom. Too many times he'd come to town looking for trouble, usually finding it, but he was big enough and fast enough with a gun, so far, to bend things his way. *Good riddance*, Hagar had thought.

Chapter Five

In Bluewater, when Luanne and Mrs. Blankenship disembarked from the stagecoach, a driver and wagon were hired to take them to the ranch. Jack Quester saw Luanne first, rushing from the Box R office, smiling shyly as he always did around her.

'Oh, it's such a surprise!' he cried. 'And so nice to have you home, Miss Luanne.'

'And good to see you, Jack.' She put out her hand as if she'd been gone for months instead of only days.

'I've got ink on my fingers,' he apologized, but she said it didn't matter.

After shaking hands with him, Jack blushing furiously at the contact, she realized it was the first time they had touched except at those rare school dances when his hands and brow seemed unusually moist – embarrassed to be dancing with the so-called queen of Box R, she supposed. But she liked Jack; everyone did. The same could not be said for his brother, Al.

Kelly Boyle had told her once that, when he had first moved on Diamond Deuce, Jack Quester and Al as neighboring ranchers had come visiting. Al, who was a great joker, had made some disparaging remarks about Carl Tripp's looks, which led to a fist fight between the two big men. Kelly Boyle had to break it up, and Jack was upset and apologized for his belligerent brother.

She withdrew her hand, her heart pumping wildly as she said: 'Jack, would you send somebody to Diamond Deuce? To let Kelly know that I'm back?' She was trying to keep her voice level, but failed completely.

'I'll take word myself, Miss Luanne.' He was going home for a few days to help his brother in preparations for roundup.

Jack hurried away because the major came to the verandah, smoking a cheroot, brows lifted. 'Well, Luanne, what happened to Saint Louis?'

'I heard that Kelly Boyle had been jumped by four men and...'

'Only two,' he corrected. 'And that brought you home?'

'Is ... is he all right?'

'Not a scratch.'

They stood together on the verandah, not embracing, eyes searching. 'Tell me, Father, did you have anything to do with it?'

Major Ransom took time to put the cheroot back into his mouth, draw on it twice, before saying: 'The two men were on Box R payroll ... which you'll find out soon enough. But it was a private quarrel. At least, that's the story.' Finally he put his arms

94

around her and said: 'I'm glad you're home.'

'You might as well know that I love Kelly Boyle and intend to marry him.'

His hazel eyes appeared to be mischievous, but the Arctic whites did not change. 'What if I withheld permission?'

'We'd elope.'

'I was only trying to lighten the moment. We seem to have so few of them. Of course, you'll have my permission.' He stepped back, a hand remaining on her arm. 'I'm sorry we had such a violent quarrel about your mother. Not the first, I'm sorry to say. Or were you determined to run off to Saint Louis for another reason? And when you heard Kelly Boyle had faced death, you came flying home?'

'Perhaps.'

The major smiled. 'Maybe Kelly Boyle doesn't know it yet, but that young man will be working for Box R. And I'll build you a house, a fine one, better than I built for your mother. But not too far away because I want to be within shouting distance of the grandchildren you will provide.'

Now was not the time to tell him that her plans didn't include Texas. 'Thank you, Papa,' was all she said. She went into the house and climbed the polished staircase to her room.

Mrs. Blankenship was hanging up Luanne's clothes.

'Don't mention California to my father,' Luanne cautioned. 'Not just yet.'

At Diamond Deuce, Kelly Boyle threw his hat into the air, slammed Jack Quester on the back so hard that his knees threatened to cave, and shouted: 'The best news I ever heard!'

'You lucky, lucky man,' Jack Quester said with a sad smile.

Kelly Boyle didn't need anyone to tell him he was the luckiest of men. Two hours later on the overcast day, bathed and shaved and so excited he threatened to blow apart, he was running up the verandah steps at Box R. Luanne flew out the door and into his arms.

After several moments of tasting the tears of joy on her lovely mouth, he heard her say: 'I saw you coming and told Sarah to hurry up with a basket.'

'Don't ever, ever run away from me again.'

Presently the major carried out the basket the cook had hastily prepared. 'Not much of a day for a picnic,' he observed dryly as he handed Boyle the basket.

'Oh, don't worry, Papa, I'll be wearing my fur coat.' She was standing at her father's stiff back, looking as if she might spill over with laughter. As Boyle shook her father's hand, he felt the corners of his own mouth start to twitch, but managed to contain himself. Only when they were safely away from the house did they burst into laughter.

'You should have seen your face when I told Papa I'd be wearing the fur...'

'You should have seen *yours*. We better be careful after this. He might get to thinking about what's so funny between us and come looking for me with a gun.'

She moved closer in the wagon seat and hugged Boyle's arm. 'The only time he'd come after you with a gun is if you decided *not* to marry me. I told him I intended to be your wife.'

They talked about it, and then Boyle said: 'Just a few more months and we'll have a house built for us at Diamond Deuce.'

'If you sold out to your partner and we moved to California, we could be married right away.'

Boyle's face darkened. 'Carl could never handle the place on his own.'

'He more important than Luanne Ransom?' Her generous mouth smiled, but there was an unmistakable tautness at the corners.

'I guess it's one of my rôles in life to look after him.'

'Your main rôle in life is to look after me.'

'Agreed.' He kissed her. 'Only a few more months.'

In their favorite grove of trees as before he was always amazed at the perfection of her body, her breasts a size to be easily cupped in his hands, the long, pale slope of satiny skin

97

to hips gently rounded and at her fork the matching blue-black silk at brows and skull. In the confines of the wagon bed the disrobing was a production in itself. But once done, it was an incredible moment when she, wrapped in the bulky fur coat, suddenly flung it open so his eyes could feast. But only for a few moments because of the cold. And then he covered her, careful of his weight, knowing instinctively that gentleness was more pleasing to her than a sudden bull-like attack. That came later when she was as aggressive as he. And finally when she moaned and sobbed and her screams were muffled against his mouth, he knew the meaning of ecstasy.

When she could get her breath, she spoke again of marriage, and he countered by telling her about the promise he had made to his mother concerning Carl.

When he had finished, she drew back so that he could see his eyes mirrored in hers. 'What if I should become with child? Due to our adventures in my fur coat?' she asked lightly.

'I take precautions.'

'You and your precautions.' She gave him a playful slap, then said seriously: 'I want to feel *you*. Not part of a sheep. What is it made of, the bladder?'

'I never asked the sheep,' he said with a faint grin.

'Where do you get them, anyway?'

'Never mind.'

'There *was* another female in your life before me.'

'I barely remember her name.'

'Dozens, you mean.' She laughed softly and wrapped the furry arms of her coat around him. 'At least, you didn't leave a gaggle of illegitimate children along the Chisholm as I understand happens every time cowboys take a trail herd through.'

'That must have been quite a school you went to in Saint Louis.'

'Miss Gramercy is a suffragette.'

'Something I bet your father didn't know.'

'He'd have probably dragged me to a convent.'

'Maybe you'd have been better off.'

'And you'd have probably never known the absolute bliss of my fur coat.' Then she frowned and said: 'I suppose you're like all men, you want nothing but sons.'

'I'm not particular.'

'I am. I want no female child.' Her voice was strained.

'A strange thing to say.'

'No it isn't. I'm fortunate. My father is indulgent, and I have a wonderful, understanding person in you. But most are not that lucky.'

'Things are changing. You've said so yourself.'

'But maybe not in time for our daughter.

I've always been a rebel. But maybe she won't be and ... do you know the Shellys?'

He told her about meeting Rob Shelly on the road with his two cowhands.

'Shelly has a daughter, Samantha,' Luanne said. 'He calls her Sam. She's his foreman. Can you imagine? A nice girl, really. Her father's an old drunk. Once at a school dance in Bluewater he fell down. His daughter was mortified.'

'What else is exciting at these dances?' he teased.

'Well, Al Quester, the big lout, Jack's brother ... I got tired of Al patting me in the crowd so I excused myself and put a pin through my corset at just the right place. And the next time he patted, he yelped and sucked at a bloodied thumb.'

He kissed her laughing mouth and said: 'You're a witch ... you know that?'

'A witch who wants her man ... permanently.' She hugged him.

'If Al Quester does any more patting, I'll...'

'I'm sure he'll avoid my startlingly armed bosom in the future.'

'I'm glad you're not wearing formidable pins today.'

'As you can see, I don't even wear my clothes.'

He didn't have to be told. A second time that day he felt her warmth and passion.

Finally, completely spent, he glanced at

the leaden sky. 'It's getting colder. I don't want you to expire from lung congestion.'

'No worry about that, my love,' she said, meeting his smile. 'We'll have a long and happy life. Not like...'

'Not like who?' he prompted, when she frowned.

'I was thinking of Samantha Shelly. Her life is hard enough now, Lord knows. But one day some good-looking, young cowhand will come along, and she'll get married. And then will come the children and the drudgery. And at thirty she'll be all used up. A pity, really.'

'At thirty you'll be more beautiful than ever.'

'By then we'll have seen all the capitals of Europe. Travel keeps one young.'

'I've got to make a success of Diamond Deuce first.'

'Father would like you to come in with him,' she said tentatively.

'I'm my own man, Luanne. If I went in with your father, I'd be his.'

'Father has a way of weaving webs that trap what he wants.'

'This spider is a weaver of stronger webs,' Boyle said.

'I hope so, my love.' She blew her warm breath against his throat. 'I'd much rather live in California with you than have you work for my father.' She went into detail about climate, friendly Indians, and the raising of cattle or oranges, whichever he preferred.

He knew she was spinning her own webs, but it didn't matter. Eventually she would realize that their lives were meant to be lived at Diamond Deuce.

That day some of the Box R hands were moving cattle and had stopped in a stand of cottonwoods for a nooning. Boyle, taking Luanne home, drove right past them, pretending not to notice. To a man they turned their heads and stared at the major's daughter, sharing a wagon seat with one of the new owners of Diamond Deuce. Rex Uland's small eyes seemed to redden. 'The major ever give me the nod ... I got me a saddle rope that'll fit that bastard's neck just fine.'

A round little man who'd just been brought down from North Ranch made the mistake of laughing. 'Can see what you mean, Uland, you bein' sugar-tit sweet on the major's daughter.'

Uland's right fist, exploding in the man's face, knocked him sprawling back among the saddle horses that were pawing for spring grass.

'Go back to the home place an' get your time. If you're still there when I git back, there won't be enough left of you to fill a hat.'

It was about four in the morning of that same day that Joe Hagar was in his small office at one end of his *cantina* in Lucero. His nephew, Hiram stuck his thin face in the doorway. 'Fella to see you, Uncle Joe. Says he's got some private business with you.'

Because business, especially private, might mean anything from A to Z, Hi Hagar thought it wise to alert his uncle even though the place was closed for the night.

Hagar agreed. 'Send him in.'

Just as a precaution, Hagar placed his .45 under some papers on his desk. He hadn't expected to see Samuel Joseph Taylor, of all people. Hagar got up to greet his visitor. Taylor sank wearily to a chair, looking worse than before. Muddied, his arm in a sling, its bandage bloodied, whatever good looks the man might have had at one time were washed out by reddened eyes and a drooping mouth.

Hagar shut the office door, then sat down again at his desk, thinking that in a way the whole thing was kind of funny.

'Something amuse you?' Taylor demanded, when he caught Hagar almost laughing.

'Was thinkin' of your wife ... is all.'

'It's what I'm here for. My luck over there' – Taylor jerked a thumb at Mexico 'was rotten.'

'There's damn' little good luck over there now.'

'Had a big pot right on the table and the right cards, and then somebody yelled that raiders were less than a mile away. And the fools got scared and we ran and ... well, somebody got their hands on the money in the pot. Not me, of course. And me with a straight flush. You ever heard of luck so bad?'

'Might be worse,' Hagar said, in view of what the husband didn't know yet about his wife.

'A drink would help.'

Hagar got a glass and bottle from a desk drawer and poured. He handed Taylor a glass and put the bottle away.

'The bastards jumped me when I complained,' Taylor said, taking the drink at a gulp, then wiping his mouth on the back of a grimy hand. 'You can see I've got to move on. So I'll take the money you made off of her. I'm sure business has been brisk, with all the comings and goings from each side of the line.' Taylor put his glass on the floor beside his chair.

'Had a fine one lined up,' Hagar said. 'A rustler. Pockets sagging with money. I even dug out a bottle of French wine that I had hid away. But she didn't wait around.'

'What do you mean by that?' Taylor demanded, his chin in the air.

'She's gone.'

Taylor sat up straight in his chair. 'Explain that, sir.' He began fumbling for something in his coat pocket. Hagar tensed until he saw that it was a pipe. Taylor jammed the bit of the empty pipe between his teeth. 'Gone where? Where has my wife gone?' The words slurred not only from whiskey but from trying to speak with the pipe in his mouth.

'I can't put it any plainer.' Hagar was annoyed, no longer amused. 'She's left town.'

Taylor drew a deep breath, the flabby shoulders sagging. He put the pipe back into the pocket of the stained coat, seeming reluctant to withdraw his hand. His bloodshot eyes never left Hagar's small face. Out in the saloon someone was mopping the floor with a rattling of a pail, a thumping against mop boards.

Taylor said suddenly: 'Mister Hagar, I think you're a liar!'

'Careful.'

'Yes, a liar, you god-damn' pimp!'

'A man who peddles his wife has got names to call other men?' Hagar said scornfully.

'You, the scum of Lucero! I want you to know you are talking to a gentleman. Now hand over the money. She's always earned big. And she wouldn't fail me in Lucero. Even as much as she detested the place, she loves me too much for that. Now, I demand an accounting.'

'Get out,' the diminutive Hagar ordered. 'Or I'll have my nephew help throw you into what's left of the river.'

Taylor took several deep breaths. 'I'm asking you in a reasonable tone of voice ... sorry I lost my temper and said things I shouldn't have. But I ask for the money because I need it desperately. And I want her because...'

'Because without her you can't make a nickel,' Hagar said contemptuously. Low on the social scale himself, he might be, but at this pre-dawn hour he had found an inferior.

The pocket where Taylor had dropped his pipe suddenly acquired a small brown hole which ejected a lance of flame and began to smoke, a sharp, cracking sound from the discharge of a small weapon. Hagar fell back in his chair, wearing a startled look. And even then, as he wavered, his hand shot to a pile of papers on the desk and the big pistol.

As Taylor's alcohol-riddled brain realized the sudden danger, the hole in the pocket erupted a second time just as a violent concussion rattled the furniture. A bullet from Hagar's .45 blew Taylor over backwards, but already the .32-caliber slug out of the two-shot Derringer had gone straight into the saloonman's heart.

Hi Hagar came pounding into the office on his thin legs. With him was the swamper whose round face was flushed with excitement.

Hagar leaned over his uncle. 'Dead,' he muttered, the corners of his mouth quirked into a borderline smile. He went to the other man whom he vaguely remembered having seen in Lucero a time or two. 'Also dead,' he announced to the swamper with some satisfaction.

Cocking his head, he listened for sounds that indicated others on their way to investigate the gunfire, but the only sounds were the distant barking of dogs. In this late 19th-Century border country, gunshots were common as salt on eggs.

'Looks like I own myself a saloon,' Hi Hagar announced as he draped a friendly arm across the swamper's shoulder. 'Barney, let's haul 'em both out the back door. An' let the boys across the river take credit for killin' 'em. It'll keep that deputy from Bluewater from pokin' his nose in where he ain't wanted. An' you'll earn a bonus. A good one. Say, ten dollars.'

Barney eagerly assisted his new boss in dragging the two bodies across sand and meager flow of water. The deceased were hidden in cattails on the Mexican side.

Weeks later the bodies were found, or what was left of them after predators. Neither one could hardly be identified as human. But on one of them was a letter, the ink not quite washed out of soggy paper, showing that he was Samuel Joseph Taylor, late of San Francisco. There was speculation that the other one might be what was left of Joe Hagar, but no one really cared. Hi Hagar's story – that his uncle had gone to do business with rustlers and never returned – had been accepted.

Chapter Six

Two days in a row Boyle neglected ranch business and saw Luanne, only because he felt something beginning to slip away and didn't know how to stop it. Only a little of their time together was devoted to their sensual pleasure. Mostly, it was Luanne's talking about California and a schoolmate now living there who wrote glowing letters. When Boyle got home, he stood in the yard, trying to make himself proud of how far he and Carl had come in life, but today it was like trying to summon up shards of last night's dream that, during sleep, had seemed so vivid but in daylight had shattered and faded to nothing.

Pete Lambourne came bowlegging up from the bunkhouse, sawed-off shotgun tucked under an arm. 'If it wasn't for you, I'd clear out,' the old man announced.

Boyle looked at the tight mouth framed by gray whiskers. 'All right, Pete, what's Carl done this time?'

'Nothin' special ... it's just that he's so damned ornery ... with me, with his wife ... everybody.'

Boyle put a hand on the old man's shoulder, remembering that, when it came time to cut down their crew to three men after driving their herd onto Diamond Deuce, Carl had cast a negative vote for Pete Lambourne.

'He's too old, Kelly,' Carl Tripp had said.

'Isn't there such a thing as loyalty? Hell, Pete's made every trail drive with us and did the work of two men. Besides, he's an expert brander. We need him.'

That had ended the matter, but Lambourne must have suspected the argument because he and Tripp got along worse than before. He had an idea what was eating Carl, a man with his looks who had managed to capture the heart of a handsome woman like Florence. And people were never letting him forget it. Boyle tried to explain to Lambourne, but the old man only shook his head.

'Hell, without you Carl wouldn't last long enough for spit to reach the puddle.'

Boyle looked around. 'Where's Carl?'

'Went up to Lucero.

'Oh, Christ...!'

'Ain't what you're thinkin'. Though, mebby wife or no wife, he'll grab hisself a bird outta the cat house. But, anyhow, he went to fetch some of his wife's things she left there.'

'You must be mistaken. A lady like Missus Tripp wouldn't be in a place like Lucero.'

'That's where Carl met her.'

Boyle gave the old brander a skeptical look. 'How do you know that, Pete?'

'Heard him yellin' it one day when him an' her was riled up ... or rather he was. I feel sorry for her. Livin' somewheres else might be easier on my nerves.'

'Pete, we've been through a lot together, and one day, when we make some good cattle sales, I aim to see that a couple of houses are built here ... with enough distance between them so our wives, Carl's and mine, will have shouting room. I want you to stay around, *compadre*, because I need a steady man to keep an eye on the kids we'll be having underfoot.'

'You still got moon eyes for that Ransom gal?'

Boyle drew a deep breath – 'I have.' – and felt a nudge of despair when he thought of their argument today. He would try tomorrow, and then, if she wasn't convinced, the campaign would have to be postponed in favor of roundup.

He had expected her to be sullen, as she had been yesterday, but her eyes were bright and mischievous, and, when they were together in the wagon, she spoke of the decadent court, so-called, of the French kings and how they found their pleasures.

'Let me prove my love,' she whispered hoarsely, and her mane of silky hair became an umbrella at his lap. A volcanic experience but he missed holding her.

'You're shocked,' she said afterward.

'Nothing you ever did would shock me.'

She nestled against him. 'Our marriage will consist of long, exciting nights. And in California with the scent of orange blossoms in the air, we'll be driven even wilder.'

'Luanne, I need a little more time.'

'How do you think I feel? ... sneaking off into the trees like a housemaid with the butler. Don't you think I want a house with a bed in it? ... and someone to keep the place clean and make our lives easy. Don't we deserve that much?'

He hadn't wanted to dig into their reserves, his and Carl's, because the cache was down to a few hundred dollars. After buying the ranch and paying expenses, there hadn't been much left, and there had been horses to buy and repairs to make. After they sold cattle, things would be different.

'All right,' he said, sitting up, 'let's see if we can't rent a house in Bluewater. There are some fairly nice places.'

'You must know more than I do, then. I've only lived here most of my life, and I recall no suitable houses.'

'You're being stiff-necked.'

'Of course, I am.' The violet eyes snapped. 'When I marry, I want to live away from my father. I won't insist on California, but...'

111

She gripped his shoulders. 'Oh, Kelly, why are you so damnably stubborn, and after I proved to you the depth of my love?'

'Luanne, I've tried time and again to explain.'

'Make Tripp buy out your share of the ranch. I'll talk to my father. He'll be so glad to be rid of me that he'll loan Tripp the money.'

'Diamond Deuce would belong to your father, even if I'd let you go ahead with it. Carl wouldn't stand a chance.'

'Isn't he ... for God's sake ... man enough to stand on his own two feet? He's older than you, isn't he? He certainly looks it. And he's bigger than you and certainly should be able to fend for himself...' Her voice trailed away under the onslaught of gray eyes. 'Oh, Kelly, don't spoil things for us. Just because your mother asked you to look after Carl Tripp ... she probably only meant when you were boys. Not grown men.'

'Listen to me once more.' Catching her by the arms, he spoke softly, urgently. 'Carl may be my half brother ... illegitimate.'

'We all have skeletons ... every family. I'm almost sure ... no, I'm positive that Major Ransom is not my father. My father was a cowboy named Sean. I never knew his last name, but my mother loved him. I haven't let it color my life. I'm standing on my own two feet and fighting for what I want, what

I believe to be right for myself and the one man in the world I'll ever love ... will love till my last breath. Kelly, let's get out of Texas.'

'You didn't let me finish,' he said quietly. He told her that in Mexico the story was that Carl's parents – the Tripps – had been killed in a runaway, Carl, a baby, the only survivor. 'Later from things my father said when I was a boy made me believe my mother had been married to someone named Tripp. But my mother never mentioned it, and the only time I heard it from my father was when Carl did something to displease him. Then one day he said my mother hadn't been married to Carl's father.'

'So he's your illegitimate half-brother ... what of it? I'm also of the same stripe, so it seems. Kelly, can't you for once be your own man?'

'My mother was a beautiful woman and rich. And I can see now that under the circumstances my father felt he had to accept Carl. When she was burning up with fever at the last, she told me she had been ... raped. At first she tried to kill the baby in her womb, but was so revolted that she went ahead and gave birth. Then she was going to give the baby away, but she couldn't. For some reason her love for Carl was almost an obsession.' He lowered his head. 'I know she loved Carl more than she did me. I guess it was pity as much as anything.'

'Raped ... my God how awful.'

'Now you know it all.'

'Give into me, Kelly. Just this once. Whether it's California or wherever, I'll be a good wife. I just want to get away from my father.'

'Yes, I can understand...'

'You have your ghosts in Carl's father and your mother. I have mine. So let's make new lives for ourselves ... away from all this.'

'If I give up on Diamond Deuce now, I lose everything.'

'I'll make my father buy you out for a hundred thousand dollars.'

'Now that's a pipe dream, if I ever heard one.'

'Yes, I guess it is,' she said after a moment, 'all of it ... *everything.* You might as well take me home.'

'Look, along with the face that Carl got from his father, whoever he was, he also got his brain. Carl isn't very smart. My mother wanted to protect him from life, and she made me promise to carry on.'

'Yes, of course.'

'If, after I get Diamond Deuce so it's a paying ranch and you haven't changed your mind about California, then I'll...' *Give up my dream for yours.* But he couldn't bring himself to put it quite that way. He did say: 'Then we'll move on to wherever you'd like.'

'Hmm'

'As long as you obviously don't want to live at Box R, then we'll find a house in Bluewater.'

'The wife in Bluewater ... the husband at Diamond Deuce?'

'Luanne, I'll buy the fastest saddle horse in the county, and you'll be surprised how many nights I'll be home.' He tried to sound exuberant, but it finally died in his throat. They sat looking at each other in the wagon, wind-flung strands of blue-black hair across her forehead.

On the drive back to Box R headquarters she was silent. No matter what he said, there was no response. Their parting at Box R was cool.

Major Ransom entered the house as his daughter was on the stairs. 'You and Kelly quarreled. What about?'

She paused on the landing. 'He told you we quarreled?'

'He told me nothing. One look at your faces when you pulled in was enough.'

'I'm used to having my own way is all ... thanks to you.'

'You've met a man at last with spurs at his heels.' He climbed to the landing where she had halted, tried to take her arm, but she pulled away.

Sunlight through stained glass, a deep rose color, made her cheeks seem flushed. 'I wish I'd gone to Saint Louis ... and stayed.'

'Let me tell you something, Luanne. Kelly Boyle is not a man you can rope and make toe your line.'

Her sculptured chin came up, and she met his eyes. 'Then, quite possibly, he's not the man for me,' she said in a dead voice.

'For his sake, you might be right.'

She turned her back, which infuriated him, and climbed to her room.

This and other events of the past few days had put him in an ugly mood. Rex Uland was waiting for him in the ranch office, wanting to know if Box R should be represented in town when the other ranchers came in to discuss roundup.

'Let 'em flounder on their own,' Ransom snapped, throwing himself into a leather chair.

'Seen Boyle's partner an' that good-lookin' wife of his in town. Sure beats all ... how a buck-toothed *hombre* like him ever got such a jewel.'

'For Christ's sake, Rex!' the major exploded. 'I don't give one damn how he happened to get her. Now clear out and leave me alone!'

This outburst caused Uland to blink, but he knew enough not to argue.

When Uland was gone, the major bolted the door, then got a bottle of whiskey. As he drank in his office, he thought back to that day in Lucero that had seen the beginning of his ruptured pride, a day when wind spat sand and grit and rolled tumbleweeds along the streets. Then her name had been Taylor. Now she called herself Florence Tripp. The mind of Major Ransom burned with thoughts of murder when he thought of Carl Tripp.

Chapter Seven

Twice Boyle rode out of the way to Box R, and each time Mrs. Blankenship came to the verandah, the round little face impassive, to say that Miss Luanne was indisposed. Whatever in hell that meant, he would try again.

He was in an angry mood when Carl Tripp said that as long as he was going to town, would he pick up yard goods for Florence?

Boyle held out his hand. 'You got money to pay for it?'

Tripp reddened. 'I done spent my last dime.'

'Yeah. How many times have I told you that monte is a Mexican's game?' He almost mentioned Tripp's journey to Lucero, stronghold of the monte aficionados.

Tripp said: 'Them grea ... some of them fellas cheat. You notice I never said greaser?'

Boyle looked into the stricken, homely face, thinking of his mother: *Aim high and take Carl with you*. Jesus! ... the chains a man was obligated to wear. Or was he? Then Boyle wiped it from his mind and said: 'What color yard goods does your wife want?'

'I'll go ask.' Carl went loping across the ranch yard. 'What color you want, Flo?' he shouted at the house.

'It doesn't matter,' she replied, sounding depressed.

That day, when Boyle stopped off at Box R, Mrs. Blankenship didn't say Luanne was indisposed. She said stiffly: 'Miss Luanne has gone riding ... with a friend.' She went into the house.

What friend? Boyle speculated a dozen times that day.

That evening at Diamond Deuce he went for a walk, far past the windmill and the pasture where their horses, rumps to the wind, were silhouetted against the hazy twilight. Trees were filled with chirping birds. He thought of his frail mother in Mexico, his father, and the grand plans that included his best friend, Montez. The many hectares of land coveted, acquired, then more land, and more, land marked by boundaries of rock walls three to four feet high, built by former owners with what amounted to slave labor. One day the *peones* would be successful against a brutal regime, but his father's dreams had vanished overnight in terror. On the chill evening, Kelly Boyle pondered the substance of his own dreams. Luanne's face floated always before him. He swore into the wind. Gone riding with a friend ... *what friend?*

The following week Boyle and Tripp were to

join other small ranch owners at the Great River Saloon to discuss plans for roundup to start in three days. In Bluewater, Tripp and his wife parted in front of the store, she going inside to shop, Carl at a lumbering walk going across the street. Boyle waited out front for him. The Quester brothers were already inside.

Rob Shelly pulled up with a slim young rider and stepped down stiffly. 'Boyle, this here's my daughter, Samantha.' He pointed at the young rider. He was wheezing badly. 'She'll give me hell if I call her Sam.'

Boyle's hat came off. So this was Sam, the tough foreman. He smiled and said: 'Howdy, Miss Samantha.'

She swung down on long legs, tied her horse, then thrust out her hand. 'Hello, Mister Boyle. I've heard a lot about you.'

'From some sheriff?'

She smiled at that. Her teeth were rather large but perfectly formed with a slight gap in front. 'Forget the Miss ... if you'll call me plain Samantha...?'

'All right ... plain Samantha.'

Her green eyes crinkled at the corners.

Then to please her, he said: 'You're hardly plain ... more the opposite, I'd say.'

'How nice, Mister Boyle.'

'Make it Kelly.'

'Why don't you come over and take supper with us one day after roundup?' she suggested. 'You can spend the night. There are spare bunks in the bunkhouse.'

'One of these days, sure.' Boyle looked her over. 'Well, well,' he heard himself saying, 'I'd heard that Shelly had a daughter, but I didn't realize she was tall and attractive.'

'Lanky and freckled is how they usually describe me.' She laughed. 'Till I was fifteen, I looked like two slats nailed to a crosspiece. But I've filled out some.'

Boyle agreed. Her flat-crowned hat was tipped back on the tight coils of braided red hair. Her shirt was checked, the work pants plain canvas. Her spurs gleamed in the sun. She gave Boyle a wave of the hand, ran across the street, and took the verandah steps of the Miller Store two at a time.

In the Great River Saloon, over whiskey, the men discussed the work ahead. Jack Quester had drawn a map of the proposed roundup camps. He explained about Box R to Kelly Boyle. 'They always keep to themselves at roundup ... in case you worry about trouble.'

'Boxer doesn't worry me,' Boyle responded, running Box R together as most of the natives did.

'Well, I thought perhaps after you killing Billy Saxton and blowing Chollmar's arm...' Jack Quester gave an awkward laugh. 'On the other hand, I guess you can take care of yourself.' Jack went on to explain that the major's crew always worked East Ranch first, then North Ranch, and finally Central, the main ranch. They always maintained their own camp, away from the others, and the major never took part in roundup.

'His branders handle any of our calves they run into and throw them in with their gather. The last few days of roundup we cut out our own.'

Boyle frowned. 'What's to keep his men from slapping Box R on our calf crop?'

Jack Quester's rather good-looking face was troubled. 'I'd rather not step on the major's toes by complaining. After all, I do work for him.'

Al Quester, who had been drinking steadily, slammed a large, hair-backed fist onto the bar top, making the glasses jump. 'Ain't a damn' thing we can do about it, Boyle. Not 'less we hire us an army.'

'Maybe have it out with the major before roundup?' Boyle suggested.

But Jack Quester shook his head. 'Let it ride till next time. Maybe we can form an association by then.'

Carl Tripp, who had remained out of the discussion, seemed to feel it was time, as half owner of Diamond Deuce, to offer an opinion. 'Seems to me,' Tripp began, 'that...'

'Wa'al, if it ain't Romeo hisself,' Al Quester interrupted. He looked Tripp over and said: 'How come it's you handsome fellas who

122

always end up with the best-lookin' wimmen?'

Tripp reddened. Somebody down the bar guffawed.

Rob Shelly, who nearly always seemed out of breath, failed to hide a grin. 'Now, boys, simmer down.'

But Al persisted, and finally Jack had to tell his brother to leave Tripp alone.

Al showed his large teeth, standing with thick arms akimbo. 'Why'd a woman ruther cuddle up to a mud fence like you,' he asked Tripp, 'than with a good-looker like me?'

As laughter swept the saloon, Tripp lunged. But Boyle caught his partner by an arm and swung him hard against the bar. 'Let's all have us a drink,' Boyle suggested, 'and stop this nonsense.'

'Good as done,' said Jack Quester, pouring into each glass.

They discussed the men needed for roundup, the distances to be covered, the probable weather. It was usually dry during roundup, somebody said, but there was always a possibility of rain. Mud could be hell on men and horses.

Bored with the discussion, Al Quester directed his cruel humor at the wheezing Rob Shelly. While the older man had his back turned, talking to Boyle, Al Quester stole his whiskey glass, emptied it into a spittoon, then refilled the glass with vinegar from the kitchen. In the hazy light of afternoon, the contents of the glass almost matched the colour of the whiskey. Al Quester tried to dissemble a look of innocence, but his mouth corners collapsed and his yellow eyes danced with amusement. Boyle missed the play because Shelly was talking about the railroad.

'Ask me, it'll be five years before rails get this far,' Shelly wheezed. 'Mebby longer.'

'Don't be too sure,' Jack Quester put in. 'Major Ransom usually gets what he wants.'

That was when Rob Shelly turned, picked up his glass, and downed the contents in a gulp. For an instant he stood at the bar with knees sprung, looking as if someone had kicked him in the groin. Then he took a great rattling breath, the wrinkles around his mouth were stretched, and he began to gag. He collapsed in a heap, then began to flop around on the floor, fighting for breath. Everyone stood around, wondering what to do. It was Kelly Boyle who shouted for someone to bring water.

Sid Bartline, the saloonman, dashed from behind his bar with a bucket of water which he started to throw into the face of the gasping Shelly. Boyle snatched the bucket and filled a glass with water. Some of it he got down the rancher's throat, but most of it was spewed onto the floor. Gradually the man's breathing returned to normal.

Al Quester was guffawing, but those who

had joined in the earlier laughter were now quiet.

Jack Quester was furious. 'Damn it, Al, one day your jokes will get somebody killed.'

When Rob Shelly realized his misery was the result of Al Quester's practical joke, he climbed stiffly to his feet and reached under his brush jacket for a gun. Someone yelled a warning. Men spun aside. But Al Quester just stood with large hands on hips, looking at the older Shelly with faint contempt on the broad face, as if daring him to draw the gun.

Finally Shelly ducked his head in embarrassment, saying – 'See you boys at roundup.' – and left the saloon.

Boyle's eyes, washed of color, settled on Al Quester. 'If he'd been ten years younger, he'd have blown off your granite head.'

Quester hunched his heavy shoulders. 'You got more to say about it, Mister Diamond Deuce?'

'It was a stinking thing to do to a man his age!'

'You don't say.' Al Quester's broad smile was meant to be disarming, for he suddenly lunged at Boyle and threw a wide, looping right.

Kelly Boyle danced aside, let knuckles whistle past his face, then drove a left into a faint pouch just above the belt buckle. A right to the jaw sent Al Quester crashing to the floor. There he lay on his back, staring blankly at the ceiling.

'Bravo!' someone shouted. 'Been waitin' years to see that done.'

Sid Bartline waved his hands, used his saloonman's soothing voice to keep trouble from spreading. 'It's all over with, boys. A round of drinks on the house.'

As Al was beginning to stir, Jack Quester leaned down, lifted his brother's gun, and jammed it into his own belt. 'He's my brother, but sometimes...' Jack Quester let it hang there.

Bartline said: 'Boys, the Lord knows there'll be trouble enough after roundup ... when everybody's wore out an' drunk. Let's save it for then.'

Strangely Al Quester didn't seem particularly angered, when he got to his feet and eyed Boyle. 'You musta hit me with a crowbar' He rubbed his swelling jaw.

'Hope it taught you a lesson, Brother,' Jack Quester said. 'Al, you head for home and get things ready. See you at roundup. I ... I have to stop off at Box R. Some ... book work I have to do for the major.' He gave Kelly Boyle a strained smile, avoided meeting his eyes, and started for the double doors. But the trouble wasn't over.

The doors parted to the banging of Samantha Shelly's elbows. She came storming up to where Al Quester was just putting on his coat.

'I heard what you did!'

'It was only funnin'...'

'You ever harm my father again, and I'll shoot you. Oh, I won't kill you. But I'll put a hole in your leg that you'll remember.' Green eyes flashing, the big saloon quiet as a church during silent prayer, she turned on Sid Bartline. 'Don't send any more gallons of whiskey out to the ranch for my father.'

'Miss Shelly, I only send what is paid for,' the saloonman said lamely, 'by somebody else.'

'Please tell Major Ransom ... no more. If he was here, I'd tell him myself.' Turning on her heel, she stalked out.

In the sudden quiet somebody said: 'God help the *hombre* that ever hitches up with her.'

Boyle thought of stopping by Box R on his way home, then decided to let Luanne get word to him if she wanted to see Kelly Boyle again. For a time he was satisfied with his decision, but he didn't sleep much that night. In the morning Carl Tripp wanted to borrow a few dollars so he could buy a tent.

'Tent for what?' Boyle demanded, out of sorts.

'Roundup. I aim to take Flo.'

Boyle was exasperated. 'Roundup's no place for a pretty woman.'

'I ain't gonna leave her home alone,' Tripp

said stubbornly.

Boyle tried to paw through the clutter of his mind, filled with Luanne Ransom and the big homely man who stood before him, and find a solution. He suggested Felicita De Gama stay with Florence through roundup.

Tripp sulked, but finally gave in.

The next morning Boyle was heading for the De Gama place to see Felicita about staying with Florence when he ran into Rob Shelly and his two-man crew. They hooked knees over saddle horns, smoked, and jawed about the ordeal of roundup, expressing hope that the weather would hold and no one be hurt. Boyle was anxious to be on his way, but out of politeness asked about Shelly's daughter.

'Sammy's fine, just fine,' the older man replied. 'Does a man's work helpin' me out. Since her ma died, she ain't had many wimmen folks around her. She looks right purty in a dress.'

'Shouldn't wonder. Well, guess I'll be on my way.'

Shelly sighed deeply, then said in his wheezy voice: 'Jack Quester buyed himself a new buggy. Seen him an' Luanne Ransom in it,' the rancher finished slyly.

Boyle felt as if someone had thrown ice water in his face. He was glad for the interruption of Chico, Felicita's young son. The boy was coming toward them across the flats on a mule. The boy waved to Boyle.

'¿*Que tal*, Chico?' Boyle sang out. Then the boy suddenly saw Shelly and the two Broken Wheel riders and altered course. He went spurring in the direction of home.

'I wonder what the little greaser kid's been up to,' Shelly mused. 'Turnin' tail like he done.'

'He's no greaser. The De Gamas are my friends.'

'Won't be your friends if you catch 'em slow-elkin' your beef,' Shelly said.

'They're hardly cow thieves, damn it.'

'I'll bet they never eat their own beef'

Boyle held himself in, knowing there was no use arguing for the dignity of a widow, trying to hold her small family together with a few head of cattle and an acre or two of maize. Obviously Rob Shelly had a blind side when it came to skins darker than his own. Boyle had had enough of the man for one day.

He was turning his horse, when Shelly said: 'I ever catch that kid around my cows, I'll beat his ass with a rope end.'

'By God, not as long as I'm around you won't!' Boyle said in a hard voice.

Shelly looked startled and started to wheeze. 'I figured you was *Tejano*. Wasn't you born here?'

'What the hell difference does that make?'

'Well, if you was, you'd know you can't trust a one of 'em.' Shelly flung out an arm in the direction taken by the fleeing boy. 'Seems you got some things to learn.'

'Tell me what,' Boyle said in an icy voice.

Shelly seemed to realize suddenly that he'd been kicking the wrong horse. He looked nervous, as if recalling that the big, gray-eyed man was the one who had done the murderous shooting down by Hank Wendover's scow not too long ago. 'If you say the De Gamas are *muy bueno*...,' he began lamely.

'I do say so,' Boyle cut in.

Shelly tried on a smile that quickly collapsed. 'They'll never have no trouble from me.'

Boyle finally caught up with Chico, and they rode together. He got Felicita's promise to stay with Florence Tripp until roundup was over. Well, that much had been accomplished anyway, he thought, as he started home. Clouds boiled in, and it turned cold, which didn't help his mood because Luanne was walking over his naked body with needles projecting from the soles of her shoes. So Jack Quester 'buycd a new buggy,' as Rob Shelly had put it. Jack was only a part-time rancher and bookkeeper. Just someone for Luanne to lean her pretty head on while gnashing her teeth at Kelly Boyle?

Chapter Eight

The next morning Boyle was about to slide a wheel onto the greased axle of the Diamond Deuce chuck wagon when Samantha Shelly came pounding into the yard on a big sorrel. She pulled up to glare at Boyle, crouched beside the wagon, her face in the shadow of a big hat brim. Her freckles seemed to have multiplied. Boyle got up, wiping his hands on a rag.

'Morning,' he said, not liking the light in her green eyes.

Swinging a long leg over the saddle, she dropped to the ground, licking the end of her quirt menacingly against the hem of her divided leather riding skirt. 'You threatened my father, Kelly Boyle,' she charged angrily. 'As a result, he was sick most of the night.'

He thought he knew what she meant. 'I didn't like hearing him say he'd take a rope end to the De Gama boy.'

'Why would he say a thing like that?'

When Boyle had finished explaining, she flicked her quirt at a weed top, clipping it neatly. 'I'm very protective of my father,' she said, meeting his eyes. 'And I get mad when people pick on him.'

131

'You proved that when you came charging into the saloon...' He broke off with a wry grin.

'I can understand why Dad said those things about the De Gamas. I know Felicita, and I like her. But my father is of the old mentality. General Santa Anna and the Alamo and the rest of it. Forgetting that this was once Mexico and that we ran them out. Maybe it's a guilty conscience.'

'I admire you for sticking up for your father.'

'You do?'

'A young girl, riding miles across lonely country, just to rage at a neighbor she thought had maligned her father.'

'You use big words. Not many around here would know what they meant. Luanne Ransom and her father, of course...'

Mention of Luanne caused him to flinch. 'You've obviously had schooling yourself.'

'Some. My mother was a schoolteacher and a great buyer of books.'

'You friends with Luanne Ransom?'

'In a way, I guess. But I had an argument with her father. So I haven't seen her for quite a while.'

'The major's not easy to get along with.'

'He sends whiskey to Dad, hoping he'll drink himself to death or get really sick. And that I, weak-kneed female that I am, or am supposed to be, will grovel at his feet and be thankful for the few dollars he'll bestow on me after I sign a quit-claim deed, then go to Arizona and live with my aunt.'

'Got a hunch the major wouldn't find you all that easy.'

'You just read my mind.' She grinned, showing her large teeth with the slight gap in front.

'Jack Quester mentioned forming an association. I think it's a good idea. One way for all of us to stand up to the major.'

'I intend to, because I'll be working Broken Wheel for the rest of my days. It's all I've got. And I sure won't trade it for Aunt Margaret and needlepoint.'

Florence stepped from a lean-to where a kettle of clothes was boiling over a wood fire. She seemed embarrassed to find another woman in the yard and wiped her perspiring face on the edge of an apron.

Boyle introduced them. While he finished replacing the wagon wheel, he noticed that Samantha Shelly was showing Carl's wife how to beat dirt out of clothes with an axe handle.

'Things I never learned,' Florence remarked in despair.

He hoped Samantha would stay for the noon meal because there were questions he had wanted to ask about Luanne that had been interrupted by Florence's sudden appearance from the laundry shed. But she excused herself, saying there were plans she had to make for roundup, the green eyes shining, a half smile on her lips as if she might be making some kind of a mystery out of it.

Kelly Boyle was checking over the remuda an hour after Samantha had left, when he had other visitors. It was the De Gamas, Jaime, the uncle, and Guillermo, or Chico as he was usually called, the nephew.

'*¡Mi hermana!*' Jaimie cried, and Boyle turned cold, thinking something had happened to his sister, Felicita. Jaime De Gama, a chunky man in his late twenties, finally managed to calm himself enough to tell Boyle in Spanish that Diego Esparza was at their *ranchita*. 'He wants to see you, Kelly.'

'Is Felicita all right?' Boyle demanded.

Jaime nodded. 'I didn't feel right about leaving her alone, but she told me to come and to bring Chico. She doesn't like him to be around rough men and hear the things they say.'

'Is she nervous, Jaime?'

'A little, I guess.'

Boyle, mounted on the fastest horse at Diamond Deuce, rode hard. Jaime and the boy, at Boyle's order, followed at a slower pace. He didn't want the boy to be possibly involved in trouble. He trusted Diego Esparza as he would a scorpion on a privy seat.

Finally through the trees he made out the small adobe house, the barn with its lean-to where Jaime slept, the corrals. Smoke drifted from a mud chimney. Several horses were in the yard, also men in big hats with crossed bandoleers on their chests. Boyle stiffened, as they watched him, but made no move toward pistol or rifle.

He dismounted. Esparza strutted up. In his *charro* outfit he looked elegant. His teeth were very white below a thin, black mustache.

'*Mucho gusto en ver le, Diego*,' Boyle said, but it wasn't a pleasure to see this acquaintance from his boyhood in Mexico.

Esparza, a year older than Boyle, insisted on the *abrazo*, as if they had been old friends. Following the embrace, Boyle saw Felicita step from the house, her proud Castilian face showing tension. Boyle lifted a hand, which she acknowledged by a tilt of her head, but he did not go to her. He said to Esparza: 'So now you threaten pretty widows, eh?'

Esparza laughed, took his arm, and walked with him away from the house and the eight men in the yard. 'I remember your father well.' Esparza spoke in English. 'He got lucky and had his own *rancho grande* with Montez. There were good times for a few years. Then they turned bad.'

'Are the bad times to come again with

Diego Esparza?'

Esparza's dark eyes assessed Boyle with mockery and challenge – eyes from his Mexican mother. There was little to indicate that his father had been *norteamericano*. 'I am told you are to marry the daughter of Major Ransom.'

'Who told you that?'

'He did.'

Boyle shrugged, said carefully: 'I wouldn't count on it too much, Diego.'

Esparza frowned, jammed thumbs into a wide belt inlaid with silver. 'What's happened?' They had halted by towering mesquite.

'Call it a lover's quarrel,' Boyle said, feeling his way.

They started walking again. On the far side of the river were knots of men and cook fires, smoke rising toward a leaden sky. An aroma of cooking meat drifted from that side of the river – Mexican *vaca* or a steer from the American side?

'Tell me about this Ransom. Is he a real major or simply a man who pinned on his own braid?'

'Real enough.'

'You are to be his partner, so he says.'

Boyle knew it best to settle the matter now, but also to choose his words. 'I told the major I want no part of any trouble across the line. I won't be his partner, now or ever.'

'I see.'

'You grew up with the trouble. I'm surprised you'd want any of it now.'

Esparza stretched out his arms, the fingers curled. 'I feel power. A wonderful feeling, Don Kelly. In order to maintain that power, I need weapons. Shipments from the east were supposed to reach me. But the cargo of a certain ship at Vera Cruz was confiscated.'

'¡Aiii! Díaz is already sending his dogs to nip at your heels,' Boyle said in Spanish.'

'Perhaps not Díaz. Perhaps a rival. I think Porfirio Díaz and I are of a single mind concerning this border country.'

'As you say ... perhaps.'

Esparza flicked a thumbnail across his mustache. 'In these days of swift changes, it is best to know which side of the river has the quicksand.'

Boyle tensed at the anger in the other man's voice. Should Esparza attempt to whistle up his men, he would ram a gun in his belly and force him to get his eight men to the far side of the river with the rest of his followers. Then Boyle would get Felicita to safety before turning Esparza loose. But on this day Esparza wasn't after trouble, only information. He wanted to know if the major was an honorable man, and in his reply Boyle again was careful: 'I've had no business dealings with him.'

'He insists you'll be with him in the business of supplying me with rifles.'

Boyle stood with right hand relaxed, fingers dangling below the tip of his gun holster. Felicita had gone back into the house. The eight men were up now, standing beside their horses. On the far side, the rest of Esparza's troop still lounged around the cook fires, smoke still ballooning above the trees.

'I won't be a part of the major's blood-letting,' Boyle said quietly.

'You are stubborn.'

'So I've been told,' he admitted coldly, thinking of Luanne.

'I take great risk to come to this side of the line just to see my old friend, Kelly Boyle.' Esparza wore a faint smile. 'You seem in good health ... for the present.'

'Don't threaten me, Diego. And, by the way, the De Gamas are my friends. If harm comes to them...' He let it hang there between them.

'They are of my blood. Why should I harm them?'

'The man who killed her husband over a horse was also of their blood.'

Esparza shrugged. 'It seems I will have to deal with Major Ransom without your help. But, who knows?' He offered his hand. Boyle hesitated, then shook it. '*Hasta la próxima vez*,' Esparza said in parting.

'Until next time, yes.' But Boyle had no intention of meeting him again.

Only when Esparza and his eight men crossed the river did Kelly Boyle relax. He went into the house where Felicita stood at a window.

'They've gone,' Boyle said, studying her face, something unreadable in the dark eyes, an unusual tension at the corners of the handsome mouth. 'Did they give you trouble?'

She sank to a chair, elbows on the table, hands together almost in an attitude of prayer. 'I thank God that Chico and Jaime weren't here.'

Boyle walked around the table and placed a hand on her shoulder, felt her trembling. 'They did treat you badly,' he said in a hard voice.

'At least Esparza didn't turn me over to his men.'

It took Boyle a minute to find his voice; most of the color had washed out of his eyes, leaving them bleak as the gray of a winter sky. 'One day, when I see him, I'll cut off both of his ears, as a sign that he is a violator of women.'

Felicita's hand flashed to his that had dropped instinctively to the butt of the holstered .44. 'Don't. It is over and done and ... and I have lived with worse things.' Her voice broke, but only for a moment, and he knew she was thinking of her dead husband.

Then he reminded her of her promise to

stay with Florence Tripp for the duration of roundup. 'Best for you to be out of reach for a while.'

'He won't come back. He has more women on that side of the line than we have gnats over here.'

'All the same, one day he'll pay for it.'

By the time Boyle was ready to leave, Jaime and the boy had reached the ranch. He told them of Felicita's temporary move to Diamond Deuce. It was agreed that Chico would stay in Bluewater as a boarder. Jaime would be working roundup.

Boyle shook Jaime's hand before he leaned down and gave Chico an *abrazo*. Then he stepped to Felicita, who had erased the hurt from her face so that her brother and son wouldn't guess. But when Boyle gave her a hug, and she kissed his cheek, he felt the heat of a scalding tear. He vowed then that one day he would cut off more than the ears of Diego Esparza.

Roundup was a time to wear a man thin not only in body but temper. Should he have been plagued all year by secret rages, at roundup they were compounded and at the boiling point. Everywhere was confusion: maddened steers, cows resenting separation from calves, a cow more dangerous because, when charging a horseman or a man afoot, the eyes were open, not closed as in the case of a bull. Kelly Boyle's crew, in addition to Carl Tripp and himself, included Pete Lambourne, Smoot, Tinkey, and Felicita's brother, Jaime. The few head of De Gama cattle would be included in the roundup.

Having Samantha Shelly at camp was a big surprise. The first day, working with her father and their two-man crew, she rode after cattle deep in the brush, strictly against her father's wishes. When she took a bad spill and was nearly trampled, a vote was taken among the ranch owners. Either she accepted a less dangerous chore at roundup, or she had to go home. Her father was delighted. After much argument, she gave in, jammed her hat down over her coils of red braids, and helped Pete Lambourne with the branding. After the first day the old man admitted she was the best helper he'd ever had. At night, when she crawled into her small tent and tied the flaps shut, Carl Tripp grumbled that Boyle wouldn't let him bring Florence to camp, but that Rob Shelly had brought his daughter.

'I don't think her father had much to say about it, Carl,' Boyle said, when they were eating steak and beans after a rough day in the brush.

'Main idea is she's here an' my wife ain't.'

'Samantha does a day's work, and all your wife could do is sit around and look pretty.

Kind of dangerous, if you know what I mean.'

'Somebody could jump that redhead just as easy...'

'The man who tried wouldn't be in very good shape to try again. Samantha knows the cattle business. She's been around rough men and knows how to protect herself. I've got a hunch your wife doesn't.'

Their luck held until the final week. After moving camp four times, it began to rain, a deluge that made the going even more hazardous because of slippery ground. All the owners agreed to knock off shortly past noon. Boyle and his crew rigged tarps in the willows as crude shelters against the downpour.

They had just finished when Carl Tripp came stomping up through the mud, looming larger than usual in a yellow slicker. He was cussing Al Quester. 'That goddamn' bastard, I'll...'

Boyle was tired, exasperated, and now he was getting an earful of the same old story of Al Quester's hoorawing. 'Laugh at him, Carl, like I keep telling you. If you don't get your back bowed all the time, he'll damn' soon get tired of the game.'

A few minutes later Rex Uland galloped up, flanked by Conover and Roone. 'Major's at our camp,' the Box R foreman said in his gravelly voice. 'Wants a confab with you,

Boyle. He don't want your partner. Just you.'

Boyle stepped from the shelter of the tarp. Rain peppered his hat. 'When Major Ransom has the courtesy to invite both partners,' Boyle said evenly, even then wondering why he was making an issue out of it, 'maybe I'll think about it.'

Uland glared, wheeled his horse, and swept down the long slant, trailed by his companions, past the holding grounds, the branding fires reduced to smoking coals in the rain.

To darken Boyle's mood, his partner was on the subject of bringing Florence to camp for the last few days. 'I'll rig a tent.'

'Your wife will keep till the end of the week.' Boyle looked at Tripp who was sipping coffee, steam from the cup rising to his homely and unhappy face. Their remuda behind a rope barrier stood with heads down, rumps to the wind-driven rain. In the willows the men huddled under tarps, looking equally as miserable as the horses. From the Shelly camp across the clearing came the muted music of a harmonica. To get away from Carl Tripp's grumbling about Florence, Boyle walked over. It was Samantha Shelly, playing the harmonica in her tent.

Boyle dropped to one knee in a patch of weeds and looked in on her. 'A lady of many talents.'

She suddenly seemed conscious of her

appearance. She put down the harmonica and rubbed at a blob of mud on a freckled cheek. 'I look a sight,' she apologized. She was sitting cross-legged on the ground just inside her tent. 'I'd invite you in, but, if I did, then others would try.'

'Well, I just dropped over to say hello. You stay warm and dry in your tent. *Adiós.*'

'Hell with that,' she said quickly when he started away. 'I enjoy talking to you. If you don't mind rain, I sure don't.' After donning a slicker, she stepped from the tent. 'We look like two yellow bugs,' she said with a laugh. 'Two tall yellow bugs.'

'We are, at that.' Turning his head, he saw that the level of her green eyes was not much below his own.

'If I ever get a husband, he'll have to come at least to eye level. Most real tall ones seem overbearing. Not all, just some.' She shot him a glance, then gave an embarrassed little laugh.

'Have you heard what Luanne's up to these days?' Boyle asked casually.

'Is she up to something?'

'I only meant if you've seen her ... or heard anything.'

'The only time I see her is if we run into each other in town.' Then she changed the subject to roundup. 'I wouldn't have come, but I worried that Dad might ... well, get sick ... be hurt.'

144

He guessed what she meant. Heavy drinking was too dangerous at roundup.

After they had walked fifty yards and back, she gave him her hand. 'That makes it appear as if we might have been talking cattle business ... in case anybody is watching.' She grinned and withdrew her hand. Boyle had expected to shake sinewy fingers and a callused palm. Instead, the hand was surprisingly soft. And for the first time he found himself speculating about the rest of her under the rough range clothing.

'I hope you'll forgive my occasional cussing,' she said. 'I've been around cowhands for so long I guess I'm not much of a lady.'

'But you are.' And his compliment produced spots of deep color on each of her cheeks that glistened from the rain.

After he had parted company with the Shelly girl, he found Jack Quester at the Diamond Deuce camp. Jack helped himself to coffee, then settled on a fairly dry clump of grass under the trees. Boyle mentioned the summons from Major Ransom.

'Thought you said he never came to roundup.'

'Never has that I know of. Till this time.' Jack Quester took a long blow on his coffee to cool it, started to speak, broke off, then tried again. 'Listen, Kelly, I ... er ... I ... seems you've got the hottest coffee in any of the camps.'

145

'Hear you bought a new buggy.'

Jack avoided Boyle's eyes. 'The major wanted some work done on his ledgers, and Luanne came down and talked, and we...'

Boyle felt a cold clutching in his stomach, was about to tell Jack to go ahead and finish it, when his brother, Al, mud-splattered and out of sorts, galloped up.

'Man rides half a mile in this weather needs half a gallon of hot coffee.' Then, as he stepped down, he saw Carl Tripp huddled under a tarp. 'Lo, Romeo. How's your balcony?'

A few frayed strands of Kelly Boyle's temper came unraveled. 'Al, we've got enough problems. Don't start that bullshit again!'

Al shot him a hard look, grumbled something, then got a cup of coffee from the pot on glowing coals. He flopped down next to his brother. He set the cup on the ground between his outstretched legs and leaned back against a willow. 'Hey, Romeo...!'

'Don't push it,' Tripp warned through his protruding, gapped teeth before Boyle could repeat his own warning.

'A good-lookin' filly like that takin' up with a mud fence...'

Jack turned on his brother. 'Like Kelly said, shut it, Al. It's childish.'

Al colored but said nothing when Jack began to discuss roundup. There had been only five or six head of cattle lost in accidents, and two men injured, neither seriously, unusual in this rough corner of Texas. Boyle agreed as rain, beating softly into the leafing trees, slid coldly down the back of his neck.

Al hitched his big behind around on wet grass, saying: 'Hey, Romeo, kind of surprised you never brung your wife to camp.'

'I figured to,' Tripp growled. 'But Kelly don't like her.'

'Hey, Carl, that's not fair,' Boyle protested.

'Romeo, you better watch your wife when her an' that good-lookin' partner of yours is alone.'

'Why, god damn you!' Tripp leaped to his feet, spilling his coffee.

Boyle angrily took the cup away and threw it into the pan beside the smoldering fire. 'I think my mare's got a loose shoe. Come on, Carl, and help me hold her while I look. See you *mañana*, Jack.'

Carl Tripp, a bear of a man with ragged hair jutting from under the soggy hat, suddenly hooked a boot toe against the handle of Al Quester's coffee cup on the ground between his long legs, and flipped it over. Al let out a scream. Scalding coffee soaked into his crotch. Still howling, he sprang up and began a jig in the mud. Men across the clearing and in the willows got up to see what all the yelling was about.

Boyle grabbed Tripp by an arm and

marhed him to their remuda. 'You crazy damn' fool.'

'I'll kill that son-of-a-bitch one day.'

'You do and you'll shake hands with the hangman!'

Hours after the incident of the spilled coffee, Al Quester still smarted from the insult, and his right underthigh was raw from the burn. He was determined to get even with Carl Tripp.

The weather cleared abruptly, as sometimes happened, and they went back to work. The wind had suddenly shifted, the rain tapering off, and, miracle of miracles, an expanding roadway of solid blue began to appear through the dark clouds. Footing was still hazardous, however. Horses fell, spilling riders who scraped off mud, clambered back into wet saddles, and went at it again.

Pete Lambourne, with Samantha building up the fires, had his branding irons laid out. Here good judgment meant the difference between top money or low for an animal. An ugly, unhealed brand from an iron that was overheated diminished its value. That was where the skill of old-timers like Lambourne was appreciated.

Working roundup on the slick ground required concentration, but occasionally Kelley Boyle glimpsed his partner, who seemed to be riding as a man possessed by demons.

Boyle shouted a warning, reminding Tripp of possibly breaking his neck and leaving behind a young and attractive widow. Tripp didn't even reply but wheeled his horse after a *ladino* that had broken out of the holding ground.

Just after supper Major Ransom rode up with Uland and glared at Boyle who was sprawled on the ground. 'How could you refuse a courteous request?' Ransom demanded. 'I sent for you.' The major's whipcords as well as his white horse were speckled with mud.

'Had to get back to work when the weather cleared,' Boyle said, hoping that would end it.

'Hardly an excuse. You're a ranch owner, not a common cowhand. May I expect you tomorrow, two hours after sunup?'

Boyle thought about it. 'Carl Tripp and I will be there.'

'Not Mister Tripp, thank you,' the major said angrily. 'I want *you*. And it's important!' Then Major Ransom rammed in the spurs and went pounding back toward his own camp through the dripping trees.

Tripp was furious. 'He didn't even *look* at me!'

Boyle, puzzled by the major's animosity toward Tripp, said: 'I don't understand the bastard. Hell with him.'

'I wouldn't go to his god-damn' camp if he

laid out Persian rugs!' Tripp snarled, his voice shaking with rage.

By morning, Boyle had cooled off enough to decide it wouldn't hurt to see what the major wanted. Besides, he ached for news of Luanne. He found Ransom in his tent, sitting with back straight, on a cot. He smoked a cigar. Cold, hazel eyes in the rather thin face surveyed his visitor. He waved Boyle to a folding chair. Even at that early hour he smelled of whiskey. Evidently he had been brooding about Tripp, for some reason or other, because he started right in on him. 'Have you ever considered it odd that a man so lacking in refinement as that partner of yours could bring home a woman from...?'

'Don't say anything against Missus Tripp' was Kelly's warning.

'Have you ever seen their marriage license that gives her the right to call herself Missus Tripp?'

'It's nobody's god-damn' business. *Nobody's!*'

'Don't raise your voice to me, Boyle. I could whistle, and ten men would horsewhip you out of my camp.'

'*Whistle!*'

Major Ransom glared for a moment. Thin lips under the trimmed mustache twitched into laughter. 'You are tough, Kelly. Or crazy.' He shook his head. 'How much you remind me of myself when I was younger. You claw

150

and kick and spit in the other man's face to get what you want in life.'

'What did you want to see me about, Major?'

'I'm willing to allow you and ... that partner of yours ... a decent profit from the sale of...'

'We're not selling Diamond Deuce.'

'I'll pay over market price for your cattle and you come in with me. We can work together, Kelly.'

'I don't think so.'

'Half of life is the deadly game of pitting your wits against the other man's. Without risk and challenge there's nothing. I was that way in my earlier years. Then one thing and another sapped my ambition. But lately I've been feeling a return of the old zest. And I realize more than ever before that to survive I need challenge. We can make a team, Kelly.'

Boyle shook his head.

'Remember one thing, Kelly. A man with a conscience can never survive in a tough game like the business of cattle.'

'Which means what?'

'No matter what debt you think you owe your partner, cut him loose.'

'You've been talking to Luanne.'

'At great length, Kelly. I'm prepared to hire you as ramrod of all my ranches.'

'What happens to Uland?' Boyle asked out

of curiosity.

'I sense you're the better man.'

'You'd fire him?'

'It would be up to you to handle him any way you see fit.' The major drew on his cigar. 'I'll see that your partner gets a fair price for his share of Diamond Deuce, providing he gets out of Texas.'

'Just what have you got against Carl Tripp?'

'It doesn't matter.'

'It matters to me.'

'Forget Tripp and listen to me. Kelly, I'm buying out the Quester brothers. Al doesn't know it yet, but Jack runs things, and Al will be satisfied. You and I will also have that place to run. We'll have the biggest spread in Texas. Doesn't the prospect of all that power fire your blood?'

Boyle's mouth was suddenly dry. 'I wonder why Jack didn't say anything about you buying him out?'

'I guess now is the time to tell you, Kelly.' Major Ransom removed his cigar, studied it a moment, then said: 'Luanne and Jack Quester are marrying next week.'

'I guess I'm not altogether surprised,' Boyle heard himself say in a steady voice, which was amazing, because of the way everything inside was being torn apart.

'They'll live near Denver,' the major said. 'I'll see that Jack gets a good start in Colorado.'

'I'm sure they wouldn't live in Texas,' Boyle said, climbing to his feet.

'Don't take it so hard, Kelly. One day you'll be thankful it was Jack who married her. Not you.'

But Boyle was already pushing his way out of the tent. He rode, hunting for Jack Quester, finding him near a hump of ground fringed with huisache. Jack and one of his crew were trying to maneuver an angry cow from her calf. Boyle rode up.

'I hear congratulations are in order,' Boyle said stiffly.

Jack flushed, wheeled away from his rider. 'I wanted to tell you myself, but the major said he wanted to do it. And I guess he did.' Jack beat a fist against his saddle horn. 'Damn it, don't look at me like that, Kelly. Luanne said you two had broken up and...'

'Sort of, I guess.'

'You're hurt, and I'm sorry.'

'No reason to be sorry.' Boyle reined away, ashamed that he had to fight down an urge to smash Jack in the face as he had his brother, Al, that day in the Great River Saloon. He rode back to his own camp, his stomach hollow. Carl Tripp was drinking from a canteen when Boyle flung himself out of the saddle.

'What'd the king of Texas want with you, anyhow?' Tripp demanded.

'Major Terrence Ransom can go straight to hell!' Boyle snatched the canteen from his partner and took a long drink of water that tasted faintly of mud and horses. Then he told him about Luanne.

Tripp pulled at the lobe of a protruding ear. 'Sometimes I look at Flo, an' I get so god damn' mad on account I know she's the reason you an' me...' Tripp stared at his muddy boots. 'Well, you an' me don't hit it off like we used to.'

'Your wife's got nothing to do with how I feel about Luanne's marrying Jack Quester.'

'I broke my word to you, when I brung Flo home.'

'Carl, let's go get a few cows out of the brush.'

A stricken Tripp grabbed him by the arm. 'I never did tell you how I met up with Flo.'

But Boyle pulled away and rode out with such fury that his horse flung great gobs of mud that Samantha and Pete Lambourne at the branding fires had to duck.

Chapter Nine

After supper, Carl Tripp stood alone in the Diamond Deuce camp, big and scowling and in a sour mood. Boyle had asked him to go with him to the Shelly camp to discuss with other ranchers a rumor that cattle prices were on the rise, but Tripp was sulking because Boyle had given him hell about his suggesting that he would get rid of Florence, just for the convenience of the partnership. Boyle had refused even to hear of such a thing.

The Diamond Deuce riders, three regulars and Jaime De Gama, were down at the remuda, jawing. While there was still some light lingering in a red-gold haze to the west, Al Quester and some of his men sneaked into the willows to hide. Some were snickering, and Al had a time shushing them. But he was grinning so hard in anticipation that his face ached. He held a gunnysack that contained a large rattlesnake, very dead.

That afternoon, Major Ransom had hunted him up and casually related a story about a loud-mouth like Carl Tripp who had worked for the old T K outfit, and how he had been laughed out of camp. An excited Al Quester had taken three of his men on a snake hunt.

Even though it was early for hibernating snakes to emerge from their holes, a few had been dislodged in the course of roundup.

Carl Tripp's back was turned as he sanded off the supper dishes – it being his turn for the chore. That was when Al sneaked up, removed the dead snake from the gunnysack, and shoved it deep into Carl's blankets, beside his saddle and rifle. He ran back to the trees, barely able to contain his laughter.

When Jack Quester got wind of what his brother was up to, he tiptoed through the trees and whispered: 'Al, that'll cause nothing but trouble.'

'Tripp'll jump high enough to grab holt of the moon.'

Jack gave his brother a worried look. 'I wouldn't push Tripp too far. I want you in one piece. You're to be best man at my wedding, remember.'

Al, not even listening, nudged his brother to be quiet. He nodded through the fringe of spindly willows at Tripp who was sitting on the ground and pulling off boots and socks. Tripp then removed his gun belt, laid it under his saddle, then slid between the blankets. Tripp suddenly stiffened, felt around with a big toe that confirmed a horrible suspicion. Somehow a snake had crawled into his soogans.

'*Yeeeeoooooowwwwwwww!*' Tripp shot out of

the blankets, rolled backwards, came to his bare feet on pebbles. Catching up his bedroll, he upended it and out popped the snake. In the half light of early evening, it looked alive. Tripp snatched up his gun and blew off the snake's head.

On the heels of the gunshot, gales of laughter roared from the willows. Only then, from the hilarity, did Tripp realize the snake was already dead. Men burst from the trees for a closer look at the spectacle, Tripp in shirt and pants, feet bare, his face the dead color of caliche, and gripping a gun. A bluish wisp of smoke curled from the barrel.

Tripp stiffened at the laughter, the sight of men slapping thighs, some with tears in their eyes, as the tensions of roundup, undammed, were roaring as down a spillway to engulf the still trembling big man.

Jack Quester stepped forward to speak. 'Carl, that was a cruel joke to play on a man. Al shouldn't have...'

That swung Tripp's narrowed eyes to Al who stood just behind his brother, still guffawing. That was when Tripp suddenly shifted the smoking gun from the dead snake and pointed it at Al Quester. In the sudden silence, there was a noisy sucking of breaths from onlookers.

Jack, looking nervous, flung wide his arms as if to shield his brother. 'Carl, put up the gun. It was a damn' fool stunt. But don't take it out on Al with a gun.'

But Tripp in his rage moved quickly to one side and fired, aiming for one of Al's thick shoulders barely visible above his brother's left ear. At the last instant Jack must have tilted his head the wrong way, because the bullet tore into his neck, just below the ear, struck bone, and was deflected upward. It blew a hole big as a dollar in the crown of Jack's hat, rimming it with bits of bone and brain matter.

As Jack collapsed near the dead snake, an awesome stillness fell over the roundup camp. Still gripped by fury and humiliation, Tripp leaped over Jack's body and tried to cave in Al Quester's skull with a wild swing of his gun barrel. But Al twisted out of reach, found his voice, and screeched: 'You killed Jack. You murdered my brother!'

Al Quester had his gun half out of leather when two men flung themselves on him, pinning his arms. 'Leave him be, Al,' one of them shouted. 'Let the son-of-a-bitch hang!'

All the yelling brought Tripp out of his blind range. And he now looked at its result crumpled on the earth that was reddened from Jack Quester's blood. Other men tried to seize Tripp, but by now survival was uppermost in the big man's mind. He aimed his gun at those advancing on him.

'I'll kill the first man puts a hand on me!'

158

Kelly Boyle was aware of the gunshots and the commotion that followed. He heard someone shouting Tripp's name, then Jack Quester's. Discussion of cattle prices with Rob Shelly, his daughter, and the muddied packing house rep who had brought news of a rising market ended abruptly.

Samantha cried: 'Oh, my God, somebody must be dead!'

As Boyle came running up the muddy slant, he saw Carl Tripp aboard a saddler, pounding off into the shadowed trees, Tripp without a hat, bare feet in the stirrups, armed only with a pistol.

'Carl!' Boyle called, but his voice was lost in the din of gunfire directed at the fleeing man. Gunflashes licked at willows in the twilight, but the shots were wild, and Carl Tripp got away.

Boyle, panting, slid to a halt and in shocked silence stared at Jack, crumpled on the ground, an ugly skull wound indicating he was beyond help.

'It was just funning,' a man said in explanation. 'Tripp went plumb loco!' And the man shakily sketched what had happened.

'We aim to hang him!' shouted a Quester man.

Boyle ran for his horse. Others were already after Tripp, Al Quester leading the pack. The tracks – what Boyle could make of them in the fast-fading light – led straight for the border. This would not end in a lynching, Boyle vowed. Carl Tripp would have a fair trial. Any rational juror would realize it had not been cold-blooded murder.

Boyle, riding more recklessly than the others, finally managed to catch up with the dozen or so men now in the light of an early moon. They were no longer able to read sign but were convinced that a man, riding for his life, would continue south to the border.

With the first heat of pursuit draining away, horses crashed through brush, climbed up-trail and down, blowing, sweated up, dripping foam, the only sounds the low-voiced curses of the men, hoofbeats, a tinkle of bit chains and spurs. Thirteen men spread out across the stark flats of northern Mexico like a cavalry patrol, chasing shadows.

Over the next two days men dropped out and headed back because of the roundup still to finish. Finally only Al Quester and his four men remained, always trying to keep Boyle in sight because of his familiarity with this country.

Finally, on the third day, when they had been hours without any sign of the fleeing man, Al bumped his horse against Boyle's weary mount.

'What you aim to do about your partner?' demanded the big, savage-looking man. He was tired as the others, twisted with frustration and grief over his brother's death.

Boyle's own nerves caused his temper to rise to a dangerous level. 'You're a great one for jokes, Al. Who put you up to that snake trick? You haven't brains enough to think it up by yourself.'

In the yellow wash of a Mexican moon, Al Quester clamped a hand to his revolver. 'Don't tell me I got no brains.'

'Go ahead and pull that gun. I've had a bellyful of you.'

Quester removed his hand from his gun. 'I got a sudden hunch that Tripp's doubled back to fetch his woman!' With that he sank spurs into the scarred flanks of his spent sorrel and started back, his men galloping in his wake.

It seemed hours later that they came in sight of the squat mud house. Boyle, who had trailed along with them, issued a warning. 'If we spot Carl, the first man reaches for a rope is dead. You hear me?'

Al Quester only mumbled something. They slowed their horses. A slender Felicita in flannel nightgown appeared in the doorway with a rifle. Dawn was already graying the east.

Al's horse had more wind left than Boyle's, and he got there first, by a full thirty seconds.

'¿Quién va?' Felicita challenged.

'¡Buscamos Carl Tripp!' Al Quester yelled, dismounting.

'*¡No aquí!*'

'What the hell you mean ... he's not here?' As he said it, Quester pushed forward toward the mud house.

As Boyle made a running dismount, rifle in hand, he saw Felicita dart before Al Quester into the house and rush to the mantel of the mud fireplace. She snatched an envelope anchored under a lamp, hiding it in the folds of her night dress. Quester apparently didn't notice what she was doing because he was eyeing the closed bedroom door. He lunged forward, had one hand on the knob, when Boyle jabbed him viciously in the ribs with the rifle.

'Get out, Al.'

Al Quester's lips twitched as he glared at the rifle, then at Boyle's tight face. 'When I finish with Carl, I'll be back for you.'

'I catch you on Diamond Deuce again, I'll see you get decent burial. But that's all.'

Quester tried to sneer at the threat. His four men stood stiffly in the yard. Felicita, dark hair to her waist, stepped to the bedroom door, opened it wide enough to show that the room was empty.

'Tripp's come an' got his woman,' Al Quester panted, heading back outside.

Boyle shook his head. 'You see a sweated-up horse in the pen? If Carl had been here, he'd take time to get a fresh horse.'

Quester had his look, rubbed his jaw

tiredly. 'I'll go ask the Mex lady about Tripp's woman.'

He started to swing around, but Boyle's voice stopped him. 'You're not seeing her again. She's likely scared half to death with all the yelling.' It wasn't true, he knew. It would take more than this to put fear in that proud face.

'I aim to talk to her,' Quester said stubbornly.

Boyle cocked his rifle. Quester stared at it for a moment. 'If it takes ten years, I aim to kill Tripp. One more day won't matter.' Al Quester gave Boyle a strange look, and suddenly his mouth began to shake. Boyle had thought the man incapable of emotion other than hilarity when someone became victim of one of his practical jokes. Tears now ran down the broad face. 'Jack was going to marry Luanne Ransom, come Monday. I ... I was gonna be best man. Damn it ... Tripp killed him.'

Quester then went to his horse, mounted. His men did likewise, and rode away on their weary horses at a walk, tired men in the saddle. It had been a long three days.

Back in the house, Boyle, half out on his feet, sat down at the table and gave Felicita details of the tragedy. She listened quietly while heating coffee, this handsome widow whose own life on the border had been mostly blood and tears.

163

'*Lo siento*,' she murmured.

'And I am sorry ... Jesus knows ... sorry for Jack and for Carl and ... and for Luanne. It'll be a shock to her. Where's Florence?' He had just remembered she hadn't been in the bedroom. Perhaps the sounds of horses approaching had panicked her.

It wasn't so. Felicita said she had left over a week ago. 'She took her things. There is a letter.'

Numbed from lack of sleep, Boyle failed to comprehend at first. 'Ran off with a man? ... while Carl was away at roundup,' Boyle mumbled.

Felicita shook her head. 'She took the buckboard.'

'A damn' thief she is, then, among other things.'

Felicita said she had to hitch up the team for her. 'She is afraid of horses.' Felicita handed him the envelope she had snatched from the mantel to hide from Al Quester.

Boyle sat looking at the envelope while Felicita poured him a cup of coffee, then she went to get on a robe, before going outside to care for Boyle's horse. When she returned, he was still staring at the envelope. To the east the early grayness had turned cottonwoods into black sticks. Boyle had been wondering if he should open the envelope or not. It was addressed to Carl Tripp in a neat feminine hand.

Maybe there are things I should know, under the circumstances, Boyle finally decided, and, now that Felicita was back, he ripped it open.

Dear Carl:
We both know it was a mistake. I'm thankful our relationship was not legal. Now we are both free of any entanglements. We won't have to slip away one day to some distant town to be married and then come home and continue to pretend we were man and wife all the time. This way is easier on everyone. I'm sure it will please Kelly that I will no longer be around to disrupt your lives. One thing, Carl, I will always be eternally grateful to you because I realize now that life is most precious. Thanks for giving mine back to me.

Sincerely,
Florence

His eyes were burning from fatigue, but Boyle reread it. Then, after eating the breakfast Felicita cooked for him, he staggered to the bunkhouse, flung himself onto his bunk, and stared up at the plank ceiling. Through his mind ran the years of hardship, self-denial, in order to achieve a dream, his and Carl's. That pale-haired Florence had ruined it. Because of her, Al Quester had gone too far with his hoorawing. And now Carl was a fugitive. In his bones Boyle felt

Carl was doomed.

Major Terrence Ransom was also thinking
of Carl Tripp's woman early that morning,
remembering how intrigued he had been in
Lucero when she wore a veil to cover her
ravaged face, and how the wind-pressed
clothing could hardly disguise a splendid
figure. The great bruiser of his pride had
been when he had subtly offered himself,
but she had chosen instead to bury herself
out at Diamond Deuce with that lout, Carl
Tripp. His plan at roundup, that had
occurred to him on the spur of the moment,
had also backfired. He had thought Tripp to
be too slow on the draw and that, when
violence erupted from the dead-snake joke,
as he had been certain it would, Tripp and
Al Quester would get into it. He had hoped
that Tripp would be dead – small payment
for destroying the plans he had had for the
woman. He hadn't counted on Jack Quester
being the victim.

Luanne came downstairs and joined him
in the library. He thought her eyes would be
swollen from weeping, but they were clear
and cold.

'I just want to say that I'm sorry about
Jack,' he said.

'Are you?'

He went over and touched her arm, but

she drew away. 'There's no reason to condemn me,' he said, watching her face. 'I had nothing to do with it.'

'I overheard Rex Uland telling Missus Blankenship about the dead snake. So I asked him right out, and he admitted that you were the instigator of the whole thing.'

'I certainly didn't think Al would try it ... knowing Tripp's volatile temper.'

Brittle laughter was her answer. She walked to a window and stood looking out at bunkhouse and a barn barely visible through cottonwoods. 'I suppose I'll be expected to attend Jack's funeral,' she said in a dead voice.

'Yes. We can go ahead with the services now. I got word from roundup that Al's back.'

'Did he kill Tripp?'

'Lost his trail.'

'I hope somebody kills him,' she said so softly he didn't hear her. 'He's ruined my life, and been an anvil on Kelly's back.'

'I sense you didn't love Jack at all.'

She turned and faced her father, chin lifted, eyes mere slits of violet behind a screen of dark lashes. 'I loved him passionately.'

'You're incapable of it,' he scoffed.

'Quite possibly in nine months ... no, make it eight ... I will give birth to Jack's child.'

He lifted a hand as if to slap her across the face, then lowered it. Some of the color that had drained his face at her blunt announcement began to creep back. 'This is a time for us to pull together, Luanne.'

'Just how?' She wanted to laugh but lacked the energy.

'Kelly Boyle's out of it. You couldn't saddle him with another man's child. Wouldn't be right. Besides, I have other plans for him.'

'You and your plans,' she said wearily.

'I'll find a husband. Some of the stockholders have suitable sons. But I'd say we have two months at best.' He was talking to a book-lined wall, not directly to her. 'You won't show until then. Your mother was barely noticeable in four months. You'll live here, of course, until I can get a house built for you.'

'Luanne Ransom, brood mare.'

'After your disgrace, why hurt me?' He waved off any possible retort. 'Let's be calm. We'll say that premature births were quite common among the women of your mother's family. Quite plausible. Has served in countless similar situations down through the ages.'

Tired of his voice, she went upstairs to her room. There she wrote a short note to Kelly Boyle, mentioning elopement and the house in Bluewater he wanted to rent. After sealing it, she walked down through the cottonwoods to find a suitable messenger. Roone of the scarred cheek was just riding in. He tipped his hat to her when she walked over,

168

handed him the envelope, and asked him to deliver it to Kelly Boyle.

'Just come from roundup. Al Quester says Boyle's at Diamond Deuce.'

'I'll consider it a special favor, Mister Roone.'

When she was walking back to the house. Rex Uland came hurrying on thick legs from the ranch office. He didn't see her because of the trees. Upon reaching the bunkhouse, Uland whistled up Conover and Roone, the latter just having dismounted to help himself to coffee.

'Major wants us to go fetch Boyle,' Uland said. 'Only part I don't like,' he went on, wide face split with a fierce grin, 'is that the major wants him brung in alive.'

Conover brushed back his cowlick and laughed. That was when Roone told Uland about the letter Miss Luanne had asked him to deliver to Kelly Boyle. Uland held out his hand, snapping his fingers. Roone dug the envelope out of his pocket and handed it over. Popping a cigar into his mouth, Uland scratched a match, and, as the flame veered toward the end of the cigar, it also touched a corner of the envelope he was holding.

'Be damned ... now how'd that happen?' he said with a grin, and dropped the burning paper onto the floor. Roone and Conover stood looking down at it until there was only ash. Then Uland stomped out the remaining flame. It left a burned place on the floor

'What'll I tell Miss Luanne?' Roone asked as they went out to get their horses for the ride to Diamond Deuce.

'Tell her about what?' Uland asked innocently.

'About the letter.'

'Damn if I saw any letter.' Then Uland gave a harsh laugh and added: 'Boyle's to home, so the major says Al told him. So let's get out there before he goes huntin' for Carl Tripp.'

Chapter Ten

After eating a second breakfast, Kelly Boyle felt better.

Felicita's warm, dark eyes searched his face. 'I'm sorry the way things turned out for you,' she said softly. 'Sometimes, I think this corner of Texas is cursed. It took my husband. And now it is crushing you.'

They were at the table. She splashed more hot coffee into their cups, then took his hand in both of hers. He leaned over to kiss her cheek, but she turned her head quickly, and he caught a corner of her gentle mouth. For an instant he wanted to put his arms around the handsome widow and let her softness draw out the pain of memory. But she was a friend, he reminded himself. Not some female to take on a whim.

'You are a good woman, Felicita. I like you *mucho.*'

She matched his faint smile. 'And I like you, Kelly. If you ever need me again...'

He gave her half the money he had in his pocket. Other money he had buried some distance from the house. It would keep. He suggested she go home. He told her he was heading into Mexico to hunt for Carl Tripp.

'I may be gone a week ... or a month.'

Felicita's face was troubled. 'You think *Señora* Tripp has left for good?'

'For good.' Boyle could barely contain a bark of weary laughter because Felicita had called her *Señora* Tripp. Hell, Florence was just a woman who had shared a man's bed without benefit of a preacher. That part was of no great importance, however. What did matter was that she had deserted Carl.

Once Felicita had left for home, Boyle roped out a horse to use as a pack animal. He loaded on beans and flour, dried beef and coffee. He got bedroll, rifle, and cartridges, thinking that, if *insurrectos* got their hands on Carl, he might possibly be kept alive – a *gringo* to be used to bargain for *yanqui* dollars. Boyle knew how to deal with that.

Before mounting up, he stood looking at the bunkhouse, at the cracks in the walls, the tilted tin chimney. His gaze shifted to the squat little house with blue curtains at the windows. He experienced a tug under the breastbone for, quite possibly, he might never see the place again – all that work, the planning, the shrewd cattle buys, the gamble on a rising market, the stampedes, rustlers, greedy politicians with moist palms to be filled with gold eagles before a herd was allowed passage. All of it could be tossed away like a handful of grit in the whining wind, all be-

172

cause of Al Quester's stupid prank.

He intended to stop by roundup camp and tell Pete Lambourne to push their cattle back on Diamond Deuce grass. If Lambourne and the men quit on him, so be it. There might be nothing left when he returned – if he returned.

He had gone no more than a mile when a team and wagon burst from a tracery of willows and cottonwoods toward the river. Reining in behind a clump of mesquite, he waited, squinting at the fast-moving vehicle. Closer now, he saw that it was driven by a woman whose hair streamed behind like a golden flag. Recognizing her, he shouted at the rising wind – 'Bitch!' – his anger so deep he tasted it. Although he had no idea why she was returning, he knew that, before resuming the hunt for Carl Tripp, it would give him pleasure to kick her off the place.

She was a hundred yards or so from where he sat his saddle and had not seen him. By the time he got his pack animal, that had drifted away, and reached the corral, he saw the buckboard team, harness dragging, far out on the flats and peacefully nibbling grass. When he brought the team in, turned them into the corral, he saw the buckboard, its tongue resting on damp ground and beyond it, crumpled against the house wall, was Florence. She lay unmoving, wind rustling hair and skirts. After tying his horse and pack animal, he walked over.

'Florence...?'

At first he thought she was dead because for the first time he saw a scarlet stain at the forehead. Carefully he looked around, eyes searching for a sniper. But by then her eyelids fluttered, and the large blue eyes flew open.

'What happened to you?' he demanded coldly, straightening up.

'I ... I called to Felicita to help me with the team.'

'I sent her home.'

She said she had tried to unhitch the team, but the horses sensed her fear and one of them spun, knocking her against the house. She got to her feet, Boyle not offering a hand. Mechanically she brushed dust from her gray dress. There was a rip down the side so that pale blue ribbons of a camisole were revealed. Seeing the direction of his gaze, she held the rent together. With the other hand she removed a small handkerchief from her bosom and dabbed at the cut on her forehead.

'I ... I hit my head an awful crack,' she explained. When he made no reply, her mouth began to shake. 'Please don't look at me that way. I was in town, when I overheard people talking about Carl's trouble.'

Then her lips whitened, and she darted into the house. After searching the mantel, she turned. He filled the doorway.

'I left a letter, Kelly.'

'Which I read.'

'You had no *right!*'

'Maybe not. But it's done.'

She brushed back her long hair, sadness mirrored in the eyes. 'Yes. A lot of things are done, I guess.'

He came deeper into the house, kicking the door shut behind him. His nerves screamed from the tension of the past hours. 'Why in hell did you come back?' he demanded.

'It's as simple as this. When I heard about Carl killing Jack Quester, I had a change of heart.'

'You've got no heart to change.'

'How unkind.'

That brought a harsh laugh as he threw his coat onto the sofa she had covered with blue cloth. 'It's because of you that Carl's in this mess.'

Her back stiffened. 'What did I have to do with it?'

Without bothering to reply, he lunged, catching the collar of the gray dress in one hand. With a sudden downward motion he ripped the front so that it hung from her two arms like a pair of window drapes. Before she could react, he caught her under one arm and carried her, kicking, into the bedroom. There he flung her onto the bed, the mattress making a crackling sound. As she tried to roll aside, he threw himself down, pinning her. Scent of her body, her perfume, was in his nostrils.

'You've ruined everything for Carl,' he said savagely. 'God knows, the same for me, likely.'

She just lay there, looking up at him out of deep blue eyes. 'I must warn you,' she said hoarsely, 'that Carl is insanely jealous. The most jealous man I ever knew.'

'Among the many, no doubt.'

'If he happened to find us like this, it could mean more tragedy.'

'I wish he would come ... to see you for what you are. But he won't. He's miles from here, and I lost his trail.' His voice faltered, and he suddenly felt the need to punish her. Or was he only fooling himself, and what he really wanted was her? His hands moved to soft flesh.

'Kelly, don't,' she whispered, trying to push his hands away. 'It wouldn't be fair to Carl.'

'You wont be here to tell him. All the damn' trouble you've caused us. And you're not even his wife!'

'I couldn't marry him. I already have a husband.'

Kelly Boyle uttered a strangled laugh against her cheek. 'Carl picked a jewel in you, all right.'

'He seemed to think so. At first.'

'What about this husband of yours?'

In a dead voice she told him about being married just before her fourteenth birthday to her father's best friend, one Samuel Joseph Taylor. 'They had soldiered together in the war. My father knew he didn't have long to live. He wanted me to be protected. So, you see I couldn't marry Carl. It would be bigamy.'

'The least of your crimes?'

'Possibly.' A sheaf of heavy yellow hair lay across the pillow. 'Kelly, why do you want to hurt me?'

'You've been bad luck for this partnership. The worst.'

'From your standpoint, I suppose.'

'What did you figure to do about this husband of yours?'

'Carl said, when he sold cattle, we would hire a lawyer to find my husband and get a divorce. But he could very well be dead because of his terrible drinking ... and other habits.' She freed one of her hands that had been trapped between their bodies and wiped her eyes. 'Sam Joe Taylor is a gambler. A lucky one.'

'The only good kind.'

'He won lots of money. Sam Joe and I moved about the West. It was exciting for a young girl who'd never received affection at home.'

'Not much of a life for a kid.'

'When he played in high-stakes games, I'd

wait in a hotel room because he wouldn't allow me to sit in the lobby or walk alone. Unseemly, he used to put it.' She laughed brokenly and ran a tongue over her shining teeth. 'We stayed a while in Chicago and then rode the steam cars west from Omaha to Frisco. That's when his luck turned sour the first time.'

'Go on.' The wind had come up; he could hear it howling under the eaves.

She shook her head on the pillow, her wet eyes not leaving his face. 'All I'll say is that one night I got tired of my life with Sam Joe and intended to end it. I stole a shotgun from the hotel in Lucero.'

'Lucero! What in hell were you doing in a place like that?'

'It's where my husband left me. Oh, he had plans for me.' She closed her eyes for a moment, then said: 'I took the shotgun to the river. I put the barrel in my mouth, but I couldn't reach down to the trigger. So I took off my shoe and had just worked my big toe into the trigger guard when someone said ... 'Don't do that, lady.' It was Carl. One second ... no, a fraction of a second ... and I'd have been dead. Carl saved me, and I ... I went to pieces.'

'What then?'

'Carl said we'd get married, and I was so upset I didn't think at first. But then I told him about my husband ... so grateful to Carl

178

I thought only of burying myself on this ranch and repaying him in any way he wished.' Two faint lines appeared between her eyes. 'Because it's Carl who made it possible for blood to sing through my veins and the scent of earth to be in my nostrils.'

While she had been talking, he was aware of a thigh pressed against his knee, felt the dampness of her tears, tasted them at her throat and a bare shoulder. When his hand found a full, warm breast, she stirred, sighing.

Suddenly he thrust himself away and got off the bed. '*What kind of a bastard am I?* he asked himself. Then aloud: 'To almost force myself on a woman against her will.'

She lay, watching him, while he went to a window to quell his self-loathing and the heat of his blood. He stared out at the hayrick, at bits of straw flying in the wind, his heart pounding. She was Carl's woman; wife or not, it didn't matter. And he had come close to violating a friendship, the brotherhood he and Carl had shared since boyhood.

He turned and looked at her, sitting up on the bed, holding the torn dress together, looking pathetic and beautiful. She *had* returned because Carl was in trouble. He had to give her credit for that.

'Tell me, Florence ... do you really love Carl?'

She gave him a strange look, then averted

her gaze. 'I made a bargain with Carl and...' A tremor touched her body, then she asked him for details of the tragedy at the roundup camp.

He told her.

'How awful.' She shut her eyes for a moment. 'At the livery barn, when I had the team hitched up, I tried to get the man to talk about what had happened. But he only mumbled and glared at me as if it was my fault that I'm married to Carl. Which I'm not, as you know.'

'I'll never let on.'

'Thank you, Kelly. Not that it matters now.'

'I had a hunch Carl might come here ... for you. But common sense tells me he's still across the line.' *Maybe dead by now*, he thought heavily, *barefoot and armed only with a pistol.*

'Poor Carl,' she mused. 'I guess maybe my coming back was a crazy impulse. Now that I look at it logically, I think Carl was getting tired of ... things.'

'Carl's strange, I admit. But he still had the same feelings for you as when he brought you out here.' Although Boyle wasn't too sure, he felt there was no use hurting her further. He'd done his share of hurting, for sure. 'I'm sorry I tore your dress.'

'You intended to rape me.'

Her candor was unsettling. 'No, you're

180

wrong. I ... I just lost my head there for a minute.'

A sheaf of long hair had fallen across her forehead so he could no longer see her wound. 'Could I go with you on your hunt for Carl?'

He shook his head. 'Too dangerous.' He told her to stay at the ranch. 'I'll stop by roundup. Lambourne and the others will be here within two days. Will you wait?'

She nodded. 'I'd better put on another dress. My things...'

He knew what she meant and went out to the buckboard and brought in a portmanteau and carpetbag. Then he stepped out of the bedroom and closed the door.

In the battered desk, willed to them by Stubblefield, he got paper and pen and ink and wrote a note for Pete Lambourne, in case the old man wasn't at camp when he arrived. He didn't want to waste time hunting him, not while going after Carl was of greater importance. The note would be there for Lambourne when he got back. If he was gone, that is. Otherwise, Boyle would tell him in person about keeping Florence Tripp from harm.

He had just finished writing the note when he heard Florence scream. Flinging open the bedroom door, he saw Bert Conover, one of the Box R segundos, just throwing a thick leg over the window sill. Conover was staring as if transfixed at a white-faced Florence hastily buttoning a blue silk dress. In that instant Conover's eyes flicked to an enraged Kelly Boyle in the doorway, hand clamped to a gun.

'Hold it, Boyle!' It was Rex Uland's voice, at his back.

Boyle stiffened, glanced over his shoulder at the towering foreman who gripped a rifle.

'You're trespassing,' Boyle said coldly.

Uland laughed. 'Yeah, ain't I. The major sent me to fetch you. For two reasons. First one is Jack Quester's funeral. You're to bring that black suit. The one you used to wear when you was courtin' Miss Luanne.' The laughter was gone now, replaced by an ugly twist of lips.

'What's the other reason the major sent you?'

'He's got word about Carl Tripp.'

Boyle tried not to show his surprise, heard Florence gasp. 'What kind of word?' Boyle demanded.

'Don't know. He'll have to tell you hisself. Now come along. We ain't got much time.'

'I tell you one thing, Uland. You get Conover off that window sill or I'll shoot him off'

'You ain't shootin' nobody. 'Less you want to risk a slug in that scared-lookin' honey ... Carl Tripp's woman.' Uland had crowded into the bedroom to stare at Florence.

Conover, poised on the window sill, said: 'She sure is a honey at that, Rex.'

When Conover tried to complete his climb through the window, Boyle lunged, caught him at the shoulders, and sent him toppling backward into the yard. He rolled, losing his hat, and came up red-faced and cursing. It brought a bark of laughter from Roone.

Then Boyle turned on Uland. 'Get out of the room. Give the lady some privacy.'

'You pull another stunt like you just done with Conover, an' you're dead,' Uland threatened.

'The major wants me alive, seems like. Not dead.'

Uland ground his teeth and stepped out of the room. Boyle followed him, slamming the door at his back. Through the open front door he could see their horses, out beyond the windmill. The same *cabrón* of a wind, now whistling across the yard, had covered their approach on foot. It crossed Boyle's mind that he might take Florence with him, but he didn't trust Uland, not around a pretty woman, and there was no telling what kind of reception the major had in store for him. Maybe the major had word of Carl, perhaps not. But he couldn't pass up any chance to help his partner.

So he got his black suit from the bunkhouse, with Uland and a glowering Conover watching him. As he wrapped the suit in his slicker and tied it on the pack horse, he thought that maybe, if he hadn't been such a son-of-a-bitch when Carl had brought Florence home, Carl wouldn't have been so on edge that day at roundup and allowed his temper to explode. But it was too late now to worry about what might have been.

He got a spare rifle and walked to the house to hand it to Florence. She stood in the doorway, pale hair blowing. 'If anybody comes around, shoot. Don't worry about spilling blood. Do it.' He gave her a pat on the arm, a reassuring smile, then mounted up.

Uland waited for him to ride on ahead, but Boyle shook his head. 'You boys riding at my back will give me an itch. You ride ahead.'

'We'll ride where we damn' well please,' Uland snarled.

'Suit yourself.' Boyle sat his saddle, waiting. 'The major sent you to fetch me.'

'Yeah, an' you'll come along whether we're in front of you or in back. On account of you wantin' to know about Carl Tripp.'

Boyle glanced at the house, but Florence had gone back inside and closed the door.

'I'm not too sure about the major and Tripp. But if you don't bring me back in reasonably good shape, Major Ransom can be rattler mean if his orders aren't carried out.'

Uland's broad face began to match the rusty shade of his hair. 'You want to ride behind, then you'll do it without a gun. Hand it over.' Uland shoved out a large callused hand.

Tired and wrought up as he was, Boyle carried it off with a harsh laugh. 'You boys remember what I did to Saxton and Chollmar. You want to take a chance, that's up to you.' It was sheer bluff, but Uland caved in, fear of retaliation from the major overriding the threat from Boyle.

It was Jake Roone, rubbing at his scarred cheek, who said casually – 'Reckon I'll stay an' keep an eye on Tripp's woman.' – giving Uland and Conover a broad wink. All three men looked at Boyle to see how he was taking it.

His response was made quietly, but there was no mistaking the warning. 'I'll personally hang the man who touches her.'

'You been pushin' your luck, Boyle,' Uland threatened. 'But the major or not, don't push too hard.'

They rode out ahead, Boyle bringing up the rear. So anxious was he to find out if the major really knew something of Carl Tripp's whereabouts, or was only bluffing, Boyle bypassed roundup camp. They went directly to Bluewater, where Uland said the major was waiting.

There was a fair-size crowd on hand for

the funeral. Major Ransom, having seen the quartet ride in, stepped from the Great River Saloon. 'Kelly, you should have been leading the troops, not bringing up the rear.'

Rex Uland flushed but had the good sense not to open his mouth to the grinning major. He and his two companions rode on to the livery barn.

'I came for one reason.' Boyle said crisply as he tied saddler and pack horse to the crowded hitch rack. 'Carl Tripp. Uland says you know something.'

'I do.'

'Tell me.'

The major shook his head. 'It'll have to wait until after the funeral.'

'I think you're lying to me about Tripp,' Boyle said after a moment.

The major's shoulders stiffened. 'I don't take kindly to being called a liar.'

Men, passing along the walk, turned to stare. Boyle felt a barrage of unfriendly eyes rake his face. If people decided to dislike him because of the tragedy, that was their business, he decided. The main thing now was to find Carl before something worse happened.

'However, in your case, I'll let it pass,' the major was saying. 'I have definite information about your friend Tripp. In his own hand-writing, I might add.'

Boyle's heart leaped. 'Then show it to me,

for Christ's sake.'

'Later.' The major met his eyes and added: 'I arranged for Sheriff Temple to remain up at Empire and to find some special task for Eli Cord to handle in the northern part of the county ... so there will be no interference from sheriff or deputy where our private business is concerned.'

Luanne hated it – people coming up and shedding tears and shaking her hand or insisting on kissing her cheek. And all she wanted was Kelly Boyle. She had seen him ride in, watched him enter the Great River Saloon. He emerged soon after wearing his black suit, looking elegant in white shirt and black string tie. *Oh, my darling.* She had to fight down an urge to flee across the street from where she was gathered with the ladies, fling off her veil, and kiss him madly. He was talking with her father. He must have seen her. He *must* have.

When the buggies arrived, she and Mrs. Blankenship entered the one directly behind the hearse with its black plumes and the casket in plain view behind the panes of glass. There weren't buggies enough for all the women. Some would have to walk.

Samantha Shelly, wearing black, came over to offer condolences. At first Luanne didn't recognize her out of her usual costume of canvas and leather and spurred boots.

Just when the funeral cortege was starting to move, Kelly Boyle threaded his way through the crowd and came to the buggy. He spoke to Mrs. Blankenship, who had a handkerchief pressed to her eyes, then, hat in hand, he turned to Luanne.

'I'm sorry about Jack. I know you must have loved him a great deal.'

She offered him her hand, but felt no special pressure of fingers, nothing in the calm gray eyes to indicate he was thinking of what she had written in the note about renting a house in town. Nothing. He stepped back, put on his hat, touched the brim, and disappeared in the crowd. *He's hurt that I'd turn to Jack, I suppose,* was running through her mind. *I'll explain that it was done sheerly on impulse.*

Boyle was thinking about Luanne and her lack of tears. Mrs. Blankenship, however, wept enough for the two of them. Al Quester in a shiny black suit stood at the edge of the walk. When he saw Boyle, his face hardened. He started to say something, but Major Ransom, standing nearby, gave an emphatic shake of his head. Quester backed away, scowling.

The spring wind had tapered off, and the sky was cleared of the mingled clouds of sand and dust from Texas and Mexico. The sun was warm.

Somebody said: 'Too bad poor Jack

188

couldn't have lived to see this fine day.'

Again Boyle felt eyes on him, as if he shared Carl Tripp's guilt, but he looked straight ahead to Luanne in the lead buggy. Just seeing her briefly made him realize how beautiful she was. But that was all, no tug of heartstrings, no heat of longing. Maybe he was just drained, he told himself. So much had happened to them all.

When Boyle saw a tall young woman walking beside Rob Shelly, it took him a moment to realize it was Samantha. Today she wore black, and her hair was not in braids but caught in a knot at the back of her head. It was the first time he had seen her in anything but a divided skirt or boy's jeans. She gave him a flutter of fingertips, and he fell in step as the funeral procession moved slowly along River Street in direction of the town cemetery.

'I'm so sorry about everything,' she said, her clear green eyes meeting his.

He thanked her, then said he had business with Major Ransom after the funeral, and, if it wasn't too much trouble, could she tell Pete Lambourne to push the gather onto Diamond Deuce.

'I'd be glad to, Kelly.'

'Thanks. I do appreciate it. There's no telling how long I'll be gone.'

'You're going after your partner,' she guessed.

189

He nodded. 'Yeah, one way or another, I'm going after him.'

Reverend Clark, a portly man with sideburns curving to a plump chin, had been summoned from Empire for the service. His voice droned on about doors closing for the deceased in one life, opening in another and better one.

Finally came the conclusion. Boyle lined up with others and tossed his clod of dirt onto Jack's coffin. And, as he peered down onto the polished wood wedged into Texas earth, he wondered if all the striving, the sweat, and heartache was worth it. You end up in a box with your friends and neighbors throwing dirt onto the lid.

When the crowd was beginning to disperse, Boyle hunted up the major, found him talking to some important-looking men in front of the Great River Saloon. Boyle got him by an arm and pulled him aside, the major's face beginning to redden.

'All right,' Boyle said coldly, 'I went through the funeral like you wanted. So now let's hear about Carl Tripp.'

The major twisted free of Boyle's hand, straightened the cuff of his fawnskin jacket. He spoke coolly of a tribute to Jack Quester to be held at Box R. 'There'll be a barbecue and perhaps some sporting events. Things Jack would have liked.'

'Sorry, but I can't make it. Major. I'm

going across the river and hunt for Carl.'

'You'll never find him.' Major Ransom bit off the end of a cigar, spat it into the street. 'I know where Carl Tripp is being held. I've been in contact with his captors.'

'I don't believe a damn' word of it,' Boyle snarled, watching the major's face. But the major only shrugged.

'You'll have to take my word for it, Kelly.'

'It doesn't do me any good, if you know where he is, and I don't.'

'In good time, my boy, in good time. But first we pay tribute to our departed neighbor, Jack Quester.'

Boyle put both hands on his arm, drew him close. 'Where's Carl, damn it?' he hissed.

'That's the second time you've put a hand on me this day,' the major said coldly. 'It's a bad habit, Kelly.' Turning his head, he said: 'Uland!'

Rex Uland materialized out of the crowd. There was apprehension on some faces at the way Kelly Boyle was manhandling the major, but when Uland, flanked by Conover and Roone, stepped forward, there were sighs of relief.

'You want somethin', Major?' Uland asked, but the eyes darting to Boyle's face had murder in them.

'Stand by, Rex. Just stand by.'

Boyle drew a deep breath, knowing he couldn't fight the three of them. Not here, with Samantha on tiptoe only a few feet away, trying to see what was going on, and Luanne nearby, and other women, and youngsters at a run, yelling in some game of their own. Releasing the major's arm, he ran the sweated palm of a hand along the seam of his black pants. 'All right, Major,' he said grudgingly, 'I'll go along with you.'

'Before our Mexican venture,' the major said softly, 'there will be some papers for you to sign.' Then, in a normal voice: 'Now, if you will be good enough to join me at the ranch.' Turning on his heel, the major walked away.

'About time that upstart Kelly Boyle got taken down a peg,' a man said. Boyle didn't even look around.

There was quite a procession of buggies and wagons and saddlers heading for Box R. Boyle kept back, letting the major and Uland ride ahead. He noticed that Uland's large upper body was bent toward the major, riding at his side as if listening, then he straightened up, nodded, and glanced back at Boyle. A smile flickered across the thick lips, then the man faced front.

Samantha rode close. She had changed clothes at the hotel, as had many of the women. 'I was afraid Uland and those other two might jump you,' she said, sounding worried.

He smiled and shook his head. 'Just the

major playing games.'

'You be careful, Kelly. Dad and I are going back to roundup. I'll remember what you asked me to tell Pete Lambourne.'

Boyle thanked her. Then she and her father spurred their horses north, in the direction of the last roundup camp.

Boyle settled down to the eight-mile ride, deciding to play along with the major, at least for now. If he crossed the line on his own, it might be a week before he located Carl, even longer, he had to admit. And the major knew where Carl was, had been negotiating with his captors. So he claimed, at any rate. Unless the major was lying.

Of the forty or fifty cowhands scattered over the three Box R ranches, some fifteen were on hand that day. Barbecue pits had been dug; meat was roasting. Tables had been set up on sawhorses under the trees.

While nearly everyone lined up for the food, eulogies to Jack Quester were offered by those who had known him well. Luanne sat stiffly in a chair on the verandah. A fiddle and concertina played mournful tunes, which only added to the gloom of the occasion.

Boyle overheard snatches of conversation that concerned a railroad to pierce the vast reaches of northern Mexico, the major talking to potential investors in his mad dream. Boyle was suddenly aware that Luanne was trying to signal him with her eyes. When he nodded that he understood, she got up and walked the length of the verandah and down the rear steps, halting near the entrance to the office where Jack Quester used to keep books for her father.

'What an ordeal it's been for you, Luanne,' Boyle greeted her.

Looking around to make sure no one had followed her, she suddenly gripped his wrist. 'Kelly, let's slip away. We can be married at Empire.'

He looked at her, then said: 'Your father claims he knows where Carl is across the line. If he's telling the truth, I've got to go after him.'

Luanne's lips slowly parted. She dropped her hand from his wrist. Smoke from the barbecue drifted into the trees. 'Carl, again, I see,' Luanne said. She captured a strand of dark hair that had come loose and tucked it over an ear. 'Maybe you didn't hear what I said, Kelly. I ... I suggested we elope.'

'I'm sorry your dreams of Colorado didn't work out.'

'I wasn't looking forward to Colorado particularly.'

'It's what you wanted. To get away from this.' He nodded at the house towering above them.

'It depended on whom I was getting away from it with.' She gave a strained laugh.

'Horrible English and Miss Gramercy would have scolded me.' Moisture appeared at the corners of the violet eyes. 'I'm literally throwing myself at you, Kelly.'

'Look, Luanne...'

'My God, it's what you wanted, isn't it? As I told you in the note, I'm even willing to rent us a house in Bluewater ... temporarily.'

'I don't know anything about any note. And I can't think of anything but going after Carl.'

'Always Carl, isn't it? Always.'

'Wait a minute, Luanne, back up. Your intended has been buried, and now you want to run away with me. I thought you were in love with Jack.'

'I liked him. It's you who has ruined so much,' she accused, her voice shaking. 'Please don't compound it!'

That stung him. 'You couldn't have loved me very much, if you could turn to Jack. And now that he's dead, you want to swing back to me.'

'Jack would still be alive, if you'd gone away with me as I wanted.' Her chin began to tremble. 'And none of this terrible business would have happened.'

'And you should have agreed to make your life at Diamond Deuce.'

'It is important that we marry,' she said, after getting hold of herself. 'So I am asking you once again to forget that partner of yours and think of me ... of us.'

'Look, Luanne, I've got to bring Carl out of Mexico. That I've got to do before I can think of anything else.'

The large violet eyes grew moist again. Tears seemed to anger her, and she knuckled them away. 'You've always thought of your own happiness. Never of mine. And because of it you put me through one of the greater ordeals of my life. Your partner, murdering poor Jack...'

'It wasn't murder.' Weariness and frustration were beginning to strip away the safeguards he had erected around his temper. And it was probably a good thing, he thought, that she whirled, picked up her black dress to keep it from dragging on the steps, and climbed quickly to the verandah. She hurried into the house. A door slammed.

It was later, with some of the guests already departing, that the major found Kelly Boyle standing alone, smoking a cigar. 'There's a speech I want you to make to my guests.'

'Everything's been said for Jack. I'm not up to a eulogy.' He lowered his voice. 'All I want is word about Carl.'

'In due time,' the major said calmly. Tumbleweeds piled at the base of poplars that lined the ranch road were beginning to stir as a breeze came up. 'Kelly, I'm hiring you as of today,' the major said with an exaggerated smile.

'The only reason I stand here talking to you at all is because of Carl Tripp. Now tell me, damn it.'

'Kelly, it all ties in. A railroad to be built. It means power. I want you to ramrod my ranches and act as my contact with Mexican *políticos*.'

'And what do I get out of it?'

'Rich, Kelly, *rich*.'

'And what about Carl?'

'He stays alive.'

'Who's got him?'

But the major wasn't ready to divulge such information yet. Soberly the major said: 'It's up to you. Kelly. Whether Carl Tripp lives or dies.'

'I want proof that Carl's alive.'

'Kelly, I'm in a high-stakes game. The biggest of my life. Gambling everything on success. I will not be thwarted by you or anyone.'

'Proof, damn it, I want proof that Carl's alive, then we'll talk.'

'First you're going to eat a little crow for the way you talked to me at roundup. I want you to address the remaining guests from the verandah. Tell them you're cutting loose from your partner. That you're going to ramrod my ranches.'

'And what about Uland?' Boyle asked through his teeth.

'It'll be up to you to settle with him.' Major Ransom gestured at the verandah;

they were at the foot of the steps. 'Now go up and make your speech like a good boy.' Teeth gleaming beneath his mustache, the major raised his voice to get the attention of his guests. 'Everybody come in closer. Kelly Boyle has an announcement to make.'

'The hell with it,' Kelly said sharply.

The major lowered his voice. 'I'm offering to let you do it the easy way, Kelly.' When Boyle just stood looking at him scornfully, the major added: 'Otherwise...'

Boyle turned his back and started to shove his way through the half circle of onlookers who had gathered to hear his speech.

That was when the major said: 'Uland. Seems like he needs that lesson, after all.'

Chapter Eleven

Boyle felt an instant icy prickle along his nape. He made a half turn to look over his shoulder at the major who was scampering up the verandah steps. At that moment Uland lunged like a maddened bull from where he had been hidden behind the chinaberry trees next to the house, crashing into Kelly Boyle on the blind side, knocking the breath out of him. Boyle found himself on the ground and heard shouts and screams of frightened women. Trying to drag in breath, he flopped over onto his stomach. Pebbles cut into his face.

Someone grabbed him by the thick brown hair and jerked his head from the ground. A boot toe, aimed for his jaw, only scraped it as Boyle jerked his head, but even so the blow was jarring. Somehow Boyle managed to reach his feet, while Uland taunted him. His legs were shaky and threatened to give way. Through a haze he saw a fist. He tried to duck, but the fist exploded against his temple like a hammer. It filled his head with lightning. For the second time he found himself on the ground.

'You got him, Uland!' became a litany.

As Boyle lay, gasping for breath, he knew that Uland's long-simmering jealousy over Luanne could end in his death. Uland, looming above, swung a foot as he would to kick a tin can. A shuddering impact against the ribs brought an outcry from Boyle. Above the tumult in the yard and the even greater sounds boiling inside his own skull, he heard the major's shouted warning.

'Boyle, if you're whipped, there's no hope for your partner. No future for yourself. Nothing!'

Up on the verandah Luanne struggled with her father, tears streaming down her cheeks. Boyle was unaware of this, or of Luanne's protests.

'You brutal man to plan a thing like this!' she cried.

'I told Kelly there might be a sporting event here.' The major's eyes were shining as he watched the two combatants in the yard below. He saw Boyle go down again, but somehow managing to escape Uland's swinging boot.

That was when Boyle seized the foreman by the leg, holding the leg and forcing Uland to hop backwards, arms windmilling. He broke through the circle of shouting men, scattering them. Uland lost his balance, fell on his rump, twisted aside, and sprang back to his feet.

This time Boyle was ready and met

Uland's rush with jabs to the face and head.

'There's the son I never had!' the major was shouting now, hands cupped to his mouth. 'You can do it, Kelly. Do it, boy!'

Luanne turned her wet eyes to the exultant older man, saying scornfully: 'As I am the daughter *you* never had!' Spinning away, when he tried to grab her, she hurried into the house.

'Stay and watch it, Luanne!' the major yelled, laughing. But she was rushing upstairs to her room. Soon he forgot about her because his attention became riveted again on the gladiators below.

In Boyle's distorted vision it seemed that a trio of Ulands, big snarling men, were bearing down on him. As the three of them rushed him, Boyle had a split second to choose his target. He lashed out at a face but struck a shoulder instead. Uland's fist tore open his left cheek, the force of the blow caving his knees. To save himself he seized the front of Uland's shirt. As Uland tried to thrust him aside, the shirt came off in Boyle's hands, exposing a tangle of chest hair the color of rusty wire.

When they broke apart, Uland triumphantly chopped away at Boyle's midsection in a series of short, vicious blows. But Boyle was backing at the time and escaped the full impact of the hammering. Even so, Boyle's legs threatened to collapse. Somehow he stiffened his knees, struck hard at Uland's belly, which brought a grunt of pain and surprise from the big man, this followed by a great *whooshing* of expelled breath, laced strongly with an odor of whiskey.

Desperately Boyle called on every ounce of reserve in following up the telling blow. His head had cleared so that there were no longer three enemies, just one. This time his blows to the face landed solidly. Without letup, he slashed away at the torn and bloodied features of the foreman. Blood trickled from a cut above Uland's left eyebrow. An enraged Uland brushed the worm of blood aside. It was a mistake, for in that moment Boyle's fists sank deeper than before into his opponent's midriff. As Uland reeled, Conover gave a yell and moved in.

'Get him, Rex!' Conover cried. A shouting weight climbed Boyle's back, nearly driving him face down into the dirt, but at the last moment he retained his balance.

Then came the major's shout from the verandah, as Conover clung, resisting all efforts of Boyle to dislodge him. 'Uland's to do it alone, Conover!'

If Conover heard him, he gave no sign. He hung on Boyle's back, pinioning the arms, and Uland was coming at a hard run, obviously intending to end it, his features smeared with blood and dirt.

Before Uland could smash into him headlong, Boyle dropped to his knees, and Con-over went sailing over his head and into Uland. Both men spilled to the ground in a tangle of arms and legs. This brought a roar from excited onlookers that beat at Boyle's eardrums.

Uland regained his feet, rushed in again. This time Boyle met Uland's wild rush with a swinging left that smashed the nose. A scream of pain and rage broke from Uland's torn lips. As Uland, sagging, made a half turn, Boyle struck him twice on the jaw. Uland reeled, eyes rolling back in his head. As Uland collapsed, the major gave a cry of delight and came running down the veran-dah steps and to the yard. Leaping over Uland's crumpled form, he seized Boyle by the arms.

'Kelly, you've won the job!' he cried. 'You're my man. Your starting salary is twenty thousand, plus a percentage of beef sold.'

Boyle's chest hurt, and his head felt as if it had taken all four wheels of a loaded wagon. Someone shoved a dipper of water into his hands. He drank and poured the balance over his head. An excited babble of voices rose in the yard as men discussed his victory over Uland. Then he allowed the major to lead him to the ranch office under the verandah.

'You put Uland up to it, damn you,' Boyle muttered.

'A test, Kelly, only a test.' And at Boyle's bitter laugh, the major added: 'My bargain concerning your partner still stands.'

Boyle flopped into a padded leather chair while the major filled two glasses with whiskey. The first drink the major handed him, he tossed off. The second one he sipped.

The major seated himself behind a flat-topped desk and tossed a folded piece of dirty paper to Boyle. 'This came yesterday. After I had made my contacts.'

Boyle opened the paper. There was no mistaking Carl Tripp's handwriting.

Dere Kelly
I am a prizoner. They gonna kill me if you don't do like the majer sez. Yur frend and podner.

The note bore Carl's scrawl of a signature.

'That proves I know where he is,' the major said softly. 'Am I right, Kelly?'

'Seems so. What's the next step?'

'A reading of a contract between two gentlemen. Us, Kelly.'

Boyle leaned back in the padded chair, sipped whiskey, and read the contract handed him by the major. It was right to the point, no excess wordage. He was to be paid twenty thousand a year for supervising the three Box R ranches. He was to sell Diamond Deuce cattle to Box R, but was to retain ownership of Diamond Deuce land.

That part of it was puzzling.

'Thought you wanted Diamond Deuce for yourself.'

Major Ransom smiled. 'It's in the form of a bonus.'

'What do you mean ... bonus?'

'You have title to the land, but I have right of trespass, of course. But over the years you can restock it. I've heard you're a man who likes something of his own.'

'I can't figure you caring whether I do or not.' Boyle's hurts from the fight were diminishing, but in rubbing a hand gingerly over his face he felt the swellings and knew he must look a sight.

Major Ransom perched himself on a corner of the desk, foot swinging. With a smile he said: 'I don't ever want to hear it said again that I have a heart as hard as summit rock.'

'Seems you like to keep a man off balance.'

'That's part of the game, Kelly, my boy.'

'Then why not let me keep my Diamond Deuce cattle?'

The major stabbed a forefinger at a clause in the contract. 'You notice that I bind you for a period of only two years. After that, you're free to go.'

Because of a deep cut alongside his mouth it hurt Boyle to smile, but he managed. 'All of a sudden you're generous?'

'I don't think you'll want to cut loose. Kelly.' Hazel eyes were bright with triumph.

'A taste of wealth can make even you forget about wanting to be your own man.' The major leaned close. 'Kelly, you'll have more power than you could ever possibly have on your own. It's a heady feeling. You'll never want to let go of it.' He stood up. 'Besides, you'll be saving the life of your partner.'

Ransom dipped a pen point, drained it in the well, then handed the pen to Boyle. But Boyle was rereading the last paragraph which stated that Major Ransom had final say in movement of cattle, of equipment, and in naming a crew.

Boyle looked up. 'What's this about the crew?'

'You run my ranches, Kelly,' the major said, almost laughing. 'But I run you.'

'The hell...'

'Read your own copy, Kelly. It's identical. Then sign, if you will. Time is running out for Carl Tripp.'

Kelly Boyle signed, laid down the pen, folded his own copy, and shoved it into the hip pocket of the pants to his ruined dark suit. The coat was torn; one knee was out of the trousers, and it was smeared with dirt and blood.

'Let's go get Carl Tripp,' Boyle said, climbing to his feet.

'Tomorrow,' the major said. 'I'll see that the wagons are loaded.'

'With rifles, I suppose.'

'Of course. A thousand of them at a time in exchange for a herd of Mexican cattle. Pretty clever of me, eh, Kelly? To pick a time of a rising cattle market.'

Boyle went to the door. 'See you in the morning.'

'There are spare bedrooms in this house.'

'Yeah, I know.'

When he went out to get his horse, there were still some of the guests lingering to talk about the historic battle between Boyle and Rex Uland.

A bearded man spoke up. 'You whipped Uland, but it don't prove nothin' to me if you still stick up for your partner. He murdered Jack Quester.'

Boyle didn't even reply. Keeping one eye open for Uland or the pair he always ran with, Roone and Conover, he hit the Bluewater road. In town he got his warbag, changed clothes, had two drinks at the Great River Saloon, a steak dinner, then went to bed in a room at the Bluewater Hotel.

No one had commented on his ravaged face. From the look in his gray eyes, they knew enough to leave him alone.

As the afternoon had worn on out at Diamond Deuce, Florence Tripp had become apprehensive. Could she actually spend the night alone at Diamond Deuce? Vivid in her mind were the three tough Box R men who had ridden off with Kelly Boyle.

She found the dress Boyle had torn, wadded up behind the bed. She spread it out, decided it wasn't worth salvaging, and wadded it up again and threw it in a corner of the closet. After washing her face, she felt better. At least, her forehead had stopped bleeding. But there was no sign of Pete Lambourne and the two riders. Had Kelly said they would be here today, tomorrow, or when? She couldn't remember. Everything was a jumble in her mind – being knocked against the house by one of the horses, Kelly finding her and what had followed. She thought back on it with a wistful smile. The hours dragged on.

Finally she panicked, transferred some of her things from her trunk to the carpetbag. Then she went to the corral and, after several tries, managed to rope out a little mare that Carl had said might be easy for her to ride. As the mare stood patiently, she tried to remember just how to place the saddle, and she finally got it straight, cinched it, and tied her carpetbag to the cantle. Then she mounted up, her dress sliding up her legs – the least of her worries.

She had a few gold coins that would provide food and lodging for several days. She would stay at the hotel in Bluewater and keep her ears open for news of Carl. After

Carl was safe, or she knew he was dead – she shuddered at the thought – then she'd move on. To where she didn't know.

It was much later that she suddenly remembered the rifle Boyle had left for her. She had gone off without it. Well, it was too far to go back for it now. She kept the mare at a fast walk that was gradually eating up the miles.

She thought of the weeks she had been at Diamond Deuce, how Kelly Boyle had kept everything going. Carl rarely did his part. She fell to thinking about Kelly, how things might have turned out differently, if he hadn't been so loyal to Carl.

All this was going through her mind when a big Texas jack sprang suddenly from a clump of mesquite right in front of the mare. So surprising was the jackrabbit's appearance, bounding away in great leaps, that the mare was spooked. It reared, neighing shrilly. Florence lost her grip on the reins, her feet popped out of the stirrups, and she was hurled backward into the road, landing with such force that she momentarily lost consciousness.

Finally her mind cleared, and she sat up. She tasted dirt and blood from a small cut inside her mouth. Climbing to her feet, she looked into the mesquite and the tall trees on either side of the road. But there was no sign of the mare.

She started walking in the direction of Bluewater. *Good Lord, let me make it before dark* was her prayer.

At his foreman's quarters at Box R, Uland treated his bruises with arnica. Then he had several cups of coffee at the cook shack and three stiff drinks of whiskey from a bottle he kept hidden under his blankets. Whiskey and his hatred of Kelly Boyle swung his thoughts to that golden-haired female out at Diamond Deuce. Carl Tripp's woman. She was out there alone. Tripp was somewhere in northern Mexico. The major had told him that much. He didn't think Boyle had gone back to Diamond Deuce, but even if he had... It hurt Uland to grin because of lips that Boyle had smashed against his teeth.

He summoned Conover and Roone. 'Let's go pick ourselves a little honey.'

Both men were eager, but at the same time wary when Uland explained. 'What if Boyle is out there?' Conover wanted to know.

'We'll kill the son-of-a-bitch.'

Roone nervously fingered the deep scar on his cheek. 'Hey, the major won't like that none ... not now.'

'Got a hunch Boyle ain't even at Diamond Deuce,' Uland said. 'He's likely crossed the line to look for his partner.'

Near the fork in the Bluewater road and the north ranch road they found a sorrel mare hung up in the brush by tangled reins and by a carpetbag tied on. It was branded Diamond Deuce, and a peek in the carpetbag showed it to be full of a woman's things.

Uland immediately guessed what had happened. 'The mare throwed her.' He began looking around for sign. He found it some forty yards south, a woman's footprints heading in the direction of town.

Florence was walking along the road, her feet dragging, hoping someone would come along in a wagon and give her a lift into Bluewater. She had no idea how far it was. It seemed that she had been walking for hours. Straight ahead, she caught a glimmer of sunlight on water through the trees. It was the river. Could town be very far?

Where the road made a great curve, she saw some riders coming across open country, leading a horse. It looked like her mare. She was sure of it, when they got close enough so she could see the carpetbag tied to the cantle. Then she froze because the big man in the lead had a misshapen face, and, when he grinned as he was doing now, he had the look of a gargoyle.

'There she is!' he shouted.

It was Rex Uland. What in the world had happened to his face? And the other two had been with Uland when they had taken Kelly Boyle away with them. She forced a

bright smile and said: 'Thank you for finding my horse. I'm afraid I'm a rather bad
rider.'

Uland swept her onto his lap with a long
arm and went spurring off into the trees.
Then he set her down and dismounted beside a towering cottonwood. His intention
was plain. He reeked of whiskey, as did the
other two. Uland tripped her, when she
started to run, flung her to the ground, and
pinned her with his weight. She screamed
and tried to fight him.

'You'll hang for this!' she cried.

'Who'd believe what you say, ma'am?' The
gargoyle face grinned down at her.

'Any decent man.'

'Major Ransom ... he wanted to know
about you ... so he hired the Pinkertons. I
seen the letter on his desk. You already got a
husband. You ain't even married to Carl
Tripp. And you was hangin' around the Rio
Vista up at Lucero. You ain't nothin' but a
whore, ma'am. An' no man ever raped a
whore. Ain't possible.' He tittered. 'We'll
even leave you a few dollars.'

She appealed to the man with the cowlick
and the burly one with the scarred cheek.
'Help me, please help me.'

They just stared and passed a bottle back
and forth.

Suddenly her hand shot out, and she
seized Uland at a place Sam Joe Taylor had

told her to grab a man that gave her trouble instead of love. Uland let out a yowl, rolled on the ground, holding himself. Leaping to her feet, she pulled up skirts and began to run. But Roone caught her, threw her to the ground. Something crashed into her face, numbing her. 'Oh, no, please ... don't hurt me.'

'Looky what you done to Rex!' he cried and hit her again.

It was Conover who drew out his heavy belt. While Roone held her, upended, skirts and petticoats falling over her face, the belt landed again and again.

Finally the punishment was finished. She could only see out of one eye, and her head felt odd. 'I ... I'll do what you want. Please don't hurt me any more.'

It pained her to lie on the spring grass because of what had been done to her with the belt, but she played a little game. As she had learned to endure on those nights when Sam Joe brought home clients, so she endured Roone and Conover and, finally, Uland. Endured them a second time.

How much longer she would have been forced to accept them she would never know because Uland suddenly said: 'What the hell! It's a kid! Over there! Get him, boys!'

She rolled her head and saw a small Mexican boy astride a mule, not forty feet away, staring with mouth open.

Roone, at a drunken run, fired three times, but the boy had turned his mule and gone spurring across the river, sand and mud flying. Roone and Conover went after him, but lost him on the Mexican side. They came back.

'Kid got away,' Roone reported.

'Hell with that!' Uland angrily adjusted his clothing. 'We'll run him down!'

They got their horses and went pounding in the direction the Mexican boy had taken. She lay, hurting from instep to her aching head. Fists and the belt had been punishing. Somehow she struggled to her feet and stood, hair hanging over her bleeding face, looking for the mare, but it had wandered off.

All she could think of was self-preservation. For if they succeeded in running down the Mexican boy and silencing him, then they would be back. Men so lacking in conscience would kill her and hide her body. At a lurching run, she headed deeper into the trees until, out of breath, she collapsed.

Because he was small for his age, Chico De Gama hoped they might think he was much younger, so young he wouldn't understand what the three of them had been doing to the woman. But he knew. Cowboys from the ranches sometimes brought girls along the river. On those other times there had been sweet sounds, and sometimes giggling from the girls. At first, because of her beaten face, he hadn't realized who she was, then recognized her as the woman he had seen in town riding in the Diamond Deuce wagon with Carl Tripp, Kelly Boyle's partner. He had crossed the river on sand bars, his mule and himself soaked, for the water was rising. It was his hope that the men would think he lived on the Mexican side. Some miles up-river he crossed back to the American side.

When he got home, Felicita stared at her white-faced young son. 'You have the look of death, *hijito*.'

'It is a pain in the belly,' Chico said, for he could not bring himself to tell his mother what he had seen the three men doing to poor *Señora* Tripp.

'How did school go this week?' Felicita asked narrowly.

'It went fine.'

He went outside, embarrassed to meet his mother's probing eyes. Tomorrow, Sunday, he would have to ride all the way back to Bluewater for another week of schooling. What if he ran into the three men who worked for Box R? The possibility turned him cold.

Chapter Twelve

The following morning, when Kelly Boyle tied his horse to the iron boy at the foot of the verandah steps at Box R, Sarah, the thin-faced cook, came out to tell him the major wanted him in the dining room. Boyle followed her inside, disappointed that Luanne wasn't sharing the long table with her father. The major, in a jovial mood, offered his hand which Boyle pretended not to notice. As Sarah filled a cup from a silver coffee pot and handed it to Boyle, the major spoke of the historic fight of the previous day.

'You hoped Uland would break my neck,' Boyle said with a thin smile from his end of the table.

'The confrontation with Uland was to make you earn your place with me.'

'Seems I earned it.'

'You did. I felt it necessary for you to prove that you were a better man than Uland.'

'By having my brains on the ground.'

'Now you'll have the respect of the crew.'

'How soon do we go and get Carl Tripp?'

'I'm having wagons loaded.' The major lowered his cup. 'By the way, you should have been here to issue the orders as my super-intendent. Oh, well, we'll let that pass. A thousand rifles at a time you'll deliver to Diego Esparza, Kelly. In exchange for a thousand head of Mexican cattle.'

'I'm surprised he doesn't want the whole ten thousand at once.'

'Oh, but he does, Kelly. He does.' The major smiled and tapped himself on the temple with a forefinger. 'But I was using my head. We'll see how he does after we deliver, say, five thousand rifles. Then, if all goes well, we'll make a final delivery of the remaining five thousand. And collect five thousand head of cattle.'

'Esparza's the one who has Carl Tripp, of course.'

'Of course.' The major pushed aside his empty plate, which Sarah collected. 'The minute I learned Tripp was probably in Mexico, I got in touch with Esparza.'

'Let's get moving, Major.'

Boyle got up from his chair, but the major made waving motions for him to sit down. 'Sarah's cooking you a fine breakfast.'

'I ate in town. I want Carl Tripp back on this side of the line. The sooner the better.'

As they were going out the door, Boyle limping slightly from the fight with Uland, the major said: 'I hope your partner has the good sense to accept an offer I will make. To get out of Texas ... and leave his woman here.'

'That's impossible. Carl loves her.'

'I happen to know they're not man and wife.'

'That has nothing to do with love.'

'I had plans for the woman. When she went with Tripp, I admit to being ... upset. Oh, well, we shall see.'

On the ride out from town, Boyle had felt that even his horse at a walk would jar his head loose and send it rolling into the grama grass. But after a few miles the pain had diminished.

'I had a talk with Uland last night,' the major was saying, 'and he's agreed to stay on as foreman.'

'You're full of surprises, Major.'

'He'll take your orders, of course.'

'I don't want him around.'

'I'm afraid you didn't read your contract carefully, Kelly. I dictate who is to be a member of the crew.'

Have it your way ...for now – crossed Boyle's mind.

When then were midway across the big yard, he turned and looked back at the house, at the second floor windows, hoping to see Luanne. There was no sign of her.

'I see your eyes hopefully search for my daughter,' the major chuckled. 'I fail to understand that girl,' he added soberly. 'But I do think the right man could mold her into shape.'

'You mean like training a horse.'

'Every woman needs a man's strong hand. My wife, Ellamae, rebelled, which was completely out of character for someone of her background.'

Kelly Boyle almost laughed, because for the first time he was thinking rather fondly of California, where Luanne said she would like to live, and he himself was getting damned sick of Texas. He could forgive her turning to poor Jack Quester, if she would be willing to forget some of the things he had said in anger. Once Carl Tripp was clear of this mess, he'd sell Diamond Deuce, and to hell with the major and his contract. The four of them, Luanne, Carl, and Florence, would make new lives for themselves. Farewell to Texas!

'Kelly, what's so amusing?' Major Ransom asked curiously, staring up into his face. 'You were smiling.'

'Thinking of the future is all,' Boyle said, erasing his smile.

'What do you think of Conover? After all, he butted into your fight with Uland yesterday.'

'I don't think much of him.'

'Perhaps, but I think he'll remain on the payroll. Unless he does something to displease me ... personally.'

Boyle uttered a bark of laughter. 'Starting in on the thumb screws already, eh, Major?'

'You signed a contract which states that I have the say concerning crew. And certain other matters. Get that look off your face, Kelly. In time you'll learn to enjoy the game as much as I do.' Then he added: 'I think a review of the troops is in order.'

They had skirted the first of the barns. The major beckoned to one of the hands wearing a leather apron. He issued crisp orders to round up every man he could reach and have them assembled at the bunkhouse within thirty minutes.

When the man pulled off his leather apron and went loping to the nearest horse, the major led Boyle through the trees to the small barn set apart from the others. Two wagons were in front. Men were loading sacks of grain over cased rifles.

'One thousand rifles, Kelly,' the major said proudly. 'In exchange for one thousand head of Mexican cattle. The beginning of our wealth.' He nudged Boyle along his tender ribs, pounded yesterday by Uland's fists.

It was hard for Boyle to contain his impatience, also his smouldering rage, directed at the martinet strutting at his side. The major halted at the wagons. He was smoking a cheroot, looking quite jaunty in his freshly ironed gray suit. He was speaking again of the riches to be taken from Mexico.

Boyle tried to turn the voice off; he was tired of hearing it. He put his attention on yesterday, how stunning Luanne had looked in black at Jack Quester's funeral. Then another image inserted itself into his consciousness – Samantha Shelly with her flaming hair, the freckles, tall and shapely. It was the first time he had seen her dressed up. Abruptly he concentrated on killdees that were making spring sounds in some nearby willows. Then he was aware that the major had turned and was speaking to him.

'You work for me those two years, Kelly, and I hope for the rest of your days. As I said, once you feel power in your hands, you'll never let go.'

'Maybe.' Boyle gave a slight shrug.

'But should you try to double-cross me...,' the major said, his back rigid as a pole. 'In that event,' he continued after a significant pause, 'I will spend every dollar, use every political influence possible to prevent you from ever again getting a foothold in the cattle business.'

'Anything else?' Boyle asked, giving the austere profile a cold smile.

'Letting you retain Diamond Deuce wasn't altogether a benevolent gesture on my part.'

'I kind of figured that out for myself, Major.'

'You won't want to ride off and leave a ranch that's in your name. And it goes without saying that, if you do try to cross me, you'll never live to buy your first cow for

Diamond Deuce.'

Boyle focused his attention on far-off California and the new lives he was planning for Luanne and Florence and Carl and for himself. He wondered what Luanne's reaction would be when Carl and Florence were finally married and she realized they had been living in what was commonly called 'sin.' The thought made him smile. Luanne as an emancipated young woman wouldn't be shocked, he was sure.

'Do you realize I could have driven you off Diamond Deuce any time I wished,' the major said.

'Perhaps.'

'But I didn't move against you, Kelly. You offered a challenge I sorely needed.'

Once Carl was safe, the major could have his loco dreams of power and railroads and the rest of it. Boyle flexed his long arms, aware of grinding pain from yesterday's battle, pain that helped to keep his temper on a hair trigger.

'But, of course, you're not going to try a double-cross,' the major said heartily, 'so we'll forget about it, eh?'

Right then, Rex Uland came stomping up the stairs from the underground hiding place of the rifles.

'All set, Major...' He broke off upon seeing Boyle, and his misshapen face began to redden, swellings and cuts and bruises.

'I told Boyle that you're quite willing to accompany him, and take his orders,' the major said briskly.

Uland grunted something, his hatred palpable. Turning on his heel, he went back inside the barn.

'If my face looks half as bad as his, no wonder Luanne didn't come downstairs this morning,' Boyle said with a sharp laugh.

'I doubt if that's the reason,' the major assured him. 'She's sulking. We had another argument last night, and she threw it up to me about her mother's ... lover ... the cowboy named Sean. Luanne has some crazy notion that Sean, not me, was her father.'

'And?'

'I finally convinced her that Sean didn't show up at Box R until two years after Luanne was born. He was a young man I took a liking to. As I've taken a liking to you, Kelly. I had my men drive him out with their rope ends. Literally whipping the clothes off his body. I could have killed him and been within my rights.' He strutted to the barn door, shouted at Uland: 'You stay here and keep an eye on the rifles. The rest of you come along.'

The men exchanged glances, but did as they were told. Others were waiting in the bunkhouse, some fifteen altogether. The major came right to the point, introducing Kelly Boyle as the new Box R superintendent. Boyle lifted a hand but said nothing. Only a few of them responded. Most looked surly.

'Rex Uland has agreed to stay on as foreman. Roone and Conover will remain as *segundos*.' The major looked them in the eye and said: 'I'm sure you'll want to be loyal to the superintendent of an outfit that pays the best wages in Texas.'

That straightened the men up, hopeful smiles replacing the surliness. The major had never been overly generous, but maybe things were changing. They looked at each other, nodding, grinning.

One of them pushed forward, saying: 'I'll work for you, Mister Boyle.'

The wagons were driven to the front yard where they halted in front of the main house. Just then, Al Quester came riding in from the ranch the major had so recently purchased.

'Where you goin' with the load, Major?' Al Quester asked.

'You'll be going along, Al,' the major announced with a tight smile.

'The hell ... I got things to do.'

Boyle shot the major a look. First Uland was going along and now Al Quester, two men who hated his guts. He stepped forward, Al seeing him for the first time, standing beside a sweated saddle horse.

'Your visit social or trouble?' Boyle drawled.

Quester peered at him, then said: 'If it was

a mule made a mess of your face, I aim to buy the critter an' pension him off on good grass for the rest of his days.' Quester guffawed. 'I hear Uland damn' near killed you.'

'Not quite.'

Quester hunched heavy shoulders. 'You an' me ever tangle, it won't be damn' near.' Then he turned, big gun jiggling at his hip. 'Major, I come for my money.'

'You're late, Al. I told you to be here early.'

'Was plumb wore out. Roundup an'... other things.' His small eyes swept to Boyle, standing spraddle-legged in the yard. 'How about the rest of my money?'

'You don't get it ... yet.'

'What you mean ... I don't get it?' Quester glared at the shorter man.

'Didn't you read the document we both signed?' The major seemed almost apologetic. 'Surely you read it, or is it a matter of failing eyesight? And you're quite young for that.'

Quester's shoulders stiffened under a blue work shirt that lye soap had faded almost white. 'Don't try no slick trick with me,' he warned.

Then Boyle heard the major state that there had been a condition in the bill of sale between Major Terrence Ransom and Alfred Quester, stating that Quester was to be available to do the major's bidding for a period of six months.

Al Quester bristled. 'Never said nothin' like that.'

'Right there in black and white.' The major winked at Boyle, who did not return the wink.

'If it was there,' Quester said, calming a little, 'I sure never paid no mind to it, Major. But I'd sure like to get my hands on the rest of my money.'

'Well, now that we have that settled,' the major said, 'I want you to accompany Kelly Boyle on an expedition to Mexico.'

'Sooner pull thorns out of a bear's nose.'

'Al, you'll go along with what I say, or you won't receive one nickel more from the sale of your ranch.'

'Yeah? Well, I'll just see the sheriff up at Empire about this,' Quester threatened.

This brought a laugh from the major. 'You do that, Al.'

Al Quester flung his hands wide. 'So you own the sheriff an' about everything else in Tyburn County.' The face with its long jaw turned red. 'But this is a damn' swindle.'

'I've already offered a fair price for your ranch,' the major said patiently. 'I could have stalled, to see if Jack had relatives who might share in it.'

'I already done told you, Jack an' me was the only ones left.'

'Your telling me doesn't make it necessarily so, Al.'

Quester fumed and threatened, while the major smiled, obviously enjoying himself.

'It's only right,' the major said, when Al paused for breath, 'that I'm able to avail myself of your valuable services for a period of six months.'

'Don't push me, Major.' Quester clamped a hand to his gun.

But the major merely smiled and gave Boyle a nod. Boyle called out: 'Careful, Al.'

Quester spun, facing Boyle. He started to splutter, but something in Boyle's cold stare from the bruised face changed his mind. He removed his hand from the gun and shook his fingers as if they had just touched a hot stove lid.

Now that Al Quester had backed down, the Box R men visibly relaxed, some of them grinning.

'You'll be well paid for the Mexican venture,' Major Ransom said.

Quester's tangle of brows twitched. 'What you call well paid?'

'You'll have to take that up with my superintendent, Kelly Boyle. He'll boss the job.'

Al Quester was infuriated but had the good sense to make no overt move. 'You mean that, if I don't go along to Mexico, then I don't get the rest of my money.'

'Next time you have a contract, read it more thoroughly. Then you won't be surprised.'

Quester swallowed. 'What I got to do in Mexico, anyhow?'

'Help Kelly Boyle escort these two wagons.'

Quester stared at the wagons. 'What if we're jumped?'

'I'm buying your loyalty. I'm sure you'll make certain that my cargo arrives safely, and that you and the others return with whole hides. Then you can collect the rest of your money.'

'Seems like you got me in quicksand up to my chin.'

'Kelly Boyle will give you your orders.'

Boyle said: 'Cheer up, Al. We'll probably come back alive. One way or another.'

They reached the river, then headed north, the major giving Boyle instructions, Boyle relaying them to the others. Boyle looked back. Roone was driving the first wagon. His saddle horse was tied to the tailgate, a mount he'd use to help herd the thousand head of Mexican cattle. The second wagon was driven by Conover. Uland and Quester rode as escort.

The major seemed to know where he was going. Boyle didn't question him. He rode with back muscles tense, almost able to feel the hatred behind him. Uland he could understand, being knocked cold yesterday in front of those who had come to pay tribute to Jack Quester. Quester he could understand, because of Carl Tripp's killing his brother, Jack. Conover seemed apprehensive, yet filled with hatred, and the same could be said of Roone. Boyle pondered as he rode.

Just a few miles south of Lucero, the major reined in. 'This is the place. Kelly, fire your gun. Two quick shots, a pause, and then a third.'

Boyle glanced at the men at his back and shook his head. 'No, Major.'

'But it's the arranged signal.'

'You fire the shots,' Boyle said. 'I just might need those three bullets.'

'As you wish.' With a faint grin, Major Ransom drew a revolver from under his coat, fired the two quick shots, then a third. An answering signal came from the far side.

They started across, the lead wagon smashing through cattails and reeds, splashing into mud holes, climbing sand banks.

'Don't let the wagons bog down,' Boyle shouted at Roone and Conover. 'Keep 'em moving!'

Quester glanced apprehensively at bleak hills and towering mesquite. 'Goddamn' major tricked me into this,' he muttered.

After making the crossing through the meager flow of water, they pulled up to rest the teams. A mockingbird swooped to their left, found a tree limb in some willows, and began to warble a protest at the intrusion. Conover, brushing aside his cowlick, swiftly drew his pistol. A snap shot blew the bird off the limb in a mass of feathers.

'No need for that,' Boyle said, spurring up. 'Scare the horses and I'll break your head.'

Conover gave him a tight smile. 'Figure to keep in practice. In case some *hombre* comes lookin' for me.'

From a corner of his eye, Boyle noticed Uland shake his head and Conover nodded, gesturing that he understood. He popped out the spent shell and reloaded. Boyle knew there was hidden meaning there, but what?

When they were a good mile from the river, there was a stirring of brush. A rider appeared, bare-headed, hair shaggy, batwing ears, protruding teeth, a little thin in the face. It was Carl Tripp, all right. Boyle felt like grinning, but held himself in. Two other horsemen, these wearing Mexican hats with curled brims, came out of the brush, spun their horses, then went pounding up a long slope to vanish in a maze of boulders.

'Kelly! Kelly!' Tripp gave a joyful whoop and came spurring up.

Now that Tripp was closer, Boyle could see an ugly gash on one cheek and that his scalp in front seemed raw and bald as if some of the coarse hair had been yanked out by the roots. Wearing the same shirt and pants, but no longer barefoot, someone had supplied him with boots to replace those left behind at roundup camp the night Jack Quester was killed.

'Carl, you made it,' Boyle said, his voice charged with emotion.

'Thanks to you I made it, Kelly.' A spate of hysterical laughter broke from the man. Then he saw Major Ransom sitting his saddle some twenty feet away. 'An' thanks to you, Major,' he called. 'I promised Esparza I'd say it.'

Down where the wagons had ground to a halt, Al Quester sat rigidly in the saddle, glowering at the man who had killed his brother. But the major spoke sharply to him, and Quester turned his horse and rode past the last wagon and sat with his back turned, staring at the sere mountains of northern Mexico.

Carl Tripp dismounted, leaned against the fine Jalisco pony, a substitute for the one he had probably ridden half to death the night he had fled across the line. 'Lucero ain't far, Kelly,' Tripp said. 'Let's you an' me go up there an' drink all the damn' whiskey they got in the place.'

'I know you've had hell over here.' Boyle waved a long arm to encompass the Mexican side of the river. 'Florence is waiting.'

'Hell with her. She's the one stirred things up between you an' me all along, *amigo*. Jeez, I've had plenty of time to think things out. Best she leaves, reckon.'

Boyle dismounted, looked into the homely

face. 'I thought you loved her.'

Tripp fingered the gash on his cheek. 'I figured you'd be glad she won't be around no more. You're better at them things than me, so you tell her, huh?'

'Tell her yourself, Carl.'

'Main thing is we can run the ranch ... without her bein' in the way.'

'There won't be any running of the ranch, Tripp,' the major said, riding up, an amused smile under the bristly mustache. In crisp tones he told Tripp about the contract Boyle had signed. 'According to the terms, I buy your share of the cattle. It will come to twelve thousand dollars. In cash.'

Carl Tripp almost fell against the barrel of the Mexican pony that had brought him from captivity. 'Twelve thousand dollars for ... for *me?*' He blinked at the major. 'Me alone?' And when the major nodded, he glanced at Boyle, his eyes shining. Then he let out an exuberant: '*Yeeeeooooowwwwweeee!*'

'Carl, listen to me...'

'First time I ever had any money of my own.'

'We've always shared,' Boyle said.

'Yeah, but with you always sayin' what we spend or don't spend. Hell, I was lucky to ever have two silver dollars to rub together.' Tripp leaned close. 'What happened to your face, anyhow? Mule kick you?'

'It felt like a mule, yeah.'

'Tell you one thing. It'll be kinda nice not to have to bust my ass on that two-bit spread from first light to last. Aw, hell, Kelly, don't look so down at the mouth. I was only funnin'.'

'Carl, you haven't said one word about Jack Quester. Jack was a nice *hombre*, and he's dead.'

'Well, he shouldn't have got in the way.'

Tripp mounted up and rode over to where Major Ransom sat his saddle, a look of amusement in the hazel eyes.

'Major, how soon do I get my money?'

'I'll have it in Bluewater by the end of the week. When I pay you off, I expect you to get out of Texas.'

'What if I don't?' Tripp was feeling cocky all of a sudden.

'A simple answer to that, Mister Tripp.' The major's voice hardened. 'You'll find yourself on the gallows for the murder of Jack Quester.'

Tripp blanched, then quickly recovered. 'Soon's you pay me, I'll be long gone from Texas.'

'Will you go alone ... without your woman?'

'You mean Flo?' Tripp rubbed his heavy jaw as he thought about it. 'I figure it's best to be shut of her. That right, Kelly? You an' me together, huh?'

'I have to stay in Texas.'

If Tripp even heard what he said, it made

no impression. 'Kelly, I figured you'd jump up an' bang your heels together when I said Flo wouldn't be with us.'

'Forget it, Carl.'

'You act like everything's my fault.'

'If you hadn't lost your temper and pulled a gun, Jack would be alive.'

'So that's all that ails you. I thought for a minute it was on account of Flo.' Tripp gave him a sudden, tight, sidelong glance. 'You acted like you were almost sweet on her yourself.'

Boyle didn't bother to answer that. His nerves were threatening to come unraveled – hurting from the fight yesterday, Tripp in one of his moods, and not thirty feet away men who would kill him as quickly as they could draw breath. To compound it, Al Quester stood rigid as a block of stone, glaring at the man who had shot his brother to death.

Tripp, being flat broke, asked the major for a loan. The major dug into his pocket and handed over three twenty-dollar gold pieces, the coins glittering in the sunlight as they lay nested in the broad palm of Carl Tripp's hand. He dropped the coins into his pocket and grinned at Boyle. 'You still mad?'

'Just kinda disgusted is all.'

'I'm the one that's suffered, you want to know. Them Mex bastards shot my hoss, an' I got some of my hair yanked out. You don't act like you're a damn' bit interested in what happened to me.'

'A lot of people have suffered, Carl. I imagine Jack had a split second of it. Just before you blew off the top of his head.'

Tripp's bloodshot eyes measured Boyle. Lips fringed in a stubble of yellowish beard twisted into a sour smile. 'Always givin' me lectures, ain't you, Kelly. But now that I got money of my own...'

'Oh, shut up, Carl. I'm tired of hearing about it.'

'Mister Tripp and I will now take leave of you, Kelly,' the major said stiffly. 'He'll accompany me to Bluewater. Won't you. Mister Tripp?'

'Hey, wait a minute, Major,' Kelly Boyle put in. 'You're supposed to deal with Esparza.'

'That's your job.' He raised his voice. 'Uland, give Tripp your gun. I want my escort to be armed.'

Uland, glowering, rode up and handed over his gun, butt first, to Tripp, who shoved it into his waistband.

Tripp gave Boyle a broad wink. 'I got to take care of the *hombre* who'll pay me twelve thousand dollars cash.'

'Minus the sixty dollars I just handed you,' Major Ransom reminded.

'Yeah. I figure to git me some whiskey an' a steak big as half a cow. An' then have me a woman. All right, Kelly, you act like you don't like the idea a-tall. Wa'al, the hell with that. It's my money, an' I'll do what I damn' please with it.'

Major Ransom had a final word for Uland and Quester. 'I'll expect the thousand head of cattle to be across the river no later than the end of the week and everybody with whole hide. *Everybody*. That means Kelly Boyle.'

Neither man spoke for a few moments, then Uland said: 'You'll have your cows, Major.'

The major swung his horse alongside Boyle's. 'Seems I read Tripp's stripes a long time before you did, Kelly,' he said guardedly. He nodded toward the four men. 'I pulled their stingers. Now the rest is up to you.'

Kelly Boyle sat his saddle, staring at the faintly grinning major. It was on the tip of his tongue to tell the man to go to hell and ride off, but the major would turn Uland, Quester, Roone, and Conover on him. Four to one. Not very good odds. And there was the major himself with a weapon. And just how far could he trust Carl Tripp? Whose side would Carl be on, now that he'd suddenly become the recipient of twelve thousand dollars? Possibly six to one. Those odds were not good at all. So, he'd go ahead with this, make the delivery of rifles, bring

236

back the Mexican beef. Then he'd have a long talk with Luanne. They'd settle things between them once and for all, and go on from there.

Having reached that decision, he felt better. Some of the tension eased off. But he was still wary. He ordered Uland and Quester to ride ahead with the wagons. Boyle brought up the rear. That way he could keep an eye on them.

Carl Tripp and the major were just disappearing through salt cedars. Tripp looked back and waved. Boyle gave a nod of his head, that was all.

Chapter Thirteen

Carl Tripp had consumed over half a bottle of whiskey in the Great River Saloon when a stubby little man, cold cigar clamped in his teeth, tugged impatiently on his arm. 'Like a word with you, Tripp,' he whispered up to the sullen face.

'What about?' Tripp demanded.

'About a friend of yours. I'm Doc Starrett.'

'I purely got no friends.' Tripp was thinking of Kelly Boyle. Sure it was too bad Jack Quester had to get killed, but it wasn't something to make Kelly's eyes turn as cold as they had been there in Mexico. And there were more cold eyes here. Carl had felt the chill the moment he entered. There had been mutterings, at first, but then Bartline had stepped from his office at one end of his bar and spoken to the patrons. Tripp could catch only the words – 'railroad' and 'the major.' After that, there had been no more muttered threats, only the cold stares. *Like I was poison*, Tripp had thought to himself. *Hell with 'em. Jack Quester wasn't the first hombre ever killed by mistake here in Tyburn County, for Christ's sake.*

The tugging was at his arm again. It annoyed Tripp, and he had consumed enough whiskey to put his temper on spring trap release. 'Speak your mind,' he snarled down into the pale face.

Doc Starrett looked nervous. 'I ... I think this should be discussed in ... er ... private.'

Starrett led him to a deserted deal table near a side window and sat down.

'Missus Tripp is at my place.' Tripp still hadn't sat down but swayed opposite the medical man, looking blank. 'Missus Tripp. Your wife. There is a matter of medical expenses.'

Seizing Doc Starrett by an arm, Tripp raised him up and walked him outside. A cold wind blew in off the river.

'What ails her, anyhow?' Tripp demanded. What he didn't need on his hands was a sick female.

'She was delirious when she managed to reach my alley door. Mister Tripp, there is no telling how far the poor woman walked. From her clothing and the condition of her ... er ... body, I gathered that she was ... er ... set upon.'

'What you mean ... set upon?' Marching Starrett to one side of the saloon, he twisted the man's arm up behind his back. Starrett cried out. 'Go on ... tell me,' Tripp snarled.

'She was ... raped.'

The word caused Tripp's jaws to tighten. The bright slits of eyes, the swelling on his cheek, seemed to make him even uglier. 'Who done it?' he demanded in a low, rasping voice.

'I ... I have no idea who the ... the assailant was.'

More pressure was put upon the arm. 'Who done it, Doc?'

'Please, you're hurting me...!'

'She say a name? Damn it, speak up.'

'The only name she mentioned was your partner, Kelly Boyle.'

'Kelly!' Tripp released the doctor's arm, and Starrett stood there rubbing it gingerly.

'Believe me, I didn't mean to imply that your partner was responsible for Missus Tripp's condition.' Starrett cringed, when he saw Tripp remove a revolver from the waistband of his trousers and spin the cylinder. Starrett's voice cracked. 'You asked if she gave any name, and his was the only one. You must remember that she was nearly incoherent at the time. When I saw you ride in, I thought we should discuss expenses. I've had to splint her arm, and there are numerous contusions.'

'So, she was beat up along with the rest of it.'

'Please, Mister Tripp, keep your voice down.' Starrett looked over his shoulder at some men coming along the walk. 'I'm trying to spare the poor soul from gossip. You, being her spouse, are responsible. If you would care to look in on her and perhaps pay a little something on her bill...'

'Let's go,' Tripp snapped.

As they were walking away from the saloon, Starrett, trying to keep pace with Tripp's long stride, said wryly: 'To establish a medical practice in a place like this is not a quick way to riches, Mister Tripp.'

Their boots made hollow sounds on the covering planks of an *acequia*. Then they reached a mud-walled house with Starrett's name on the door. Tripp had to stoop when entering the low doorway. Starrett pointed down a hallway.

Tripp found Florence propped up on a cot in a small room with one window. Her right arm was in a sling. To see someone suddenly looming beside her made her fearful. Then she saw who it was and managed a weak smile.

'Hello, Carl. I'm glad you're all right. The doctor told me that Major Ransom gave orders that no one is to bother you...' She broke off; it seemed to hurt her to speak, probably because of the swelling at her jaws.

'You sure must've put up a fight,' Tripp said.

Fear flicked across the large blue eyes. 'There was no fight. A horse threw me.'

'Doc claimed you was raped. Tell you one thing. Kelly's face looks a heap worse'n yours does.'

'Kelly's face? I ... I don't understand.'

'What'd you hit him with? A flat iron?'

What little color remained in her bruised face drained quickly. With her left hand she tried to capture his wrist, but he jerked away. 'Listen to me, Carl. Kelly had nothing ... absolutely nothing to do with it.'

'Kelly kicked me off the place. Sold out to the major, by God. 'Course, I'll get me some money out of it. But now I see why Kelly was givin' me them looks today.'

'Carl, you've got to listen.' When she tried to sit up straighter, her lips twisted in pain. 'Carl, you know that big blue roan? Well, I foolishly tried to ride him. And he threw me.'

Carl Tripp was not listening. He was thinking of the bruises on her body that the doctor had mentioned. He thought of his own needs because sight of her on the cot had aroused him. A little unsteadily he hurried along the hall to the front room where the doctor was studying some crystals he had shaken from a vial onto a piece of white paper on his desk. Tripp asked the doctor if Florence could be moved to the hotel.

'I'd suggest waiting a few days.' Starrett licked his lips. 'Do you have a little money, Mister Tripp, that could be ... er ... applied...?'

'*Sheeeeiiiitttt!* If I gotta pay money, it might

242

as well be to a female who ain't black an' blue an' who ain't got a busted arm.'

'Mister Tripp, I suggest you keep your voice down. You're understandably upset by your wife's ... er ... accident.'

'Woman got herself manhandled. Hell, they might fight an' claw at first, but all the same they likely don't mind too much.'

Starrett, looking worried, got to his feet to stand with his back to the peeling plaster on one of the adobe walls. 'I shouldn't have told you of my suspicions, Mister Tripp. I had no idea you'd react in such a manner.'

'What the hell'd you expect?'

'I really don't know. I'm at my wit's end, and this has all been quite a strain. No sooner do I open an office here than trouble starts across the river. I treated three gun-shot wounds this morning and so far have received not one dime.'

'Kelly Boyle's marked up bad as she is. They must've had a helluva fight before they fucked.'

Doc Starrett was shocked at the word Carl Tripp used so loudly that Mrs. Tripp was bound to hear it. When Tripp had gone lurching out, the doctor hurried to see to the welfare of his patient.

'I don't want to see him again, Doctor,' Florence said.

'I'm sure he didn't mean anything. He's been drinking.'

She looked up at rain spots on the ceiling. 'I vowed I would never tell. Because I was afraid Carl would go after them. Or Kelly would.' She touched a swollen lower lip. 'Or somebody would seek revenge, and they would end up dead. Oh, my God, what a mess.'

'Go after whom?' Starrett asked. 'What are you talking about, Missus Tripp?'

'A horse threw me. I want you to remember that. What's happened can't be undone. And there's already Jack Quester's death because of me.'

Starrett was shocked. 'But that was hardly your fault.'

'I was told that it was.' She was thinking back to the horror with the three men under the giant cottonwood along the river.

'No one could possibly blame you.'

'All my life I've been a coward. Well, no longer. Now I could even face up to *them*, if need be.'

'Face up to whom?' He leaned down, but she had closed her eyes. He tiptoed from the room.

The poor woman had refused to name her assailant – were there more than one? Yes, she had referred to *them*. Starrett sank into his swivel chair, removed a bottle from a desk drawer, and took a long pull. Whether he liked it or not, he was trapped in Bluewater. At least for the present. All his spare cash had been invested in business lots along River Street, which were expected to quadruple in value once the railroad reached here and then pushed into Mexico. A sinking coldness came in his stomach as he wondered if, as usual, it would be the ones already rich like Major Ransom who would make the big killing in a boom?

Recalling the wildness in Tripp's eye, Starrett shuddered. What would happen if Tripp returned for his wife? Much as he needed money and detested firearms, Starrett decided to buy himself a second-hand pistol.

Earlier in the day Kelly Boyle had come up behind Uland, Conover, and Roone in time to hear the last say: 'Well, she ain't said nothin' so far. Likely she'll keep her mouth shut.'

At sight of Boyle, they broke apart. Boyle didn't give it further thought.

On the following day they reached the village of El Zapato, beneath the towering rock in the shape of a shoe that had given the place its name. There Diego Esparza rode out to meet Boyle. Hoofs of his fine black horse shot pebbles as he reined in. He was dressed in *charro*. He eyed the wagons creaking to a halt. Boyle told his men to wait with the wagons in the shade of cottonwoods near some smoke-blackened *casas*.

'Did you encounter any trouble?' Esparza inquired.

'I had an eye cocked for *Federales*.'

Esparza laughed. 'They are busy else-where.'

'You'd see to that, I suppose.' Boyle smiled, visualizing Esparza without his ears. He was remembering his vow to Felicita.

Esparza studied Boyle's ravaged face and said: 'A fight?'

'A fight.'

Esparza asked for no details, and Boyle offered none. Instead, Esparza spoke of Carl Tripp. 'You and he must have a strong friend-ship.'

Boyle shrugged. He didn't feel like dis-cussing Carl, either.

'When I first realized your friend had a certain value,' Esparza continued, 'he was given better treatment. I secured for him a virgin of fifteen. You never saw a man so impressed.'

'Carl looked like he'd had the hell scared out of him.'

'But that was before I received word from Major Ransom to be on the look-out for this man.'

Esparza's men were everywhere, all heavily armed, dark faces under the brims of big hats. Boyle rode with Esparza some three miles to where the herd was held. From a rise of ground Boyle made a rough eye tally of the herd, noting that the animals seemed in fair enough shape, and the count seemed close enough, as nearly as he could tell. He had no intention of staying in Mexico long enough to make a full tally. A dozen *vaqueros* were with the herd.

Boyle suggested the herd be started north toward the village. 'Once you make sure of the cargo I've brought, I'll take over the herd.'

'I'm disappointed I'm not getting the full ten thousand rifles at once,' Esparza complained. 'Maybe you can hurry him.'

'I can try.'

Esparza signaled to the man in charge of the herd, thickly built, with vicious eyes in a pockmarked face. As the man cantered up, he gave Boyle a curious, sidelong glance. Then, upon receiving Esparza's orders to move the herd, he wheeled his horse and galloped back to the herd.

'Somehow that one is familiar,' Boyle mused.

Esparza was watching the broad back of the man clad in a stained white cotton shirt. 'Don Kelly, how many gold *onzas* would I have to pay for you to desert the major and work for me?'

Boyle tried to contain his surprise. He was being forced to deal with Uland, Quester, Conover, and Roone, any one of which would delight in seeing him dead. And now this new threat. Esparza would expect him to be flattered by the offer. And if he refused...?

'I have a pact with the major,' Boyle said, shrugging elaborately.

'I will pay a princely sum. You will have women. I will send to the far corners of this state ... which I will soon control ... for the fairest.'

'You're afraid of that pockmarked *hombre* who took your orders about the herd. Am I right?'

'And there are others,' Esparza admitted. 'Every passing year slows the heartbeat of Porfirio Díaz by that much.' Thumb and forefinger were held a quarter of an inch apart. 'When he is finally escorted heavenward by the *santos*, blood will flow deeper than our Río Bravo at flood tide.'

'Let's hope not.'

Women, beating clothes on rocks by a trickle of water, turned to stare as he and the slim young dandy in *charro* passed them.

'It is best to have a strong right arm at your side, Don Kelly. We all die, that is true. But to postpone death until a time when you find reading a book in bed is more interesting than having a woman ... that is my one great hope.' Esparza's face, in shadow under the broad-brimmed hat, was unreadable. 'What do you say?'

'I gave Major Ransom my word.'

'No other Anglo would have such a fine offer as the one I just made you. You should be flattered.'

Boyle thought carefully of his reply to this arrogant young *rico*. If crossed, Esparza could turn savage in an instant. 'You have paid me a great compliment, Don Diego,' Boyle said in formal Spanish. 'I'll keep your offer in mind.'

'Take it now or forget it!'

'If I broke my word to the major, you wouldn't trust me any more than you do the rest of your men.'

'Your fool moralizing angers me.'

They rode half a mile in silence.

'When you deliver the next rifles, be prepared to stay on this side of the border. Working for me.'

Boyle turned his head, his hat brim cutting the blinding sun. 'Well spoken,' he said, and forced a smile. He had no intention of delivering more rifles. His obligation to Carl Tripp had been discharged, and Major Ransom, contract or no contract, could go straight to hell. He and Luanne would have that house in Bluewater, and, when he sold cattle, he'd repay the major for the money given Carl. One day, Boyle was sure, Carl Tripp would come crawling back. That he'd deal with when it happened.

'Come, we will drink.' Esparza gestured at a flat-roofed *cantina* next to some trees scorched from the fighting when the village was attacked. 'A bottle of French brandy.'

In the dimness of the *cantina* Boyle was

alert for trouble, pausing just inside the slatted doors, smelling the dried mud of thick walls, the damp dirt floor, the pungent odor of *sotol*. His hand rested on the wood grips of his gun until shadows became faces and a bar and a few tables. A girl with a comb in her dark hair smiled at him.

An aproned fat man hurried up to their table with bottle and glasses. 'Always a pleasure to serve you, Excellency,' he beamed.

'Keep your tongue quiet, or I will slice it. Find for my friend here' – Esparza tilted the high crown of his hat at Boyle – 'the youngest and the prettiest of your *muchachas. ¡Andale!*' Esparza clapped his hands together, then laughed as the man scurried to the bar.

But Boyle waved a hand to the man. 'Do not bother, *señor*. I have no time for such luxury.'

The fat man turned and looked at him in surprise. Then he looked at Esparaza who shrugged and poured from the bottle.

Esparza lifted his glass. '*Salud*, Don Kelly. To our new agreement.'

Boyle's broad wink was meant to convey acceptance.

The brandy was fine. Boyle felt it course warmly into his stomach.

'It is different on this side of the river, as you know from your own youth,' said Esparza, between sips of brandy. 'I clap my hands, and you can have whatever you wish.

Nothing is against the law unless I deem it so.'

'You have the power, it seems,' Boyle said, meeting the arrogant eyes.

'Not even murder ... unless I deem it so.'

'There is still *ley de fuga*,' said Boyle with a tight smile.

'Law of the fugitive. I see you remember.'

Esparza sat with his back to a mud wall where someone had scratched – *Viva Fuentes* – who some years ago had been a general strutting and with plans for empire. Fuentes and his associates were stood upright in holes deep enough so that only their heads were above ground, and then the horses of Esparza's uncle had been ridden across the field of heads. Afterwards the horses had been ridden to a creek to wash blood from the hoofs. Boyle had witnessed it when he was ten years old.

Esparza said: 'There is a quality of leadership in you. You have a look in your eye that lets a man know you mean what you say.'

'You make me out better than I am.'

They went outside. Blackbirds screeched atop an adobe wall, avoiding bits of embedded broken glass. It reminded Boyle of Conover's blowing a mockingbird to bits. Loyalty could be purchased, Major Ransom was out to prove. If the theory failed, then Kelly Boyle could end up very dead.

251

The herd reached the village. Esparza had ordered the squat, pockmarked *segundo* to open gun crates at random, also boxes of ammunition. Esparza lifted out an occasional rifle, shiny with grease, and nodded his satisfaction.

'The count appears accurate,' he said finally. Then he added: 'I will tell you something in confidence.'

One thing Boyle did not wish were confidences from this young dandy. 'Yes?' he said politely.

'You come in with me, and we can make our own country.'

At last the truth. All Boyle wanted was to get the cattle back across the line, himself in one piece. Boyle pretended interest in what Esparza had to say. The man's eyes glittered with ambition.

'We can throw out that pig of a governor. We will declare us independent of Mexico City.'

'You would need a fortune,' Boyle said cautiously.

'And what you *yanquis* call guts. What do you say to that?'

Boyle knew this was no time for blunt refusal, not with Esparza's men nearby with their carbines and bandoleers and the squat one with the pockmarked face whose hard eyes now and then swung to Boyle. 'A grand plan you have, Don Diego.'

'Do not trifle with me,' Esparza warned.

Boyle gave a laugh to indicate such a thing was impossible. He visualized Esparza's ears nailed to a barn door to show the world that he, among other things, was a violator of women. Boyle shook Esparza's soft hand, mounted up, and ordered his men to take over the herd from Esparza's *vaqueros*.

He set Uland and Art Quester at point, which caused the latter to give him a mocking smile. 'Afraid of us at your back?'

Dust rose higher into the clear sky. Why couldn't it rain as during roundup, to kill the dust which was like a flag? Anyone for miles around could spot the movement of the cattle. Did Esparza have the situation as firmly in hand as he bragged? What if *soldados* appeared, demanding to know why cattle were being driven toward the border. And in exchange for what?

The hours ground along. Pausing by the drag in clouds of dust, Boyle took a moment to wipe the sweat band of his hat with a bandanna. It was when he was repositioning the hat that he noticed a figure on horseback emerge from a tangle of green mesquite on a rocky slope. Boyle's first reaction was to reach for a rifle. Then he recognized the rider.

He ordered the men to keep the herd on the move. Boyle let them get on ahead, obscured now in boiling dust. Then he whirled his horse and sent it running upslope where he drew rein in a shower of gravel.

'Carl, for Christ's sake what're you doing back on this side of the line?'

Boyle was aware of a wildness in Carl Tripp's eyes. Carl's shirt was dirty; he needed a shave and smelled strongly of mescal. The neck of a bottle jutted from a saddlebag. Carl Tripp sat his saddle, scowling, a rifle clamped under the right arm.

'Heard you was still over here,' he grunted.

Boyle nodded at the Winchester locked under the heavy arm. 'What you aim to do with that?'

'It was always you the big auger, Kelly.' Tripp drew back his lips.

'What's eating you?'

'Always you, Kelly. Tellin' what time we get up, how far we ride. How much we put in the bank.'

The two horses stood flank to flank. Insects droned at Boyle's sweating face. He brushed them aside. Tripp was obviously drunk. In his eyes was more meanness than Boyle had ever seen before. The herd was out of sight now where the ground dipped.

'Come on, Carl, let's get some shade and set a few minutes.' Boyle pointed to a sheer rock wall out of the sun, rode a few paces, then realized Tripp wasn't following. He halted and turned his horse so that he sat facing Tripp again.

'You sold me out to the major, Kelly,' Tripp accused.

'Can't you get it through that mud-brick head of yours that I did it to save your life?'

'Mud-brick head. Yeah, that's what you always figured.'

Boyle debated whether to be placating or tough. He chose the latter. 'Carl, you boot that rifle. Or I sure as hell will shoot it out of your hands!'

'Didn't want me to have Flo. Oh, no. But when my back's turned ... you son-of-a-bitch, you took what you wanted!'

'Hey, Carl, that's going too god-damn' far. I don't know what you're talking about.'

Boyle saw the rifle barrel shift, saw Tripp's big thumb draw back the hammer. 'Carl!'

Something smashed into Boyle's chest, knocking him sideways in the saddle.

Even the split second before the rifle spat its dim flame in the bright day, Kelly Boyle's reflexes were operating. His pistol was out, firing. His intention was only to wing Carl Tripp. But he had done otherwise. Both shots were accurate, one of them lethal.

Within minutes two riders came pounding up the slant to rein in and stare.

Uland gave a bark of laughter. 'Killed each other, by damn.'

'Boyle's breathin', looks like.'

'Lets get the hell out before that Esparza bastard comes along!' Uland gave a worried glance toward the south.

'I'll make sure.' Quester drew his revolver. 'Koop de grass, I think they call it.' He fired from the saddle. Blood ran down the side of Kelly Boyle's skull.

As the two riders went tearing back down the hill, it proved to be no *coup de grâce* – because Boyle opened his eyes and began to crawl.

Chapter Fourteen

The news of the death of Kelly Boyle was received in stony silence by Felicita De Gama. The moment the bearer of the grim tidings had gone, she drove to Bluewater and took the ferry on one of its first crossings of the season across the river to Los Milagros. There, at the church, she lit a candle and prayed for the eternal salvation of the soul of Kelly Boyle.

When Doc Starrett brought the news to a recuperating Florence, regret welled in her as she thought back to the day Kelly Boyle had thrown her on the bed. She would live with what might have been for the rest of her life.

Luanne Ransom listened to her father raving in his office and finally went down to ask him what was the matter. He told her, his mouth shaking.

So Carl Tripp had won, after all. Instinctively her hands pressed at her abdomen. *Your mother didn't show for four months.* Wasn't that what her father had said? She looked at her father, snarling his grief and disappointment. Should she let him select for her a husband from among the sons of stockholders in his railroad? Or should she make a move that he would utterly despise?

That same day she began actively to court Rex Uland.

Major Terrence Ransom had a long talk with one of his friends and stockholders, Onslow Byles, regarding the mating of his son with Luanne. Young Byles, who had managed to hold Luanne's warm hand during school dances and place the palm of his other hand against her supple back, instantly came alive with erotic dreams. They were soon quashed, however, because, when the major made the announcement to Luanne, rubbing his hands together, saying – 'Our problems are solved.' – she told him calmly that she was marrying Rex Uland.

Quickly spending his rage against an implacable daughter, the major reluctantly gave his permission. As he witnessed the simple ceremony at Empire, he supposed that Luanne did, after all, find a certain fascination in Uland with his thick barrel of a body, bowed legs of one born to the saddle, broad nose that had been flattened by the fists of Kelly Boyle in that historic fight, and eyes pale in a massive face. Just thinking of Kelly Boyle brought a twinge of mingled regret and anger. Boyle had let him down by allowing himself to be trapped by that fool, Carl Tripp, only at the last possible second trying to shoot his way clear, costing him his life. At first, the major had regarded the story told by Uland and Quester as possible fabrication, thinking they might have disobeyed his orders and gunned down Boyle themselves. But the more he questioned them, the more certain he was that it had happened as they said. Boyle and Tripp had shot it out, and both men had died.

Uland had engaged a suite at the Empire Hotel for the honeymoon. He stayed downstairs until well past midnight, accepting congratulatory drinks from a cadre of sudden friends. By marrying the daughter of Major Terrence Ransom, he was heir apparent to Box R. He came staggering upstairs finally and lurched over to the bed, pulled down the bedcovers, and lifted her night dress.

'*Don't!*' She tried to push his hands away, but it was like trying to move iron embedded in rock.

'You're my property,' he said, slurring his words, 'an' don't ever forget it.'

He hurriedly undressed, letting his clothing fall in a heap in the middle of the floor.

As he came to her, she tensed. Just once would she allow him to touch her. Just once, to make everything right, so that she could give birth to her child and hold her head high. She had expected the equivalent of rape, but he was surprisingly gentle, and she found herself responding, not to him especially but to her need, never realizing until that moment how much she had missed the times with Kelly Boyle in the wagon. Her association with Jack Quester had been only a rather pleasant interlude, but it could have resulted in disaster when Jack was killed and she was left with no prospective husband.

This brought her mind swinging back to Kelly Boyle. Why couldn't he have given in? Gone away with her? Instead, he had kept to a stupid code concerning Carl Tripp, and it had cost him his life. Oh, Kelly, Kelly...

'That's more like it ... show a little life.' It was Rex Uland's hot, whiskey-laden breath against her mouth.

For an instant she was revolted, then found herself responding again to the great tireless engine of his body, until at last the steady rhythm became frenzy, and she felt herself whirled aloft like a leaf in a high wind where she collided with lightning and was sent smashing back to earth.

'A husband teaches his wife things,' Uland said, sitting up in bed, huge and glowering. Moonlight spilled through lacy curtains so she could see the cruel twist of his mouth. 'But you know it all,' he went on. 'Who taught you?'

'Go to sleep.' She tried to turn over on her side, but his fingers cut into a shoulder and pushed her back.

'Kelly Boyle, he's the one, ain't he?'

'Don't ask questions.'

She saw the broad callused palm of his hand streaking toward her face and tried to duck. It crashed into her, exploding lights in her skull, bringing a taste of blood to her mouth.

His two hands pinned her, his heavy legs trapping her flailing feet. A second time he had her, but there was no response from her. She vowed that for the duration of their marriage it would be thus. He fell asleep on her, and she had to shove him aside. To the darkness she said silently: *Kelly, Kelly, what have you done to us?*

Three days later, when the swelling of her cheek had subsided, they left for home. Her father dispensed his own brand of punishment for her rash deed of marrying against his will. He called them to the ranch office. When Luanne saw Al Quester of the shaggy brows, glittering eyes, standing beside the desk, a smug look on his large face, she sensed what was coming.

'Rex, I've appointed Al Quester my superintendent. You'll take your orders from him.'

'But ... but I'm your son-in-law,' Uland spluttered, his face matching the rust color of his hair.

Major Ransom smiled thinly under his military mustache. 'So you are.'

'Uland, round up Diamond Deuce cows and drive them to railhead,' Quester said.

'I'll arrange for a packing-house rep to meet you there.'

Rex Uland's mouth worked, and he glared for half a minute, then said: 'Yeah, I'll do that.' Turning on his heel, he walked out.

They could hear him clumping up to the rooms set aside for him and his bride on the upper floor of the great house.

When Luanne started to follow him, the major said: 'Wait.' Then he said: 'That'll be all, Al.'

Quester bobbed his head and walked out.

'What happened to your face?' the major asked bluntly.

Luanne started to grope for a lie, then decided on the truth. 'He hit me.'

Instead of the indignation she expected, the major only lolled back in his leather chair and said: 'What did you expect? Kindness from such a lout?'

'You haven't made it any easier for me by demoting him.'

'No demotion ... not at all. Uland is still foreman. I just decided to give Al Quester Kelly Boyle's job.'

'I see.'

He eyed her midsection. 'I suppose, when the baby comes, Uland will strut and brag at what he produced.'

'I suppose you'll tell him the truth.'

'That would bring disgrace to the family name.'

She laughed and left the office. But she was determined of one thing: to get rid of the baby. Her father had said Rex Uland would strut and brag at what he had produced. Never would she allow that. She recalled discussions of pregnancy at school. Jumping off a barn roof, one of her classmates had said, was infallible.

Luanne in the cool of twilight tried it twice from the low roof of the small barn set apart from the others. The second time all she did was to sprain both ankles badly. She was in bed for a week.

A question asked by many in Tyburn County at the time was the reason why Kelly Boyle and Carl Tripp had shot it out across the border, the consensus being that it had something to do with the golden-haired woman whose name up at Lucero had been Taylor. The remains of a corpse bearing Taylor's name on a letter had been found in river reeds some weeks before.

No matter what they said about her, Florence remained aloof. Because she knew yard goods and was quick at figures, she got a job in the Miller Store. At first, the ladies of Bluewater were cool but soon relented, when she helped them with patterns and was able to inform them on the quality of fabrics.

Most males of the town were preoccupied with the future, which depended on the railroad. According to surveys, the railroad would head straight for Bluewater. It would become a border metropolis. Cargo from Mexico would mean riches. 'If only them Mexicans would quit fighting each other' was a frequent complaint heard in the Great River Saloon.

Major Ransom appeared in town regularly, would drink, then go about his personal business, which caused men to wink behind his back. Even the mighty, it seemed, were vulnerable to female flesh. These days the major seemed drawn and rarely smiled.

One day in the Great River Saloon, his bottle of Colonel's Choice on the bar, he was staring absently through the front window. He saw Rex Uland, Conover, and Roone ride in. They dismounted and stood on the walk in front of the Miller Store, their heads together. The major wondered idly what they were talking about. Him, perhaps. They had sold off the Diamond Deuce cattle last week and seemed to accept taking orders from Al Quester. But the major sensed a smouldering resentment in Uland. Thinking about it produced a spare smile.

At that moment Florence Tripp stepped from the store and looked around. Even in a plain brown work dress there was no hiding her class. She was calling to a woman who evidently had left a package in the store. She hurried to the walk, handed the woman the package. She turned to go back to the store and was suddenly face to face with Uland, Conover, and Roone.

Uland started to laugh, but something in the way she stared into the face of each man in turn seemed to freeze them completely there at the edge of the walk. As she continued to stare coldly, Uland shifted his feet. The three, wearing hangdog looks, stepped around her and shuffled over to the saloon.

Uland was muttering, when they entered, but broke off when he saw the major at the bar. Ransom turned his back, refusing to acknowledge the presence of his son-in-law. Finally he jerked a hand at Conover who came over, looking wary.

'What was behind the icy stare that woman gave you?' the major demanded.

'She's a cold one,' said Conover, not meeting the probing gaze.

'I never want to hear of you saying one word to embarrass that lady. And I mean *lady*.'

'You'll never have to worry about nothin' like that from us. No siree, Major, not us.' Then, with ear lobes reddening, he hurried back to where Uland and Roone were waiting.

The major couldn't get Florence Tripp out of his mind. The following day he sent Uland, with Luanne, over to run East Ranch. When that was done, Luanne sullen about it, he visited the Miller Store where he engaged Florence Tripp in conversation.

'You can have the run of the big house for as long as you want,' he said, coming right to the point.

'Until you tire of the arrangement, I suppose.' She arched her pale brows, smiling. 'Thank you, no, Major.'

Two other times he made his proposition and was turned down politely but definitely. He began to steam. Hell with her.

He tried to get Florence Tripp out of his mind by paying more attention to his regular town woman. Two weeks later, after a few drinks at the Great River Saloon, he climbed the outside stairs to Annabelle's quarters. When, inside, he saw her sitting on the bed, all ripe flesh, smile etched in bright lip paint, unlacing her corset while throwing him seductive glances across the room, he suddenly felt disgust.

Why did his favorite whiskey these days no longer have its old flavor? Why did the woman on that bed no longer stir desire? Why did he lie awake nights in that monstrous house? Night after night in the big bed alone. Not even his daughter's footsteps pattering about these days. Only the servants who, he suspected, hated him.

Who would shed a tear at his grave? Oh, the *políticos* he had made might look appropriately saddened because their futures without him would be so uncertain, but no woman, not even his own daughter. He was the first to admit he had killed her love. How about Annabelle, across the room on the bed, whose corset was off at last, who now was rubbing at the red marks left on her flesh by whalebone edged in lace – would she weep?

Suddenly he snatched up his hat, causing Annabelle to wail: 'Where you going, Terry sweet?'

Without replying, he clattered down the long flight of outside stairs and marched to the Miller Store.

'I want to speak to Missus Tripp!' he thundered at Miller, who nervously wiped small hands on an apron.

'Gone. She's gone, Major.'

'Where, damn it, where?'

'Miss Morgan ... she got married and her husband took her over east to live. An' Missus Tripp ... well, she could read an' write, an' had some education, an' – well, how could we get a teacher to come 'way out here when things is so unsettled? She's at the school, teachin'...'

The school was rambling, of adobe, with two dozen pupils of various ages. They were at recess, when he entered. She looked elegant, sitting behind the desk, hair done up. He was thinking of their last meeting when he had practically ordered her to come home with him, reminding her of his initial offer up at Lucero when she had worn the veil, before she had gone with Carl Tripp. She had looked him in the eye and said calmly: 'I am no longer afraid, Major Ransom. You may tell everyone what you know about me, if you wish. But I'm sure it's hardly news to almost everyone in town.'

All along there had been rumors and head shaking, but to get another regular teacher took money, and these days all spare cash was being put into the railroad. Today she was about to pick up her hand bell to summon pupils back to class. He looked older, she noticed. Lines at mouth corners, some of the arrogance seemed to have washed out of his hazel eyes.

He said bluntly: 'I could go to Austin to find a woman, or New York. Or any place in this world. But there has probably never been one day I haven't thought of you.'

'I've already given you my answer.'

'Because of you, I changed my whole life.'

'I find that hard to believe,' she said with a small smile.

'I couldn't sleep nights, thinking that you had turned from me to that ... that Carl Tripp.'

'Don't revile the dead.' She gripped the bell in her two hands, staring coldly from behind the desk. 'If you will leave now, Major...'

'I want you to come to Box R. I'm sick of being alone.'

'How will you threaten me this time? Oh, there has been talk. If the railroad survey comes through here, then the town will be assured of its future. A new teacher could replace one so morally corrupt.'

'Florence, I'm asking you to be my wife.'

She stared at him a moment, and, when he repeated it, she dropped the bell. It rolled, clanging, under the desk. She would not capitulate, because she had her pride and she did not love him. What was love? Kelly Boyle had asked her. But she was alone in the world and in two years would be twenty-five, the division point between available young female and spinster. And what of the years following?

Within a week she had nearly made up her mind, but with reservations. Was Major Ransom really sincere? He had been accused of so many vicious deeds over the years. Finally it came to the point of discussing Luanne.

'Will she accept another woman in her house?' she asked.

'Not her house, yours.'

It was a day he had brought a picnic basket in his buggy. The sun was warm. Florence wore a blue dress, a scarf over her golden head.

She said: 'I'd want my husband to be liked, to be satisfied with what he has, no longer to

269

crave more land, more cattle, and to juggle the lives of other men.'

He was turning the buggy toward willows along the river where a towering cotton-wood speared the sky.

She suddenly caught his arm. 'Not there ... please. Not *there!*'

He pulled in the horse, staring in surprise at the tree. 'You have bad memories of this place. Why?'

'It ... it's nothing.' She shuddered against him. 'We passed a place a mile or so back. There was grass, and we can picnic...'

'But there's no shade.'

'Please ... Terry.'

'Something happened there along the river. Tell me what it was.'

'It's just a feeling I have. Will you give into me this once?'

Her fetching smile swayed him. 'I expect in years to come I'll be giving into you quite a bit.'

They were married three weeks later. Luanne had declined the invitation. She was still living at East Ranch and used as an excuse complications of her pregnancy. Many *políticos* came from as far as Austin. There were Chinese lanterns in the yard and music and dancing and enough whiskey, someone remarked, to float the house and the several barns. Major and Mrs. Terrence Ransom were at home.

Kelly Boyle got details of what had happened from his cellmate, Cipriano Delgado. Still weak from his double wounds, he would pass the time by asking Cipriano to tell him again of the tragic day when Kelly had regained consciousness to see this burly, pockmarked man squatting beside him, the eyes no longer vicious but filled with compassion.

'You did not remember me,' Esparza's segundo would tell him. 'In the old days I rode for your father.'

Boyle did not remember. There had been so many. Water from a canteen was cool against his parched lips.

Presently there had been sounds of hoofs and the raging voice of Esparza. 'Get away from him!' he screamed at Delgado.

'He is badly hurt.'

There was the hiss and crack of a quirt. Cipriano Delgado, bleeding from a cut across the cheek from the quirt, continued to give water to Kelly Boyle.

'I will say who is to receive pity from us!' Esparza screamed. 'Not you!'

'It is not right to leave him to die.'

Esparza looked down at Boyle, face and shirt soaked with blood. 'You are of no use to me now, Don Kelly. Spilling your blood. You let that cabrón *of a partner get the drop on you! By letting him shoot you, I can see you had already lost your greatness.'*

The next thing Boyle remembered was being awakened in a jolting cart. A harsh sun burned through his clothing. He desperately needed water. His wrists and ankles were chained. Jammed next to him in the cart, also chained, was Cipriano Delgado. The viciousness had returned to the eyes.

Later Kelly Boyle was vaguely aware of being in a great domed building. At first he imagined he was inside a church, but there was no altar, no candles. A harsh voice was speaking his name, but Kelly Boyle failed to respond.

He fully regained consciousness in San Cristóbal Prison. Delgado, in a patchwork of shadows from a small barred window in a stone wall, said that they had been sentenced, the two of them, for the murder of one *Señor* Carl Tripp. In seventeen years they would be free. They were fortunate not to have faced a firing squad.

'Of course there is always *ley de fuga*,' Delgado finished with a shrug.

Over the weeks, Kelly Boyle chinned himself on the bars, leaped about to keep his legs in shape. His hair had grown back where one bullet had grazed the skull. The second bullet by good fortune had passed through his body and not lodged behind bone or sinew to fester and kill at some later date.

One day Diego Esparza came to his cell. He was thinner, seemed harassed, and his uniform was dirty. He was white with rage. 'I have set a reasonable price for you which Major Ransom refuses to meet.'

'What do you call reasonable, Don Diego?'

'One hundred thousand dollars for your return ... plus the remainder of the rifles and ammunition. Three times I have sent a messenger.'

'Let me write to him.'

Permission was granted. Boyle was taken to another room, given pen and ink and paper. He composed what he thought was a reasonable plea.

While awaiting a reply, he was able to evaluate Esparza, who was making his first visit to the prison of San Cristóbal. Things had been going badly for Esparza, he gathered. Money and weapons were needed desperately.

Within three days Kelly Boyle had his reply from the major. Esparza came storming up to the cell door, trembling in his fury. 'He says not for one dollar would he ransom you.'

'Let me try again.'

'And he has turned from me to Emilio Casas ... thinking that fool can guarantee his railroad will be built. Hah!'

'I can show him the error of his ways,' Kelly Boyle said patiently.

Esparza bared his teeth. 'Tomorrow at sunrise you are to be shot!' Turning on his heel, gold spurs making a tinkling sound in the prison corridor, he strode away.

'At least now you know,' said Cipriano Delgado.

'I hope he's close enough so I can spit in his face.'

When at last gray light seeped through the prison, he heard the sound of boots in the corridor. He shook hands with Cipriano.

'*Vaya con Dios,*' said the Mexican. 'I will be next.'

The moment the cell door was opened, Kelly Boyle was slammed against the wall by three burly soldiers. His arms were bound. Then he was marched to the court-yard and his upper body tied to a post that had been damaged by bullets and stained from the blood of previous victims.

He worked a mouthful of saliva, but the captain, thick in the neck and very dark, knew the trick. He whacked him on the back. Saliva spurted from Kelly's lips to the ground. 'Where your blood will soon be,' said the captain through his mustaches.

Boyle was blindfolded, the world cut off as it would be permanently in a matter of seconds. As Boyle braced for the shock of bullets, he heard the voice of Esparza.

'You came close to death, Don Kelly. You are frightened?'

'No,' he lied.

'You *are* frightened. Your voice shakes. This time you are to compose a letter to Major Ransom that I will dictate. Before you did not beg for your life. This time you will.'

Somehow Kelly Boyle managed to laugh. 'I'll never beg that bastard for *anything*.'

Esparza swore and ripped the blindfold away, his face twisted. 'You will do as I say!'

'I'll never beg!'

'My ancestor was with Cortés!' Esparza screamed, the whites of the eyes showing. 'He knew how to force the *indios* to do his bidding. I will use his methods. You will write what I tell you, or I will make you pray for death quickly.'

'The Indians should have drowned Cortés in his own blood!' Kelly Boyle shouted.

Esparza spun around to shout at the captain. 'Bring me a whip! One with lead tips! I will strip the skin.' When a soldier was dispatched to get the whip, Esparza came close, glowering. 'I will teach you.'

Kelly spat into his face and at the same time lashed out with the right foot. A great screech of pain burst from Esparza as the foot caught him at the groin. He sank to his knees, clutching himself, groaning in his agony. Some of the soldiers started forward to help him, but fell back at a signal from the captain.

As the captain of the guard stared impassively, offering no sounds of pity, Boyle said to him: 'You are *indio*. His ancestors tortured yours. You heard him brag of it!' Kelly Boyle sweated, his heart pounding, as he awaited the captain's reaction.

At last the man spoke through his mustaches. 'As you said, hearing him tell of the torture of my ancestors by his does not amuse me.'

He gave an order. Boyle was cut free. Boyle rubbed his arms. Esparza still screamed, now rolling in the dust, very pale, his face drenched with sweat. Soldiers leaned on their rifles, regarding him curiously as they might a bug that had been stepped on.

'General de Varga and troops from Mexico City are a day away,' the captain mused gravely. 'It is time I announce my allegiance to Díaz.'

'No wonder Esparza is desperate.'

'A lesser man than you facing certain death would have soiled himself. Yet you were able to curse Esparza and kick him where he moans that his ability with women is impaired.' The captain smiled thinly. 'I will repay you for your valor.'

'Whatever you do for me, *el capitán*, do likewise for my friend Cipriano.'

The captain looked at him for a moment, then nodded. 'It will be done.'

'To be unarmed in Mexico during these

times a man might as well be dead from *ley de fuga*,' Boyle said earnestly, waiting tensely

'Two weapons will be left just beyond a wall.'

'*Mil gracias.*'

The captain barked an order. A trooper, a rifle in each hand, trotted across the courtyard and dropped the rifles over a low wall. He came trotting back.

'Understand one thing,' the captain said gravely. 'After I give you a head start, I will do my best to kill you both.'

Kelly Boyle looked deep into the Indian eyes, but there was nothing there to read. 'It is understood.'

When Cipriano was brought to the courtyard, the captain said: '*Ley de fuga.* It is better than wondering what fate awaits you with General de Varga.'

'*Señor* Kelly Boyle, awaiting your orders,' Boyle said formally. From a corner of his eye he saw Esparza, who had been silent these past minutes, clamber to his feet and seize a rifle. Boyle suddenly spun about, giving Cipriano Delgado a mighty shove and crying: 'Run! *Run!*'

Then they both were sprinting toward the low wall at the far end of the yard. Without breaking stride, Kelly Boyle flung himself headfirst over the wall. There was a sharp crack from a rifle. Delgado grew limp on the wall, the back of his head shot away.

Desperately Kelly Boyle groped about on the ground, found one of the rifles in some weeds. He came up with it, saw Diego Esparza screaming his rage in the distance, Esparza in his stained uniform, holding a rifle. In that split second of time, Boyle aimed for the gleam of Esparza's teeth, fired, saw them explode. Esparza dropped suddenly from sight behind crouched soldiers with their carbines.

Whirling about, Boyle ran, hearing the whistle of bullets, the slap and *thonk* as they slammed into adobe walls or screamed in ricochet. He raced to an alley where a burro loaded with firewood was spooked by his sudden appearance. For half an hour he ran, his pace slowing rapidly and always behind him the drumbeat of running footsteps. He hadn't realized how weak he was from his wounds. His legs felt leaden. Dogs barked and children squealed as their mothers shouted warnings at them.

On a high hill crowned with rock slabs, as if from some prehistoric cataclysm, he flung himself down. His heart pounded, and sweat ran coldly from his body.

When he started out again, he felt unbearably cold. His teeth chattered. Weeks of convalescence, poor medical attention, bad food had sapped him.

Finally he was conscious of a lemon rind of moon starting its slow climb into the stars. He remembered no prayers from his youth, but he did say aloud in Spanish to the night breeze that he wished the soul of that *mucho hombre* Cipriano Delgado to find rest.

Because the threat of recapture or the quick death from *ley de fuga* was ever present, he pushed on. At the first hint of dawn he hid in mesquite, trying to put his mind from food and water so desperately needed.

He found his mind wandering and thought he was fourteen again, and he and Carl were running from Mexico. *Carl*, he called. *Carl, speak up. They killed my father, and they'll have us next.* Then his mind swung back to the present, filled with the image of Major Terrence Ransom whose residence was over a hundred miles to the north. *At your service, suh. No, you at mine now, definitely you at mine. You-son-of-a-bitch!*

At last he came to the river's roaring, and almost flung himself down and wept at this new hazard. But he somehow seized his remaining strength and waded in. Almost instantly he was swept off his feet. A barrel flashed by, which he grabbed. Gradually he kicked his way to the far shore. He was half a day lying in the reeds before he had the strength to move.

He turned north and, staggering like a drunk with his brain afire with mescal, swayed through brush and bumped into trees. Felicita De Gama, hanging up clothes, saw him first. Then Chico and Jaime came running.

The last thing he remembered doing was falling into Felicita's soft arms and whispering: 'No one must know I am back. Not until I am ready.' Then he passed out.

Chapter Fifteen

At East Ranch, the foreman's quarters Luanne shared with Uland were spare. Luanne smoldered in hatred of her father for allowing this to happen, but what could she do about it? At night she hated herself for allowing her need to transcend an intense dislike for her mate. Already her gowns were on the point of binding her at the midsection. How many more months, dear God? She counted them and felt her despair.

One night Uland drunkenly made love to her, then began muttering about her father humiliating him by giving Al Quester a job that should have gone to the son-in-law. 'I could take every one of them god-damn' rifles an' shove 'em.'

'What rifles are you talking about, Rex?'

He unburdened himself, but in the morning, remembering, he cautioned her never to repeat what he had told her. 'Mebby they've been carted off to Mexico by now,' he said thinly. 'Little I know what goes on at Central these days. But you keep your mouth shut about 'em all the same, hear?'

'Yes.' She managed a straight face, but her violet eyes held a strange glow.

Later that week she announced she wanted to go to Central to visit her old friend, Mrs. Blankenship, and to see her father, of course. She filled a pocket of her dress with matches.

Uland was busy but sent along two men to act as escort. She drove a buggy the long weary miles to Central Ranch. Mrs. Blankenship was overjoyed, flattered that she'd come so far just to see her, which Luanne assured her with a straight face was the case. She also met her new step-mother who ran into her on the varnished staircase.

'Why didn't you let us know you were coming?' Florence said after recovering from her surprise.

'I made up my mind on the spur of the moment.'

Florence glanced down and then up at Luanne's face. 'How are you feeling these days? Everything progressing naturally?'

'Very.'

Luanne was pleased to note that her regal stepmother seemed ill at ease. 'I'm sorry you couldn't be here for the wedding,' Florence said.

'I understand it was quite a spectacle.'

'It was rather grand, yes.'

Luanne excused herself, saying she needed rest after the long trip. In her old room she made her plans. Her father was in Bluewater for the night. A meeting of railroad stock-

282

holders, Florence had said, that caused Luanne to think: *dear lady, is the novelty wearing off so soon?* She knew it was probably true in her own case, having noticed the quick interest in Rex's eyes when she announced a trip home for a few days. He would be by now no doubt prowling the sin alleys, such as they were, of Bluewater.

That evening she had Mrs. Blankenship bring her supper to her room. When she was finished and the dishes taken away, she told Mrs. Blankenship she was going to bed. She listened to the woman going down the stairs, then quickly went through her closet, searching for a long dark cloak she remembered. It wasn't there. Possibly she had given it away in a Christmas basket for the poor across the river. All that was left was her fur coat.

Reluctantly she put it on. The coat was dark and would blend with shadows. Thankfully there would be no early moon. After midnight she crept down the back stairs and to a storage area at the rear of the house where a large drum of coal oil was kept for the lamps. She found an empty five-gallon can, filled it nearly full, and stepped out into the quiet night. Crouching beside the house, she listened, but there were no sounds to indicate anyone about.

Keeping to a row of trees, she carried the can, sloshing and bumping, against her leg.

It grew heavy, and she had to pause to get her breath, then shift the can to the other hand. She pressed on, trying to remember the exact location of the smaller of the three barns. Over the years she had paid little attention to it, only knowing that it was set apart and used for storage. At least that was what she had always been told.

With her heart pounding, she stepped through a barrier of thick trees and saw it silhouetted in the center of a clearing. Some distance away a night light from the bunkhouse shone through another line of trees.

With each step the can grew heavier. It was frustrating not to find the barn entrance right away, but she had to make a complete tour of the barn before finding it. Large double doors were locked on the inside by a heavy bar. She could barely see through a crack, but part way along this same wall was a smaller door with a large padlock. The lock was a further frustration. She should have realized that doors wouldn't offer an invitation by being unlocked.

Her father had the key to the padlock, of course. Perhaps she should have searched his office desk. But knowing him, he probably carried the key. She blew at a lock of hair that had fallen across her forehead and tried to decide what to do. Stooping, she felt along the bottom of the door and found a half-inch gap. That decided her. She tipped the can and let the coal oil trickle against the door. Some of it vanished under the door, but most of it made a great puddle on the outside. Fumes from the coal oil upset her stomach.

She scratched one of her matches against the barn wall and, as it flamed, let it drop into the pool of coal oil. Instantly there was a flash of blue flame, moving so swiftly that she had to run. Because she had expected to use more than one match, it caught her by surprise, and, even now, it was engulfing the barn wall. Sparks leaped skyward. For an instant she stared in fascination at what she had done, then she began to run. By the time she reached the rear steps of the house and started to climb, there was a wrenching pain. She doubled over, gasping, her face drenched with cold sweat. Somehow she made it to her room and closed the door quietly. Then she lurched over to a window and stared out at a dull yellow glow through the trees.

As she got out of her clothes and flopped into bed, she was barely aware of yelling in the distance. How long she lay there she never knew. Someone rapped on her door, opened it. Mrs. Blankenship put her head in.

'Don't be frightened, lass,' the older woman said, 'but one of the barns is afire. The men has formed a bucket brigade, so I've been told. They'll have it out soon.'

'Thank you for telling me. I ... I did wonder about all the shouting.'

Luanne felt despair. The fire would soon be out, all her work for nothing. And it had brought on pain, such pain as she had never experienced.

'Are you all right, lass?'

'Yes.'

'You seemed to be a-moanin'.'

'I ... I'm quite all right.'

'I'll bring a pot of tea.'

Mrs. Blankenship was barely closing the door when the first of the eruptions took place. In the distance a man yelled hysterically: 'It's goin' off. The whole damn' thing!'

There were wild yells now, the sounds of men running. Luanne, despite the pain, came to an elbow and saw the shooting stars through a window. Something struck the side of the house. A window was smashed. Beyond the door, Mrs. Blankenship was screaming. Then, as Luanne watched, the whole barn seemed to erupt in a great shuddering roar that shook the house.

Florence suddenly flung open the door, etched there with lamplight at her back. She sprang into the room, swept Luanne from the bed to the floor.

'Keep down, keep down,' Florence gasped. 'It's ammunition going off. Missus Blankenship, poor thing...!'

She didn't finish it. Luanne lay huddled

against her stepmother as the awful bombardment continued.

'Is ... is Missus Blankenship wounded?' Luanne finally brought herself to ask.

'I don't think she ever knew what hit her.'

'Oh, my God. My God!' Luanne buried her face in her hands and began to weep. Tears spilled through her fingers.

Florence laid a consoling hand on Luanne's shoulder. 'It certainly wasn't your fault, my dear.'

Great sobs wracked Luanne. 'Not my fault...?'

Finally the sounds diminished, and the pelting against the side of the house became less frequent. At last, after what seemed a very long time, there was silence.

For a time, Luanne was too frightened to notice the pain, but with the quiet it returned. Luanne bit her lips. Finally she managed to sit up without crying out.

Florence now stood by a window, looking down. The air was so thick with smoke it was still hard to breathe.

Despite all the commotion at the ranch as a result of the fire, Luanne insisted on going home. She had to get away, *had* to. The buggy was brought by one of her escorts. She climbed in and took the reins in trembling hands, trying not to look at the gouges in the side of the house, the smashed windows, or the stumps of burned trees, and, beyond, the great heaps of smoking ruin. She had already seen the dark smear at the top of the staircase where Mrs. Blankenship had been standing when hit by one of the random bullets. This had brought on a period of retching that further weakened her.

'You all right, Missus Uland?' one of her escorts asked with concern.

'Perfectly,' she snapped, and slapped reins across the back of the dun horse in the buggy shafts. It took off with a rush, perhaps spooked by the long night of shouting, the clouds of smoke that still stained the air.

Midway across the yard, Luanne lost her grip on the reins and numbly she huddled in the seat, watching them dragging beside the frightened dun. Her escorts spurred, trying to catch the animal, but it veered suddenly, and the buggy went up on two wheels. Luanne screamed as her grip on a seat brace was torn loose and she was flung onto the hardpan of the yard. She lay, stunned, hearing the yells as the men brought the dun under control, seeing the upended buggy, one wheel smashed. Lying in the tangle of bloodied skirts was a bit of flesh that she knew was hers. She fainted...

Major Ransom took the news hard. He had counted on a grandson sired by the late Jack Quester, had raised the baby's uncle to a

place of prominence at Box R. Rex Uland
came over from East Ranch upon hearing
the tragic news. In his office the major
listened to the big man moan about his lost
child. He felt like telling him the truth, but
decided it would be unfair to Luanne.

He was seated in his leather chair with
Uland standing, twisting a hat brim in his
large hands, close to tears.

'Enough about the baby,' Major Ransom
said abruptly, unable to tolerate further
anguish from his foreman. He fixed Uland
with a hard hazel stare. 'Tell me. Rex ... did
you ... to get even with me for raising Al
Quester above you ... seek to get even by
firing my barn?'

Uland came up on his toes, his mouth
dropping open. 'Me? You figure *I* done it?'

'Somebody did. That's for sure.'

Uland fidgeted, started to speak, sweated,
then finally admitted a misdeed. 'I was all
night at ... I hate to say it, Major.' The large
face writhed under a new anxiety. 'Ain't a
thing a fella likes to tell his father-in-law,
but...'

'Speak up, for Christ's sake.'

'I spent all that night at Belle's place in
Bluewater.'

This brought the major straight up in his
chair, but the rebuke died on his lips. He
had been unfaithful to Luanne's mother.
Could he expect any less from a son-in-law

toward his own daughter? He slumped in his chair, thinking about it, while Uland continued nervously to twist his hat brim.

'I been thinkin', Major, that the two of us oughta do everything we can to make Luanne happy. To get her mind off losin' the baby.'

'By you spending less time at Belle's, perhaps?'

Uland colored. 'It'd make her mighty happy if her husband was to be top dog around here again.'

'You're speaking of Al Quester.'

'I am,' Uland said through his teeth.

'Challenge him for the job, if you want it so badly.'

'What d'you mean ... challenge?' Uland leaned forward, hands no longer busy at his hat brim.

'With a gun.'

Uland's smile was quick. 'I can blow that son out of his boots.'

'Done when I give the word. Done where I can see it happen. No back-shooting. No Conover climbing his back as happened the day you fought Kelly Boyle.'

'Wasn't my doings that day.' Uland grinned fiercely. 'Me an' Al Quester. You give the word, an' I'll have the job you shoulda give to me in the first place.'

'Earn it, then!' The major waved him out of the office.

With the loss of the baby he had no further tie with Al Quester as a potential uncle. And so, as far as Uland was concerned, the major suspected everything was over between Rex and Luanne. He'd send Luanne to St. Louis where he suspected she'd be eager to visit.

'Then we'll see who's the better man, Uland or Quester,' he mused aloud.

Thinking of pitting one man against another sent a dash of warmth through his body. It was something to look forward to.

Meanwhile, he'd find out who had fired his barn. Some disgruntled former hand? Or had it been the work of Diego Esparza? Retaliation for ignoring the ransom demands for Kelly Boyle?

Well, he no longer needed Esparza. His new contact was a man of much higher caliber, Emilio Casas, who already had sufficient weapons. All Casas wanted was a share in the new railroad. A very sensible man.

Because it was expected of him, he ordered ten of his men into their Sunday best and headed for town with his wife. Luanne was too ill to go. But it was politically expedient that Box R put in an appearance at the funeral of a faithful servant, Mrs. Blankenship.

After the service, while the women chatted at the Miller Store, the major walked to Belle's and there questioned the portly owner of the town's brothel about Uland's all night visit. She assured him that the big foreman had, indeed, spent the night.

'Reckon you heard the news about Kelly Boyle, eh, Major?'

Ransom had been turning away but now swung back. 'What news?'

'Boyle's hangin' out at the De Gama place?' Belle jerked her blonde head in that direction.

'Just how do you know that?'

'Two kids got in a fight over at the school, the De Gama kid an' Billy Simms's boy. Seems Billy's boy said somethin' about Kelly Boyle's bein' shot dead by the Mexicans an' the De Gama kid said otherwise. Well, they went at it, and in all the yellin' an' carryin' on the De Gama boy said that Kelly Boyle was alive an' livin' out at his place.'

'Well, thanks, Belle.' The major walked away, thinking about it.

Bert Conover had come over from East Ranch with Uland and was one of those in town for the funeral. The major found him in the Great River Saloon, got him aside, and gave him an order. It was still early in the day, and school was in session. 'Go over to the school and get the De Gama kid. I think his name is Guillermo. Here, give him a dollar.' The major handed over a silver dollar. 'Tell him I'd like to see him.'

Conover hurried away.

Miss Marpleton, a scrawny woman with

glasses and a raspy voice, had taken over when Florence married Major Ransom. She looked exasperated when Conover, hat in hand, came shuffling in to ask about one of her pupils. But mention of the magic name of Major Ransom soothed her. She beckoned to a small, dark boy who had been staring at Conover with open mouth.

'Guillermo, you are to accompany this gentleman.'

That was as far as she got before the boy bounded to his feet and fled the schoolhouse, producing guffaws from older boys, titters from the girls. Through the side window the boy could be seen running as if for his life along a side street, to disappear beyond some buildings.

'My land,' Miss Marpleton exclaimed, 'what's got into that boy!'

She turned and saw that her visitor had turned pale and seemed on edge. He quickly bowed his way out of the classroom and hurried to the saloon. There he reported that the boy wasn't in class and returned the dollar. Watching his chance, he slipped out and rode hard for Box R.

Conover found Rex Uland out behind the last barn, practicing a fast draw and firing at a tree some thirty feet away. Quickly Conover told him about the boy.

'Sure as hell it's the kid that seen us that day we done in...' – Conover, sweating,

293

looked quickly around, saw no one in sight, then finished it – 'done in the gal the major married.'

Uland's heavy jaw dropped. 'Jeezus Keeryst! If that kid opens his mouth, the major will hang us sure.'

Chapter Sixteen

One day when Boyle was feeling better, although still resting in bed, Felicita had come into the room. There was a sudden sound of a fast-moving animal.

She turned, her face frightened. 'It is Guillermo's mule. I know the sound. Something's happened. He does not come home until Saturday.'

Quickly she stepped from the room, closing the door.

Boyle rose and dressed hurriedly, hearing the boy's distraught voice, Felicita trying to make sense of what he was saying.

'Those men ... I try to keep out of their way. Whenever I see the three of them, I hurry away.' The boy was panting, as if out of breath and terrified. 'But today. One of them came for me ... to take me away.'

Boyle came into the front room. Felicita cast him an imploring glance. 'I do not understand him. Perhaps you...?'

Boyle knelt down. 'Chico, what is it? Tell me.'

'I ... I can't.'

'Guillermo,' his mother reproved, 'Don Kelly is our friend. Answer his question.'

But the boy fled the house and went out to the yard and stood next to the lean-to against the barn, staring into the distance. Boyle went out to talk with him. The boy was obviously frightened. 'You mentioned three men to your mother. What three men?'

'I only know one of them. The big redhead. His name is Uland.'

'What did they do to you, Chico?' Boyle's voice was suddenly harsh.

'It is not what they did to me. It is what I didn't do. I should have had a pistol. I could have gotten the drop on them and saved that poor woman. But I ran like the coward I am.'

Gradually he got the rest of the story out of him.

'One more score to settle against Box R,' he said grimly. And he knew it was time to move. A little sooner than he would have liked, but time nevertheless.

There was a problem. His clothing was ruined and Jaime's didn't fit. Felicita had a suggestion. Rob Shelly had died some months before; he had been a big man. Perhaps Samantha had some of his things around the house. It was worth a chance. She wrote a note. Kelly added a postscript.

Then Chico was bounding away on his mule, glad for the chance to take his mind off the man who had come for him at the schoolhouse that day.

When the boy was gone, Boyle told Felicita what he had learned. 'From what I could get out of him, he witnessed a rape.'

'Who was the woman?'

'My dead partner's ... widow.'

Felicita's hand flew to her mouth. 'The one who married Major Ransom!' she cried.

It was the first Boyle had heard of it. He turned and looked at Felicita. 'Married the major? Well, I'll be damned. She aimed high, that girl.'

Just before dark, Samantha and Chico arrived. Samantha, carrying a bundle of clothing, burst into the house. 'Why didn't you let me *know!*' she cried at Kelly, 'letting me think you were ... dead.'

Then her mouth began to tremble, and she flung herself into his arms. He felt her tears, tasted them. Then she turned her face, the large wet green eyes nearly on a level with his own. 'Oh, Kelly, Kelly...'

That evening at supper she told him how her father had finally given up, gone to live with his sister, Samantha's aunt, but died soon afterward.

He was glad to hear that Samantha had hired Pete Lambourne. 'I felt sorry for him,' she said. 'And we worked so well together at roundup.'

The following day, Boyle left his horse in the cottonwoods at Diamond Deuce. Gun in hand, he cautiously skirted the barn. Two horses, bearing the Box R brand, were in the corral. A glance through the bunkhouse window showed a broken chair. Tumbleweeds had blown through the open door. Rusted tin cans were scattered about. An empty whiskey bottle lay in a pool of sunlight.

As he started toward the house where he and Carl had had their bachelor quarters, a lank man, wearing a faded shirt, came to the door to empty a pan of soapy water. Upon seeing Boyle, he dropped the pan and made a pass at his holster, yelling – 'Mike!' – to someone inside.

Boyle fired through the door, the bullet clanging against an iron pot on the cook stove.

'The next one'll be in you,' Boyle warned. 'Mike, show yourself!'

A squat, bald man peered out the door.

Boyle told both men to lift their hands. '¡Alto mas!'

They raised them higher.

Boyle disarmed the pair, threw their weapons across the yard. 'You've got five minutes to get off this ranch,' he told them.

When they were gone, heads hanging in humiliation at having been driven off by one man, Boyle dug up his rusted money box. After removing two hundred dollars, he reburied the box.

Then he rode back to the De Gama place

and forced a reluctant Felicita to accept a hundred dollars. 'Little enough for the time you spent on me.' He patted her cheek. She seized his hand and held it in both of hers.

'Be careful, Kelly,' she urged.

'I want you to go across the river. You've got relatives over there. Stay until things quiet down over here. Will you do that for me? And take Chico and Jaime with you.' Finally he wore down her insistence that she would be all right where she was. 'I'll keep an eye on your place,' he promised.

At supper that evening Florence took a sip of wine, then said: 'Is Mister Uland going to live here at Central permanently?'

The major was in a bad mood over the loss of his grandchild, the burning of his barn, and the destruction of rifles and ammunition. 'What difference does it make to you?' he demanded, glaring through the candle glow.

'I like it better when he's at East Ranch.'

'Why?'

'Just a feeling is all.'

That was all he could get out of her, but the next day he got Uland aside. 'Tell me something, Rex. Have you ever had a run-in with Missus Ransom?'

Uland's face with its scars left from Kelly Boyle's fists was innocent. 'Never a word, Major. A real lady, she is.'

'Nobody around here ever better forget it,' the major said roughly, and stalked away.

Later that morning, Uland, Conover, and Roone had a conference.

'She ain't never said nothin', and my guess is she won't,' Conover offered.

'I still figure we oughta clear outta Texas,' was Roone's contribution. 'If she ever did talk... *Cristo!*'

Uland calmed him down. 'Now that she's got the major in harness, she ain't about to kick it to hell by yellin' that she rolled in the sand with us three.'

'But how about the kid?' Roone wailed.

'I hear he lives with a couple in town,' Uland mused. 'Goes home Saturdays. He could have an accident on the way.'

'Yeah, figure he could.' Roone agreed. 'But what if he's told his ma?'

Uland thought about that. 'Major's been wantin' to move 'em off, anyhow. An' they just might put up a fight.' He flashed a wink and a hard grin.

But they had no chance to perfect their plans for the major ordered the three of them back to East Ranch, *pronto*.

'My wife seems uneasy with you three around,' he finished coldly before walking away.

After Felicita agreed to do as he asked, Kelly Boyle rode north to the Shelly ranch. Upon his arrival he found Jaime De Gama breaking horses. Samantha and her cowhands were away. He told Jaime of the agreement he had reached with Felicita.

'I worry about her and the boy,' Boyle finished.

Jaime nodded that he understood and got ready to leave. It was then that Samantha and her riders appeared. At sight of Boyle, Pete Lambourne gave a whoop of joy. It was a time for back-pounding. The old man had tears in his eyes as he backed off and took a long look.

'Got to put some meat on your bones, son,' the old man said.

Samantha paid Jaime what he had coming. Then, with a wave of a dark hand, Jaime De Gama rode away.

'Stay the night, Kelly,' Samantha urged, coloring, and then with a little laugh added: 'In the bunkhouse, of course. I'll cook you a meal.'

While she went into the house to prepare supper, Boyle took a walk with Pete Lambourne. The old man filled him in on what had been going on in the months he had been away.

'Story got out you was bein' held in a Mex prison, an' I tell you that gal ... that Samantha ... she wrote the Texas Rangers. An' when they said they couldn't do nothin', she wrote the U. S. Army. But nothin' ever come of it. Main thing is ... she tried.'

'And I appreciate it, Pete. I'll remember to tell her. By the way, you still got that sawed-off Greener?'

'Sure have.' The old man cranked his head around to look up at Boyle. 'Why you ask?'

'Want to borrow it.'

'Why for you want a double-barreled shotgun?'

'You said once it'd kill a mule in his tracks.'

'Two mules. One for each barrel. You ain't told me why you want it, son.'

Boyle patiently explained that he was carrying an unfamiliar gun that had belonged to Teodoro, Felicita's late husband. 'I don't know just how good I'd be with it in a pinch. Your Greener could be the old equalizer.'

'You let me stand up with you, an' I'll handle that ol' equalizer.'

Boyle shook his head. 'I want you to keep an eye on Miss Samantha.'

They walked a dozen or so paces before Lambourne spoke again. 'Tell you the truth, Kelly, she ain't got the chance of a spitball in a bonfire of makin' a go of this here ranch. Her pa let it run down all to hell. And the major's Box R outfit's been givin' her fits.'

'In what way?'

'Some of 'em from North Ranch run off a

bunch of her cows. It was what we was doin' today, chasin' 'em back acrost the Box R line.'

'I want everybody to just sit tight. A lot of the major is just bluff and bluster. I aim to get some things settled.'

He washed up at the bench outside the bunkhouse and ran a damp comb through his hair. After studying his thin face in a piece of looking glass nailed to the wall under the eaves, he decided this night he could make no further improvements.

He walked up to the house and knocked on the door. A smiling Samantha met him, wearing green that matched her eyes. Silver hoops were at her ears. It was the first time he'd seen her in a dress since Jack Quester's funeral.

'Come in, come in, Kelly. Don't just stand there with the door open. You'll let some of my favorite flies escape.' She gave a little laugh.

'I was admiring you is all.' He came in and closed the door. Aroma of cooking food filled the house. Although it was not quite dark yet, she had lit a lamp. There were bearskin rugs on the floor.

'Dad had a jug of wine put away for some occasion. Poor Dad, his occasion never came.' Her eyes clouded for an instant, then were merry again. 'Ours has.'

The wine was mellow, the steaks perfect.

Finally Boyle realized Sam was eating little. 'You're only picking at your food,' he chided.

'I'm too nervous. Having you under my roof is the most ... most stupendous thing that's ever happened to me.'

'I'm flattered.'

'I mean it, Kelly.' Her voice broke. 'Having you here alive ... weeks ago there was a rumor that you'd died in that prison ... or been killed.'

'People tried to put me under, but they didn't make it. Pete told me about you trying to get me out.'

Tears glistened in her eyes. 'But no one would listen. Damn them.' She choked on it. Boyle reached across the table to give her hand a squeeze. She clung to it a moment, then said: 'I feel better now. I can eat.' And she did joyfully.

He helped her clear the table, remembering he had done it for Florence a lifetime ago. When he thought of the chain of events that had led to Carl Tripp's trying to gun him down, his jaws tightened.

A perceptive Samantha noticed the change. 'Something upset you.'

'It was nothing.'

'Tell me, Kelly. My father used to say that I had the best pair of listening ears in Tyburn County.'

She poured more wine from the jug and suggested he kick off his boots and make himself comfortable. He sat at one end of the sofa in the parlor, she at the other, her long legs stretched out.

He began to talk, telling of the day Uland and Conover and Roone had come to Diamond Deuce to fetch him for the major, how he had warned them about Florence after one of them had made a bawdy remark. 'Near as I can tell, they caught her out alone. They beat her and raped her.'

'How terrible,' Samantha gasped. She sat on her feet and moved closer to his end of the sofa. It was very quiet in the house. One of the lamp wicks smoked slightly. 'You know for sure they did it?' she asked when he sat silently, sipping wine.

'There was a witness,' he said. 'Carl Tripp got a crazy idea in his head that I'd been the rapist. I tried to talk to him, but he wouldn't listen. He ... he shot me and in that flash of time I acted instinctively. I drew my gun and I ... I killed him. I'm reasonably sure that he was my own half-brother.'

He put the cup of wine on the floor between his sock feet and held his head in his hands. Samantha reached out and placed a consoling hand on his shoulder. 'How terrible for you, Kelly.'

'So ... until I'm told otherwise ... I hold Uland and the other two accountable,' he said in a dead voice. 'Not only for the assault on a fine lady, but for the chain of events that led me to commit a murder.'

'It wasn't murder, Kelly, it wasn't.'

After a minute he said: 'No, I suppose ... technically ... it wasn't. But I feel guilty all the same.'

'You must get over it, Kelly,' she urged. 'Cleanse your mind of it.'

'Easy to say.'

'You must.'

Her voice was louder, and he realized suddenly that her warm breath was against his earlobe. Turning his head, he saw her shining eyes, so close, saw the moist red mouth, the lips slightly parted, the curve of a breast under green silk. Then he shook himself and said: 'Cleanse the mind. Yes, I must do that.' He leaned away from her and picked up his cup and took a long swallow of wine. It trickled, slightly tart, down his throat to mingle with its brothers that had gone before and formed a delightful pool in his stomach.

Her fingertips played with his lips. 'You have a strong mouth, Kelly,' she whispered.

'You keep on tantalizing me this way,' he said hoarsely, 'and I won't be very strong.'

'It is my intention.'

She waited stiffly, her back arched, watching him out of round green eyes. And he thought: *She's lonely and so am I. Why not?*

Leaning forward, he kissed her gently. After a moment her mouth opened. He felt the thrust of her warm tongue. And then she nibbled his lower lip as he leaned forward awkwardly. 'I'll get a crick in my neck,' he said finally.

'We'll uncrick it.' She came into his arms.

He felt body heat through her clothing. 'Wine fires the blood,' he heard himself say.

'Yes, doesn't it.'

She lifted her chin to expose a long throat. His lips pressed soft flesh; his hand found it through a gap in her dress, miraculously unbuttoned.

'I'll probably live and die an old maid cattle rancher,' she whispered. 'But I want one taste of love in my lifetime.' Her eyes misted, then she exposed her strong teeth, slightly gapped. 'Don't look so astonished, Kelly Boyle.'

If he hadn't consumed so much wine, her remark might have made him back off, but he wasn't thinking too clearly. All he knew was that he had unlocked his soul and exposed its raw side with his talk of rape and Florence and Carl Tripp. And there was the nearness of this delightful female to obliterate it from his mind.

'Undress me, Kelly. I'm too nervous to do it by myself.'

He found the rest of the buttons, helped her draw the dress over her head. Some of her red hair came undone and fell across her moist brow. She blew it away, her eyes dazzling bright. She was long-limbed and strong, yet surprisingly soft. He had expected a sprinkling of freckles, but her body was unblemished marble. Reaching out, he cupped a lamp chimney and blew out the flame.

In the darkness he got out of his clothing. Then every centimeter of her body reacted to his lips and the caress of fingertips.

Finally she whispered that it was time. 'Do it to me, Kelly, do it!'

For a moment he was blocked. It was something he hadn't expected. With Luanne he had, and been vaguely disappointed. When he started to draw back, Samantha gripped him in her strong arms. Trembling, she pulled him against her sharply which caused her to give a little cry, but suddenly the obstruction was gone.

She clung to him and gasped and moaned alternately. In his exuberance they rolled from the sofa, he breaking her fall with his body against one of the bearskin rugs. There the gentle fury continued until she cried out and lay limply in his arms.

At last she spoke in a voice so low he could barely hear her. 'Many nights I dreamt of this and wondered if reality could match a dream. And it did.' She stroked his face. 'I dreaded possibly going to my grave as a girl. Now I can go as a woman.'

'You're too young to talk of graves.'

'Not in Tyburn County. One learns to live

for the day, the moment. And I have. Thank you, Kelly.'

When he got back to the bunkhouse he had a hard time falling asleep. In one way he had enjoyed himself immensely, but in another he felt that he had walked into a trap.

In the morning, wearing jeans and shirt, she came to the bunkhouse to eat breakfast with them. No coy glances cast his way, no gentle pressure of hands. Just straightforward ranch talk.

When it came time for him to leave, she said: 'I hear you're taking Pete Lambourne's shotgun. That worries me.'

'It's only for effect. I enjoyed myself, Samantha. Thanks for the supper and the wine.'

'It was an enjoyable evening,' was her parting remark. She waved to him when he looked back.

A strange young woman, for sure. Mighty cool in view of the tumult they had stirred up together last night.

Chapter Seventeen

Kelly Boyle arrived in Bluewater the following day, a Saturday. Clothing of the late Rob Shelly fit him reasonably well. His sombrero was Chihuahuan. Strapped around his lean waist was the revolver that had belonged to Felicita's husband. On the way he had done some more shooting and was getting used to the feel of the weapon. Also he had looked over Pete Lambourne's Greener which he carried in a saddle scabbard opposite the one holding his rifle.

After leaving his horse at an end spot of the hitch rail, he started walking. It took a little time before he was noticed, he had thinned down so, but suddenly a gasp went up from those nearby. 'Kelly Boyle ... back from the dead.'

He started to ask if the major was in town, then saw his daughter, alone, in a buckboard in the Miller turn-around. She was thumbing through a newspaper.

A woman said – 'First time she's been in town, poor thing.' – and told him the rest of it.

Boyle walked over, removed his hat. Luanne looked up, the violet eyes startled, then unreadable.

'You seem reasonably happy,' he said by way of greeting.

'Reasonably.'

'I just heard about the baby. I'm sorry.'

'One learns to recover from ... 'most anything.' Now her eyes were bitter, accusing.

'You act like everything is my fault.'

'No, I blame my father ... because by now I'd be happily married to Jack Quester and living in Colorado.'

Boyle wondered why he wasn't hurt or angered by what she had said, putting Jack Quester before him, but it seemed all drained away. 'Your father didn't kill Jack. Carl did.'

'It was my father who gave Al the idea to put the dead snake in your partner's blankets.'

'I shouldn't be surprised, I guess.'

'But it was a pretty low thing to do, even for him. Knowing Tripp's temper. He hated Tripp because of the blonde.'

'You talking about Florence. But why should he hate Carl?'

'Who knows why my father hates? Something I could never understand. Why he should have been interested in such an obviously low-class female...'

Boyle bristled. 'No reason to insult her.'

'No, I suppose not. But isn't it reasonable to assume she was hiding from something? To bury herself out at Diamond Deuce with a man like Carl Tripp?'

'I understand she's now your stepmother.'

Luanne showed her teeth. 'Unfortunately, yes. Frankly, I'm surprised you didn't steal her away from Tripp. But, of course, I'm forgetting your great bond of friendship with Tripp that transcended all else.'

Not trusting himself to speak, he touched his hat brim and left her.

When he had gone, she thought: *Why did I act like such a damnable bitch?*

Uland came thumping out of the store, took a look at her. 'Why're you cryin'?' he demanded.

She blamed it on something sad she had read in the newspaper. Uland drove her out of town, heading in the direction of East Ranch where they were still living.

It was strangely quiet in the Great River Saloon. Sid Bartline came from his office, small and worried-looking, and poured Kelly Boyle a drink. 'Mebby you can tell me how things is across the line,' he said confidentially, 'you havin' been there a spell.'

'A spell, yeah.' Boyle gave a short laugh.

'Bloody as usual, I hear. Though we don't get much reliable news. I got money in that damn' railroad. Kelly, you figure it'll ever be built?'

'Not by Esparza, for sure.'

'But he's top man down there.'

'I guess news does travel slow. He's dead.'

Bartline had a wad of tobacco bulging a cheek. Boyle's statement made him forget to chew. Tobacco juice slid down to his small chin. He wiped it off and spat into a cuspidor. 'Jesus Christ, you sure about Esparza bein' dead?'

'I killed the son-of-a-bitch ... after he murdered a friend of mine ... and to settle other scores.' He was thinking of Felicita.

'You sure you killed him?'

'Unless somebody found a way to put his head back together.'

Boyle drank his whiskey, one eye on the double doors.

'That's bad news.' Bartline sounded depressed. 'Railroad up here ain't been goin' so good, neither. Main line will go over east to Del Norte is the latest rumor. All we can do is run a spur line here to Bluewater.'

'The major been around today?'

Bartline shook his head. 'We still might get rich off a spur line. But it's already cost us dearly.'

'You boys have listened to the major too long.'

Bartline peered up into the bitter, dark face. 'Tell you what, Kelly. I figure me an' the boys can raise a little more cash. When you head out, you let us know where you'll be, an' we'll send it along.'

'Pay me? For what?'

'Sort of a bonus for leavin' here ... without

313

blowin' everything to hell. You already run two fellas off Diamond Deuce, an' the major's just bidin' his time. So I reckon you know which way the wind's blowin'.'

'What gave you the idea I'm leaving Texas?'

'My God, you ain't fool enough to hang around an' try to buck Box R.'

'Forget trying to pay me to leave. I'll be at Diamond Deuce.'

Bartline shook his head. Down the bar men were staring. 'You oughta know better'n to cross the major,' Bartline continued in an awed voice.

'Something I never learned. Rex Uland been in?'

'Was in earlier. He's livin' over at East Ranch.'

'How about Conover and Roone?'

'They're with him. Al Quester's been ramroddin' Central an' North.'

'Seems the major had to sweep the stable floor to find a ramrod.'

'Holy Keeryst, don't let Al hear you say that.'

Boyle gave him a cold smile.

There was a sudden clatter of boots on the outside stairway of the adjoining building. Through a side window Boyle had a glimpse of Major Ransom stomping up the stairway.

Bartline sighed. 'Reckon he ain't heard that Annabelle Tyce left town last week.'

314

'Seems the major doesn't spend much time in his own bed.'

'Takin' a new wife did settle him down for a spell.'

In a minute Major Ransom rammed a shoulder between the swing doors and entered the saloon, his face reflecting an inner turmoil. Whatever had been eating in him now flamed tenfold in the hazel eyes as he saw Boyle at the bar. 'I'm surprised you'd have the guts to come back after such a miserable failure.'

'Thanks for paying my ransom.' Boyle came up within two feet of the major, his hard eyes raking the older man's face. 'We've got an agreement, Major.'

'It is null and void,' the major said coldly. 'You voided it by shooting it out with your great friend, Carl Tripp.'

'You don't know a damn' thing about friendship. Or loyalty.'

'Get out of Texas!'

'I understand you sold off my cattle. So I'll expect payment in full.'

'You can go straight to hell!'

'I'll take you to court. We'll let a jury decide.'

The major showed his teeth under the mustache. 'You'd pay hell winning your case.'

'Just maybe this time you can't pack a jury or buy a judge. People are getting damned sick of you, Major. They've put their hard-

315

earned cash into your railroad. And you've spent most of it on your political friends in Austin. Oh, I've been nosing around.'

The major looked nervously at the silent patrons of the saloon, then snapped: 'Boyle, I'll give you a thousand dollars for a quit-claim deed to Diamond Deuce.'

'You owe me roughly twenty thousand dollars for my cattle you sold.'

'I'm speaking of nuisance value. A thousand dollars to be shut of you!'

'You honor our agreement, and I'll be your ramrod. Superintendent, I guess is the fancy title you gave me.'

'Never!'

Ignoring him, Boyle said: 'But this time *I* deal the cards, Major. Uland and Conover and Roone are off the payroll. Also Al Quester.'

'You're not dealing any cards. I made you an offer. Do you accept it or not. I don't give much of a damn, either way!'

'No!'

Major Ransom shook his fist. 'God damn you, Boyle!'

The temper that the major seemed to have been fighting to control finally broke. He grabbed for a gun under his coat, but Boyle drew in such a blinding reflex action that his weapon roared first. Concussion beat at the eardrums in the Great River Saloon as the major's gun spun away. A bright red streak appeared across the back of his right hand. His gun struck the front of the bar, then clanged against a spittoon. In the ceiling a film of dust hovered about one of the rough beams where a bullet from the major's gun had made a small, dark eye in the wood.

Men sprang up from deal tables, ready to run if the fight continued. Along the bar others were poised, every eye on the pale, enraged features of Major Ransom. In the stillness, he glared at Kelly Boyle as he wrapped a linen handkerchief around his wound. Instantly the linen was stained.

'I'll kill you for this, Kelly,' he whispered, then whirled and strode from the saloon.

Bartline wiped his face with a dark blue bandanna. 'That was a damn' fool trick. Pullin' a gun on the major.'

'Better I let him shoot me?'

'You got to admit you sure riled him, Kelly.'

'He'll be a lot more riled than this.'

Major Ransom stormed into Doc Starrett's office for treatment of his bullet wound.

'How is Missus Uland these days?' the doctor asked as he bandaged the flesh wound.

'She's gone back to East Ranch with her husband,' the major snapped.

When he got home Florence confronted him, saw his hand, and demanded to know what had happened.

'You preached conciliation,' he said thinly. 'But there's no dealing with Boyle.' He held up his bandaged hand. 'This is the result. A wonder he didn't kill me.'

'Are you sure you tried to talk peace with him, Terrence?'

But he wasn't listening. In his office he scribbled a note, his hand hurting, and put it into an envelope that he sealed and marked: Personal. Summoning one of the cowhands, he told the man to deliver it to Uland at East Ranch.

When the man had hurried away, a suppressed excitement threatened to set the major's nerves humming. This was the war all over again, the grand challenge, lives of men dependent upon the snapping of his fingers. He would hang Kelly Boyle, he decided, not from a tree but from the tied-back tongue of a wagon. Put him on a box two feet high and kick it out from under and let him dangle. He hoped Boyle's eyes remained open to the last and that he would be conscious of the fact that he had forfeited life for betraying his benefactor because of that senseless shoot-out with Carl Tripp.

Kelly Boyle bedded down in the trees, instead of the house, because he expected visitors. He had them the next morning, but not those anticipated. Samantha Shelly and Pete Lambourne came roaring into the yard.

318

Lambourne gave him a worried look, and Samantha seized his arm and walked him out by the corral. 'I heard what you did, Kelly. I sent Curly to town for supplies, and, when he came back, he told me about your shooting the major. You could have been killed'

'But I wasn't,' he assured her with a tight grin.

'How in the world did it happen?'

'One thing just led to another. Samantha, there's going to be trouble. Why don't you go to Arizona and stay with your aunt?'

'No!'

'Then, at least, go to town until this is over.' Boyle shook his head at the obstinate green eyes.

'Kelly, let's face facts. These aren't the wild lawless days of the Republic. This is late Nineteenth Century, the age of reason, of law. We're not going to stand by and let Major Ransom spill the blood of innocents.'

'A noble speech, but this age of reason and law hasn't quite reached Tyburn County.'

'I love you, Kelly. I want you alive, not dead.'

The simple declaration touched him, he had to admit, but he brushed it aside and told her to head for home.

'Know what I intend to do, Kelly?'

'From the look in your eye, probably something I won't approve of.' He gave a hint of a

319

smile when she declared she was going to send for the Texas Rangers. 'This is the U.S., not Mexico. This time they'll *have* to listen to me.'

He told her what he had heard in town, that politicians had whittled the ranks of the force, that what was left of the Texas Rangers had been drawn south because of trouble near Laredo. 'Let me do it my way, Samantha,' he urged.

Finally after arguing for five minutes, she reluctantly agreed to go home – but not to town, not to her aunt's.

'You walk easy,' was Pete Lambourne's parting advice.

When Boyle saw Samantha riding off, her back straight, braids bouncing to movements of the horse, he had an urge to shout that he'd go with her, give up this crazy idea of bucking Box R, but it died in him almost instantly. After they had gone, he saddled up and started for Box R. He had gone about three miles when he saw a buggy approaching. Drawing the sawed-off shotgun, he waited beside the road until he saw it was a woman driving. Florence Ransom. He was still sitting his saddle, shotgun across his thigh, scanning the trees, when she drove up.

'I see you've overcome your fear of horses,' he said.

'Overcome my fear of a lot of things,

Kelly. What are you going to do with the shotgun?'

He told her he was on his way to Box R for a showdown with the major.

'A showdown is what I want to prevent. It's why I slipped away and was coming to see you.' She wore yellow, from a broad-brimmed hat to her dress and shoes. Her hands were gloved. The roan horse stood patiently in the buggy shafts. She said: 'Terrence is … the major is furious that you shot him. I'm making one last try ... to appeal to both of you.'

'He'll never listen to you. Are you happy with him, Florence?

She shrugged. 'Sometimes I think he was born to be unhappy. He told me once that his greatest pleasure in life was the war. And then he thought that you and he...' She shook her head. 'He says you had to spoil things for him by allowing Carl to shoot you.'

'Poor Carl.'

'The major told me once that the first time he killed a man in combat was the same as having a woman. Can you understand such a mind?'

'I'm past trying to understand him.'

'It was terrible, your having to kill Carl. Will you ever get over it?' She looked at him anxiously.

'I can't sort it all out. Not yet.'

'I don't know whether he was your friend

321

or not. At times, he seemed to resent you terribly.'

'It makes no difference now,' Boyle said in a dead voice.

She stared off at trees being stirred by a spring breeze. 'I feel guilty only because at one time Carl did so much for me.'

'Saved your life, so you said.'

'Could anyone do more?' Her deep blue eyes looked into his face. 'Now I want to save your life. Please, go back to Diamond Deuce and wait until I can convince the major...'

'Tell me, Florence. It was Uland, Roone, and Conover who assaulted you?'

'It doesn't matter,' she said quickly.

'There was a witness. But I want to be sure. When you go to hang a man, you don't want to make any mistakes.'

'Yes, it was the three of them, but I say again ... it doesn't matter.'

'I'll go to East Ranch and dig up those three and hang them.' His voice shook.

She gasped, a hand going to her throat. 'Kelly, you haven't a chance.'

'With this I have.' He touched the stock of the shotgun he had booted. His roan stomped the ground nervously.

'I'm not worth avenging Kelly.'

'Any woman is.'

'Let me tell you about myself. In San Francisco is where Sam Joe's luck turned sour. My late husband I'm talking about.'

'You don't have to tell me anything.'

'But I insist you listen. When the pot was empty, he ... he expected me to help. Do you understand?'

'I understand,' he said after a moment. 'But there's...'

'At first I was reluctant. But only at first. I suppose you could say I didn't have much pride. But I was afraid of him, for one thing.'

'You're tearing yourself apart with this, and it won't change a damned thing.'

'I could have run away, and I didn't. The humiliation of expecting me to help him once again at Lucero was too much. He knocked me down, then said all he wanted was one week. Then we'd leave. It was a high-stakes game with some American mine owners. I always wondered if I'd meet someone who'd remember me. I never remembered any of them. It's why I jumped at the chance for a sanctuary such as Diamond Deuce. Well, after Sam Joe left, I saw the shotgun behind the hotel desk. You know the rest of it.'

'I know, yes.'

She looked at him, her eyes brimming with tears. 'Now you can understand why it isn't necessary that you defend a whore. That's what Uland called me that day.'

'I swore to hang them, and I will.'

'You'll make Luanne a widow.'

It had crossed his mind, but he had always thrust it aside. But hearing her say it weighed heavily on him. 'All the same...'

'Please think of others who ... who might care for you ... when you take such awful chances.'

He rode with her back to the Box R line, she arguing for him to hold off until she could talk to the major. At one point she said: 'His health isn't good, and he's lost a lot of money. I sense he doesn't want a showdown with you. Please, please give me a chance, Kelly.'

'I'll see,' was all he said.

He sat his saddle and watched her drive rapidly along the ranch road, a classic figure in yellow, until swallowed up by the willows.

For a long time he remained where he was, thinking. What she had said about making Luanne a widow was like a barb on his conscience. Carl had cheated her out of marriage to Jack Quester by killing him. He'd give Florence twenty-four hours, he decided at last. If by some miracle she could arrange a peaceful settlement, then lives would be spared. Quite possibly his own, although he didn't dwell on that. If things didn't work out, he'd go after Uland and company, then settle with the major.

On the way home he thought of what Uland had done to Florence. *Which made Carl Tripp come after me with a gun,* he thought. *And I killed him. Because of you three* hijos de putas *I killed him.*

Major Ransom's messenger intercepted Rex Uland, Conover, and Roone a dozen miles west of East Ranch. They were on their way to finish the business with the De Gama boy once and for all.

The messenger thrust the envelope at a scowling Uland, who tore it open and read the contents quickly. It was a summons to Central Ranch.

He showed it to Roone and Conover. 'We'll go see what he wants. You get outta here,' he added to the messenger who went pounding away.

'I still say we oughta get shut of Texas,' Roone said worriedly.

The other two ignored him.

Felicita De Gama listened to the firing across the river, diminished now from what it had been earlier. Her brother, Jaime, came to stand at her side. 'What do you think?'

She shrugged. 'Who knows? But from the sounds it seems that whoever was shooting over there is moving on. I say we wait another day to make sure.'

Jaime laughed. 'Good. It will postpone one day my seeing cousin Maldonado. I owe him money, and he will ask me for it.'

'Why do you owe our cousin money?'

Felicita asked sharply.

'A monte game. I lost.'

'As usual,' she chided. 'When will you ever learn, Jaime?'

There was only sporadic firing now on the far side of the river. Raiders, she supposed. Times were unsettled.

Chapter Eighteen

An hour later Uland faced the major in the Box R ranch office.

'I want Kelly Boyle ... alive,' Major Ransom said bluntly.

'He might bleed a little, but he'll be alive,' Uland assured him.

'We'll clean this range of trouble-makers once and for all.' Cursing his injured hand, the major started to write out instructions to be delivered to the sheriff at Empire, via the deputy, Eli Corn. 'I'm requesting twenty deputy sheriff badges.'

'Don't figure we need to wait for that,' Uland said, watching the major's face. 'Boyle's been stayin' at the De Gama place.'

'I discount what that fool De Gama boy is supposed to have said one day at school.' Then the major fixed him with a cold stare. 'How do you know Boyle's at the De Gama place?'

'Ear to the ground.'

'I see.'

'Me an' Roone an' Conover can take him easy.' Feeling he had an opening, Uland plunged on. 'We could move off the De Gamas at the same time we grab Boyle. You been wantin' to get shet of 'em for quite a spell.'

'You're right, Rex.'

Al Quester came in without knocking, which caused the major to frown. 'Major, you sure you wanna sell two thousand head of beef with the market down like it is?'

'I thought I made it clear, Al.' The major's voice was cold. He needed the money because of funds he'd shipped across the line to his latest hope, Emilio Casas. And damn Quester for making an issue out of it.

Quester noticed Uland for the first time. 'Mind getting out, Uland? I wanna talk to the major in private.'

Uland, sensing tension between the major and Quester, decided to press it. He was remembering what the major had told him about gunning for Quester's job which could come later, after the De Gama business was settled. 'I'll move when I'm damn' good an' ready.'

'Mebby you forgot,' Quester said, his heavy face angered, 'I run things now. Not you

Uland's smile was malicious. 'I happen to be the major's son-in-law. Somethin' mebby you forgot.'

The major yelled at them to shut up and, in the silence, stared at a book-lined wall, turning over in his mind what Uland had said about getting the bloody business done now, not later with deputy badges to back them up. Maybe Uland's way was best, after all, in case the sheriff balked about sending the badges. Delay in the laying of tracks toward Bluewater had turned Sheriff Temple cool; he was a stockholder. But on the other hand, with his men deputized, he could move off the De Gamas who had been squatters for years. Then he'd go after the Shelly girl, who certainly had more spunk than her late father. In this corner of Texas spunk bought nothing but heartache unless it was backed by power.

'I'll get Boyle for you, Major,' Uland said, and started for the door. It was obvious that the major didn't want him to have a showdown with Quester today, so Uland was anxious to be on his way.

Al Quester reddened. 'I got ideas of my own how to handle Kelly Boyle. We'll take a dozen men...'

Uland stiffened at the door. Witnesses he didn't want. 'It's a personal thing with me, Major. Me an' Roone an' Conover can handle it fine.' He watched the major for reaction, while Quester grunted and snarled under his breath.

As usual the major had his own ideas. 'Rex, take Al along with you.'

'But...?' Uland wanted no Quester along to witness what they would be forced to do for survival. If the major ever found out what the three of them had done to the woman he later married ... He didn't finish the thought – just that much passing through his mind turned him cold.

Quester seemed equally unhappy at the arrangement and argued for a show of force, but the more he argued, the more the major balked.

'Get going,' the major demanded. 'By the way, Rex. You boss the job.' And he gave Quester a nasty smile.

'Sure thing, Major,' Uland said with a grin.

Quester didn't know it, but the way things were turning out Uland expected to be top dog again at Box R. That would give Luanne something to think about, and get her over any ideas about going back to St. Louis for an extended visit. Since losing the baby she'd been cold toward him. Well, that would change. If necessary, he would get her by the hair of her head and teach her some manners, in bed and out.

The major called to Uland as he was closing the door. 'I'll be in Bluewater. When you catch Boyle, one of you ride in and tell me where you're holding him. Then we'll finish it. Good luck, Rex.'

'Thanks, Major,' Uland called and closed the door.

Conover and Roone questioned him with their eyes when Al Quester, wearing a black scowl, rode out with them, but Uland gave them a slight shake of the head. And because he seemed to be in a jovial mood, they felt their own tensions begin to fade.

The minute Uland had left, Florence entered the office. 'Terrence, I want to talk to you.'

'Later, later,' he said, waving her away.

'You sent Uland after Kelly Boyle.' She drew a deep breath and studied her husband slouched in his big leather chair behind the desk. 'I was outside. I overheard part of what was being said in here.'

'You had no right!' he thundered, finding in her a vent for the accumulated frustrations of the past weeks.

She withstood his glare, matching it with her own. 'I want you to send someone to bring Uland back.'

'Now you give orders?'

She approached the desk, leaned against it, peering down at him. 'Terrence, this can be solved without bloodshed. It must be.'

'All of a sudden you have a place in your great heart for Kelly Boyle,' he sneered.

'And so should you. The way you've treated him...'

He waved the bandaged hand at her. 'You expect me to forget *this?*'

'No doubt you provoked him.'

He pointed. 'Go to your room!'

'All right, I'll go after Uland myself.' She turned for the door, but he sprang up.

'Don't touch me,' she warned.

But he did, viciously, a wide-swinging backhand that crashed into her cheek and knocked her down. As he stood over her, enraged, she came to her knees, her face bleeding.

'What you have done ends our marriage, Terrence,' she told him, her voice shaking.

'I'll let you know in my own good time when it ends.'

Seizing her by an arm, he half dragged her upstairs, the servants wise enough to keep out of the way. He locked her in her room, then got his gun and his hat, and started for Bluewater. He had made sure there was a rifle in the boot before heading out. There was no telling how this mad day might end.

Uland and the others cut along the ranch road, then branched onto wheel tracks that led to the De Gama place down near a bend in the river. At last they came within sight of it and reined in to study the squat adobe house, the lean-to built against the barn, the corral. Pepper trees in front and on two sides had been planted by Felicita's grandfather when a young man.

'How the hell do you know Boyle is inside?' Quester grumbled as he stared at the house.

'I don't,' was Uland's sharp reply.

'Then what the hell we doin' here?'

332

Quester glared at him.

Ignoring him, Uland raised his voice: 'Hey, kid. Step out here ... want a word with you!'

'Go away,' came the strong voice of a woman in Spanish. 'You are trespassing.'

Roone said nervously: 'Why don't she talk English, for Christ's sake?'

'Send the boy out here!' Uland shouted. 'I want to talk to him!'

'You want to hurt him,' came the woman's voice from the house. Felicita was shouting, and switched now to English. 'Because of what he saw you do to the woman.'

'What woman she talkin' about?' yelled Al Quester, leaning over the saddle horn, heavy jaw outthrust.

But Uland's big rifle exploded, the sound washing over whatever else was shouted from the house. Rifles opened up from a window and rear door. Powder smoke ballooned into the pepper trees.

'Son-of-a-bitch!' cried Quester, sawing his horse around with such savagery that it squealed.

'We got to protect ourselves,' Uland yelled, and spurred to put the barn between himself and the house. He was about to shoot Al Quester in the stomach, in fact had his rifle pointed, with Quester half turned in the saddle toward the house, but right then Conover, his horse coming at a hard run, pitched headfirst out of the saddle. The crack of a rifle came from the house an instant later. Conover's foot was jammed in the stirrup, and the panicked horse dragged him, his head bouncing over the uneven ground.

Uland muttered an oath and went after Conover, Roone right behind him. Roone caught the runaway horse, and Uland made a flying dismount.

Conover was already dead from the bullet. Uland pulled his foot from the stirrup, felt sick at what the ground had done to Conover's face, then straightened up. More rifle fire erupted from the house. A bullet whanged off a piece of metal in the yard. Another came dangerously close to Uland's hat brim as he mounted up and raced for the protection of the barn where Quester waited.

'How in the hell is this gettin' us Kelly Boyle?' Quester demanded angrily.

'He finds 'em dead, an' he'll come lookin' for them that done it. Us.'

'Kill the woman and the kid?'

'You ain't got stomach for it, Al, you better cut an' run for Box R. It's how things is gonna be done.'

Uland debated whether to put a bullet in Quester now or later. Savage gunfire Uland hadn't counted on, and Conover's getting gunned down gave him pause. It would likely take the three of them to silence the De Gamas.

Felicita De Gama wished now she had

gone across the river as Kelly Boyle had asked. But there had been the shooting over there, and besides the river was high, and she had delayed going to Bluewater and taking the ferry. She called to Jaime and Guillermo. 'I will go and talk with them. The minute I am gone, you two slip out and get away.'

Jaime gripped a rifle, the boy a pistol that it took both hands to hold.

'No, *hermana*,' Jaime said bluntly. 'I go and do the talking. You and Chico slip away.'

But it was too late. A big, vicious-looking man was coming at a run toward the front of the house. Jaime fired his rifle, but the man was untouched. The man raised up and fired through the front window. Jaime gave a low gurgling sound and collapsed.

'Run, Chico!' Felicita screamed at the boy. But more gunfire came suddenly from the rear of the house. Something smashed into her, driving out all sight and sound.

Uland came stomping into the house. 'How about the kid?' he said to Roone.

'Dead, looks like.'

'And the woman?'

'The same,' Quester answered. 'I say we get the hell out before somebody comes along.' His large face was gray as the enormity of what they had done struck home.

They heard sudden firing from the far side of the river. It decided them. They hurried away.

Kelly Boyle had dismantled Pete Lambourne's sawed-off shotgun to give it a thorough cleaning. There were traces of rust in both barrels. Evidently the old man had not taken the best care of his favorite weapon. He had just reassembled it when he heard someone call his name. It came from such a distance and was so indistinct that he couldn't recognize the voice.

Alert for any ruse, he drew his gun and stepped from the house. What he saw was Chico up by the windmill, astride his mule. The boy just sitting there, slumped over.

Then Boyle took in the rest of it, bloodied face and shirt. He began to run as Chico lifted a hand, and then doubled up and toppled to the ground. The mule shied but stood his ground.

'Chico, Chico!' Boyle cried, kneeling down.

'*Mi madre*,' the boy gasped.

'What about your mother?' Boyle asked anxiously, but the boy had passed out.

Boyle carried him down to the house, placed him on the sofa. Then he tore up some old shirts to make a compress for the boy's twin wounds. A bullet had caught him in the chest and made an exit wound. By the time he had fashioned a crude bandage, the boy had revived and told what had happened. As he listened, Boyle's face drained of color. Because he couldn't risk leaving

336

the badly wounded boy alone, and there was a chance the mother was still alive, he tied him to the saddle and started out.

It seemed hours later because of the slow pace he was forced to keep until he saw the house in the pepper trees. Crossing the plowed field, he came upon Conover's body, then to the house, dreading what he might find. He felt sickened as he stumbled over Jaime's body, saw that he was dead. Then he felt a pressure of tears quickly blocked by his fury as he saw Felicita crumpled on the floor. She lay across a carbine. The right side of her dress was stained with blood. As he knelt down, her eyes opened and her lips stirred.

'Thank God,' he murmured, close to tears again.

'*¿Mi hijo...?*' Her pain was forgotten in concern for her son.

'He lost much blood. He came all the way to Diamond Deuce to fetch me. Oh, Felicita, why didn't you get out like I told you to?'

She seemed not to comprehend, saying instead: 'Did you kill those men?' Her eyes were wide, anxious.

'No, but I will,' he vowed.

'You know who they are?'

'Chico told me.'

He found an *olla* and gave Felicita some water. As nearly as he could tell, she had been shot twice. He tore up some of her underclothing to make bandages, then went to work. She had been shot under the right breast. Another bullet had torn through her left thigh. She also had lost much blood.

'They ... they thought we were dead,' Chico gasped, having come to lean weakly against a door frame.

Kelly Boyle knew that the boy and his mother needed medical attention, and soon. He got a team hitched to a light wagon. Then he stripped the house of blankets, placing them in the wagon bed. He carried mother and son to the wagon and covered them.

Starting the team, he wondered if either of them would survive the rough trip to town. As he drove, Boyle had a hard time keeping his hands from trembling. Never in his life before had he felt such rage as he did on this afternoon as he drove for Bluewater with his two badly wounded friends.

Chapter Nineteen

Samantha Shelly had taken it upon herself to get word to the Texas Rangers. She rode to the Forks, caught a stagecoach to Empire, and sent a telegram. She fidgeted for most of one afternoon before receiving a reply. Giving a whoop of joy when she did, she caught the southbound, got off at the Forks, changed into riding clothes, and galloped home.

'Pete! Pete, look what I've got!' she cried triumphantly, and waved a telegram under Lambourne's nose.

He read it, looked up, his bearded lips in a faint grin. 'Cap'n says he'll look into the matter. Don't mean he's gonna kick the major where he sets.'

'It's a start, Pete!' she exclaimed. 'We can settle this without bloodshed. I feel it strongly.'

Leaving her two cowhands to look after things, she and Lambourne headed for Diamond Deuce. They found Lambourne's shotgun, but no Boyle. He had evidently left in a hurry because the house door was wide open.

Major Terrence Ransom was standing at the bar in the Great River Saloon when Pete Lambourne shuffled in, the gray-bearded face twisted with worry. He went directly to Sid Bartline at the far end of his bar.

'You seen Kelly Boyle today?' Lambourne asked.

'Haven't laid eyes on him,' said the saloon-man. 'Something the matter?'

'Plenty.' Then Lambourne spotted the major midway down the bar, turned on his heel, and hurried out to the street.

Bartline came over to the major. 'Wonder why he's in such a sweat to find Kelly Boyle?'

'Boyle doesn't interest me one damn' bit,' the major said coldly. But he was interested, very. He wondered what Uland and Quester and the other two had managed this day.

He was thinking of going up to Belle's, now that Annabelle had left town and his own marriage was at an end, when he saw through the window Samantha Shelly emerge from the Miller Store across the street. She looked first one way, then the other, and hurried out of sight, her braids whipping in the wind. The roar of the river came faintly through the saloon walls.

Standing there, he clenched and un-clenched his sore right hand, mindful of what Kelly Boyle had done to him. He'd kill time while awaiting Uland's report. Just as he stepped out, turning for Belle's place, he heard a shout. Uland came pounding up on a sweated horse. Behind him were Quester and Roone. Only Conover was missing, not Uland or Quester, which caused a stab of disappointment in the major that the pair had not shot it out.

Uland began to explain excitedly that they had thought Kelly Boyle was holed up at the De Gama place. 'When we yelled for him to come out, they opened up on us. We had to do the lot of 'em in to save ourselves.'

'The woman, too?'

Uland nodded. 'An' her brother an' the kid.'

'I see. Where's Conover? Didn't he go with you?'

'They killed him right off. That's when we had to move in on 'em.'

'Where's Conover's body?'

'Left it there.'

'That was smart thinking,' the major said sarcastically.

'We just figured to get the hell away before anybody come along.'

The major smoothed his mustache that lately he had neglected to trim. 'We'll say that some Box R cattle strayed onto the De Gama range, that, when you went after them, the De Gamas opened up on you. Even the kid. He's old enough to hold a pistol.'

'Boyle was close to them,' Uland said.

'When he hears about it, he'll come lookin' for us.'

'Yes, thanks to the calling card you left,' the major said dryly. 'Conover's body. You sure you didn't leave any live ones out there?'

'Dead. Shot all to hell.'

Quester spoke for the first time, his heavy face turning red. 'You shoulda listened to me, Major. An' took fifteen men an' got rid of Boyle once an' for all. Instead of that, we kill a woman an' a little kid for no damn' good reason that I can see ... unless Uland *wanted* 'em dead.'

Uland clamped a hand to his gun. 'Careful, Al,' he warned.

But before Quester could respond to the threat, there were sudden sounds of a fast-moving team and wagon. Roone, shading his eyes against the westering sun, yelled: 'It's Kelly Boyle!'

Boyle and the wagon swept down a narrow back street, scattering dogs and chickens. From a doorway someone cursed him loudly. Another sharp corner with the wagon skidding, then Kelly Boyle pulled the spent team up before a small house. Doc Starrett's sign swayed in the spring wind.

He was shouting for the doctor as he got the team tied off to a stump. Instead of the portly doctor, a thin woman holding a feather duster came to the door. She looked surprised at all the excitement.

342

'These people are bad hurt!' Boyle cried, and ran to the rear of the wagon, to come up short when he saw Felicita so still in the blankets. Her eyes, wide open, were filmed with dust. A moment of sadness was instantly replaced by a renewal of his rage. People were coming at a run to see why he had entered town so recklessly.

'Doc ain't here!' cried the woman in the doorway. 'Gone to the other side.' She jabbed the feather duster in the direction of the river a block away. 'Likely be gone for hours.'

Kelly Boyle, panting, made another quick decision. From where he stood, he could see the ferry tied up on the Bluewater side of the river. Snatching up the boy and also his rifle, he started trotting toward the landing.

He had gone no more than half a block, when he heard Samantha call to him. 'Kelly, Kelly, wait! Pete Lambourne and I have been...'

'Haven't time,' he gasped, not looking around but continuing, now at a run.

But she came in at an angle on her long legs. 'Kelly, listen to me. The Texas Rangers...!' She was waving a telegram at him. Then she suddenly realized what he carried. 'What happened to the boy?' she asked in a more hushed tone.

'Kid's bad hurt. Doc's across the river.'

Boyle could feel Guillermo's blood soaking into the front of his shirt. At each running step the boy's head bobbed. He knew the boy should be handled more gently. But how could he gently prolong a life ebbing so swiftly away?

As he neared the river, it seemed even higher. Wavelets slapped the prow of the beached ferry. Tall poplars swayed in the late afternoon wind that ruffled feathers of mockingbirds chirping in cottonwoods.

Tornillo thorns slashed at his boots as he plunged down a twisting path. He shouted at the ferryman who was staring. 'Know where Doc's gone?'

Hank Wendover nodded. 'The Morales woman. In labor and in bad trouble. Triplets, mebby, is the way I hear. What's that you got there, Kelly?'

'Guillermo De Gama ... Chico.' Gently he placed the boy down on the planks of the scow now awash in the flood. Even here, where the river was relatively quiet, he could feel the tug and push of the powerful current. He placed his rifle beside Wendover's carbine on a shelf under a tarp.

Just then Samantha Shelly bounded onto the ferry and knelt beside the boy.

'Don't come with me!' Boyle yelled above the river's roar. 'Too dangerous crossing over!' He tried to take her arm, but she jerked away, her concern for the boy.

'He's so pale,' she said, shuddering.

'Lost a lot of blood.'

To Boyle's right, upriver, water pouring over the dam shot spray into the wind, filling the air with moisture. Driftwood boiled over the dam, the dripping lengths shining in the sunlight. A log whipped past, rolling end over end to crash into a chicken coop washed away from some place upriver. Wendover lashed up the landing platform.

'¡*Vamanos!* Let's go!' Boyle had to shout to make himself heard above the howl of a river swollen with runoff from distant mountains, made even more treacherous by a series of cloudbursts farther north.

'We're a-goin'!' Wendover cried, and heaved powerful shoulders against the winch. They began to move, agonizingly slow, it seemed to Kelly Boyle, out into the flood tide, along the taut rope stretched bank to bank, each turn of the handle bringing a screech from the winch. Now current caught the ferry and sucked against planking, tossing the prow. Water boiled across the deck. Driftwood hammered the scow on all sides.

'Chico, hang on,' Boyle pleaded to the unconscious boy.

Samantha stroked Chico's brow. 'Doc will know what to do for him.'

'Let's hope.'

She smiled encouragement and said: 'No matter what some claim, he's a good doctor.' Kneeling in the muddy wash of the planking, she knuckled her eyes, then adjusted the

345

bandage Boyle had applied to the boy's chest. 'Who would do such a thing? What about Felicita and Jaime?'

He had to yell it, the screeching of the winch having put his teeth on edge. '*Cristo*, what people!'

Samantha stared in disbelief. 'Not the major. Bad as he is, he couldn't do such a thing!'

'What a child you are, Samantha,' he said roughly, and watched the far shore edge ever nearer in the flood tide.

'Uland, maybe, or Al Quester, but not the major.'

'Drop a stone in a puddle and it makes ripples. Major Ransom, god damn him, dropped the stone.'

'We're about to make it!' Wendover yelled. Water poured over the prow. He had to duck a sheet of spray.

A moment later they were grounded on the far bank. Wendover unhooked the slats at the prow and allowed them to crash into the mud. The scow shuddered.

'Hank, you know the Morales house?' Boyle cried, scooping up the unconscious boy.

Wendover gestured wildly to the right of a ruined plaza and at a house larger than most.

Samantha started after Boyle, but he turned with his burden, blocking her. 'Go back to the other side,' he ordered.

'But I want to be with you...!'

'They'll be after me. I don't want you here!'

'But maybe I can help.'

'*Do what I say!*'

Wendover was straining at the winch where the rope had become twisted. 'Have it fixed in a minute,' Boyle heard him say to Samantha. But he was running now, Guillermo a dead weight in his arms.

Oh God, he prayed, let me salvage one life at least out of this terror. Dogs barked, and there were staring eyes from behind shuttered windows as he came tearing along a street where there were crater holes from artillery fire. At last he reached the house Wendover had indicated. A door was open to a court-yard where there was a tall mesquite and a path of tiles. From inside the house came multiple squalls from infant throats.

Doc Starrett, looking weary but wearing a faintly triumphant smile, was just rolling down his shirt sleeves when Boyle came bounding into the house. The doctor looked startled, when Boyle laid his burden on a sofa.

'Doc!' Gasping for breath, Kelly Boyle explained. Then – 'Help him!' – gesturing at the boy. 'His mother and his uncle ... dead. Don't let certain sons-of-bitches rake in *all* the chips.'

Starrett didn't know what he was talking about, could only make out some of it, but his professional eye noted the death shadow on the boy's face. It caused him to dash to another room and reappear a moment later with a medical bag. It was at that moment that Kelly Boyle remembered leaving his rifle on the ferry.

Major Terrence Ransom had seen Kelly Boyle from a distance, running toward the ferry with a burden. 'What's he carrying?'

'The De Gama kid,' said Al Quester, giving Uland an angry glance.

Roone licked his lips.

'Why is he carrying the boy?' the major demanded.

'We told you about them gettin' shot...,' Rex Uland began.

'You told me *nothing!*' the major snapped, giving him a look. They sat their horses in a screen of willows on the Bluewater side of the river, watching Boyle carry the wounded boy aboard the ferry and begin the treacherous crossing.

'Better for us all around,' the major said with a fierce smile.

'How you mean?' Uland asked dubiously.

'We can hang him high. Nobody on that side of the river will even lift an eyebrow.'

'With this De Gama business,' Al Quester said darkly, 'we sure as hell better never give

348

him a chance to make a gallows speech over there.'

'I say shoot him to rags,' said Uland.

'Main thing now is to shut his mouth,' said the major, sounding excited. 'It's been put right into our hands. Let's go get him.' The major started down the slant, but Uland gave the churning river a nervous glance.

'We better wait till the ferry comes back,' he suggested.

The major gave an exuberant laugh. 'We'll swim our horses!'

Al Quester shared Uland's skepticism. 'River's too damned high.'

'Hell, can't you boys accept a challenge? What else in God's world so fires the blood? Not even a woman!'

The three of them gave him a curious look, then exchanged glances. Already the major was urging his reluctant chestnut saddler into the swirling, brown flood. Holding his rifle high in his right hand, he jerked his head at the three men to follow him. Only Roone did, right then, getting in behind the major who was expertly steering his swimming horse so as to avoid driftwood and debris being swept along by the muddy tide.

Rex Uland stared, hoping the major would be swept under. When the major was nearing the far side, Uland turned to Quester. 'Go see if we got any men in town. Chick an' a couple of others was comin' in today.'

'You givin' orders now?' Quester demanded, leaning over in the saddle, his broad face tight.

'Seems I'm related by marriage to the old bastard. You ain't. Let's save somethin' for ourselves, Al. What you say?'

Fighting down his rage, Al Quester saw the wisdom of making sure something was left to salvage. Kelly Boyle alive was still a threat to them because of the botched De Gama business.

'See you in *Méjico*,' Uland sang out, and forced his horse into the water.

Quester galloped to the saloon, rode his horse onto the walk, and shouted above the slatted doors. 'Boxer! *Trouble!*'

In the scurrying and shouting of surprised patrons, four Box R men appeared, only one too drunk for combat. The three more sober ones ran for their horses.

Chapter Twenty

Hank Wendover finally got the rope untangled so the winch would turn freely once again. 'Here we go, Miss Shelly!' shouted the ferryman. 'Hang on!'

By the time Kelly Boyle came at a run from the Morales house, the scow was already several yards out into the flood.

'Wait, Hank!' Kelly Boyle cried. But the squealing winch was apparently all that Wendover could hear above the pounding throb of the current. Sluggishly the ferry moved toward the center of the turbulent river.

From the bank Boyle ruefully watched the scow bouncing about but moving unerringly toward the U. S. side. Whatever trouble developed now, he would be without a rifle.

At this end of the village were mostly ruins of *casitas* and buildings ravaged during Esparza's bid for power. Most of the surrounding wall of a weed-grown plaza was knocked down. The bandstand lay in ruins. Hearing a sudden rattle of hoofbeats, Boyle turned to his right. He saw horses pounding in his direction from downriver, muzzles foaming, hides slick from the swim to the

Mexican side. Hoofs smashed through cattails, throwing great gouts of mud.

Boyle's throat dried as the riders came at a hard run, only a hundred yards away in lengthening shadows. Each appeared to be soaked by river water to mid-chest. Three Box R men in the vanguard brandished rifles. Two he vaguely remembered. Behind them by a dozen yards or so came a bareheaded Uland, coarse, reddish hair flying in the wind. Slightly to his rear were the major and Al Quester. And behind them was Jake Roone.

As they neared, the major shouted something, which caused the cavalcade to abruptly rein in, horses rearing. Al Quester stood in the stirrups, fired a rifle in the direction of the river. Turning, Boyle saw Hank Wendover abruptly fling arms upward as if beseeching heaven. He lurched, then toppled away from the winch and into the muddy boil of the river. For a few seconds his head bobbed and dipped in the swells like a leather ball, then disappeared.

As Boyle watched in horror, the scow being tossed about, he saw Samantha work her way to the winch and try to turn the crank, but she lacked the strength, or the lines had become fouled.

'Hang on, Samantha!' Boyle cried, knowing his voice was lost in the roar of wind and water. The ferry, pitching wildly in the treacherous current, sawed against its rope now fouled with brush and driftwood. On the far bank some men watched helplessly as the girl, a mite in all that rush of water, tried to get the ferry going again.

When Boyle turned, he no longer saw his enemies, and sprinted for a low wall, part of a courtyard that looked as if it had been blasted by cannon. Taking shelter by a solid piece of wall, he tried to spot the Box R men. Someone scrambled over the wall at his back. Boyle whipped around and saw an older Mexican gripping a big Remington revolver.

'That boy, Guillermo,' the man said grimly as he knelt beside Boyle. 'My cousin ... very distant ... but still of my blood. I am Maldonado, and I have come to help you.' He crouched down, teeth bared under a half moon of graying mustaches. They shook hands.

'Welcome to hell's back door,' said Kelly Boyle.

During a lull in the wind, he heard the cavalcade again at full gallop along a side street. Coming to his knees, he aimed for the lead rider he thought was Uland, but at the last moment the hard-running horses swerved into an alley. His shot missed Uland but caught one of the lead mounts squarely in its dappled gray breastbone. Its forelegs collapsed, the hindquarters flipping up before the rider could kick free. He was smashed to the ground. One of his hands fluttered briefly from under the oddly twisted head of the gray horse, then it fell, limp as a shot bird. The others coming at full tilt avoided a pile up by swinging wide of the downed horse and then swept behind a windowless warehouse across an alley from where Boyle and Maldonado had taken shelter.

As the thunder of Box R horses ceased, Major Ransom's shrill voice challenged from the empty building. 'Boyle, are you listening...?'

'I'm listening, you murdering...'

'You and that girl have exactly ten seconds. Or she joins Hank Wendover in the river. Al, draw a bead on her. All right, Kelly Boyle, put down your gun. Climb over that wall with your hands in the air. Al, you got her in your sights?'

'Dead center,' sang out Al Quester loud and clear.

Boyle felt his despair. By carefully lifting his head, he could see Samantha bravely clinging to the winch as wave after wave crashed into her, a girl so vulnerable to a marksman like Al Quester. 'All right!' Boyle shouted. He put down his gun and stood up, hands lifted. 'Leave her alone!'

'Good sense, Kelly,' came the major's triumphant shout.

To Maldonado, Boyle said: 'Keep down and don't try to fire. Soon as I'm gone, run for your life.' But even as he spoke, seeing Major Ransom with a broad grin at the corner of the building, there sounded above the rumble of the river a woman's dim but unmistakable scream of terror. A horrified Boyle risked a glance just as a great tangle of tumbleweeds, weighted by splintered drift-wood, bounded across the ferry to catch Samantha in the chest. The force of it broke her hold. She slid almost gracefully into the river and from sight.

Boyle was stunned, but grief was twisted into rage. 'Major you just lost your ace!'

Already he had flung himself flat behind the low wall. He blinked at a sting of tears. The agony of watching Samantha engulfed by the torrent turned him into a madman. Snatching up his pistol, he rose and fired at the spot where he had last seen that tri-umphant grin, but the major's face was gone, and the bullets merely chewed bits of adobe from the building corner. A foolish waste of ammunition, he warned himself. More such recklessness with ammunition in short supply would leave Samantha and the De Gamas unavenged and himself shot to pieces before he could get a one of them.

Trembling, he fumbled cartridges from his belt. Maldonado's voice suddenly rang in his ear. The Mexican, crouched, had seized him by an arm and was pointing downriver. A limp, bedraggled bundle of clothing and red braids clung to a log being carried by the flood current toward the shore on the American side.

'The *santos* have smiled on her!' cried Maldonado. 'Truly a miracle, *señor!*'

Boyle felt a sudden lift of spirits, but what happened next was no miracle of life. One of the Box R men, lank and bearded, had clambered to the roof of the building across the alley. He and Maldonado fired simultaneously, but the Mexican, with a soft sigh, dropped his old Remington revolver that had toppled the Box R man, arms waving, yelling his terror headfirst into the alley twenty feet away.

A rifle bullet screamed past Boyle's ear. He ducked down before a second one could shatter his skull. Reaching out, he extracted the Remington from under Maldonado's body, holding it in his left hand, his own .44 in his right. He glanced at this man he had barely met, who had given his life, crumpled now in a dusty smear of blood. '*Compadre*, I will avenge you,' he promised in Spanish to the dry wind.

Lifting his head slightly above the broken top of the low wall, he risked a glance at the river. No longer was there any sign of Samantha in the churning flood. Hoping she had made it to the other side, he sucked in a deep breath, vaulted the low wall, and started running along the alley. He skirted the body of the Box R man who stared at the twilit sky, a bone, like a bloodied stick, jutting from his neck.

Someone shouted from inside the warehouse. 'There goes Boyle!'

A gun opened up. Boyle fired at a gunflash, heard a yelp of pain. Another rifle spat from a corner of the building, spraying him with adobe chips as it slapped into another low wall to his right. Another gun started up. Caught in the open, Boyle flung himself over the wall. With his legs in the air, his left was suddenly numbed as a rifle crashed. He felt the impact clear to his hip and fell headlong. At his back was what remained of a *casita*, one of the smaller houses in the village of Los Milagros.

When he tried to stand, the numbed left leg refused to support his weight. He fell among ashes and bits of broken pottery. More gunfire erupted from the warehouse.

'Damn you, Rex...!' It was Major Ransom's stricken voice.

This was followed by a roar, too heavy for a rifle. Someone screamed.

'Roone, you hit?' It sounded like Al Quester.

'God damn Pete Lambourne an' his scatter-gun ... can't see ... blood in my eyes.'

Silence clamped down.

Boyle didn't try to figure out how Lambourne happened to be on this side of the river. That he was here was a miracle. At that moment what Kelly Boyle wouldn't have given for the man's sawed-off shotgun. He yelled: 'Pete, you all right?' But there was no reply from the deepening shadows.

A sound to his right at a break in the wall caused Boyle to spin around. Through this someone crawled. He felt his boot warmed by his own blood. Holding both pistols, he pointed them at the crawling figure of Major Terrence Ransom. The major was bareheaded, face drawn, the mouth under the mustache thin as a saber cut.

Surprise in Boyle gave way to fury. As he stared, unable to speak, he concentrated on trying to interpret each sound coming from the warehouse. Someone moaned; he could make out muted voices but no words. A horse neighed some distance away. Dogs barked, and there was the constant roar of the river.

Major Ransom halted a few feet away, on hands and knees. 'I wondered if they had the guts to try for me,' the major said, breathing hard. 'Seems one of them did.'

'Sleep with rattlesnakes ... what do you expect?' Boyle said contemptuously in Spanish.

'Kelly, why didn't you leave my dear son-in-law dead last year in Mexico?'

'Nothing much works out as planned.'

'You were my whole life, Kelly.'

'The hell.' Boyle laughed bitterly.

Ransom fell to a sitting position, back to the wall, careful that his head was well below the top. 'To inject danger and adventure into my later years,' the major continued, straining for each word, 'at a time when most men turn to soft chairs and early sleep, you were to be the catalyst, but you turned out to be about as tough as a paper rope. Letting Carl Tripp...' He faltered.

Boyle looked toward the shadows, saying: 'Seems like I've got my ace now. As you had yours. A helpless girl on a raft.'

'I wouldn't have let Al kill her.'

'Maybe. But I've got *you*.'

'They couldn't give a damn, Kelly.' The major seemed unutterably weary. 'There's no bargaining power in my hide.'

'We'll see.'

'It's you and me together. We'll battle them to the end. The way it was destined.'

Boyle started to laugh against the twilit wind, but pain was gradually replacing the numbness in his leg.

The major said: 'I don't like the look I see in your eyes. Don't hate me.'

'You son-of-a-bitch!'

The major's face, seen in the shadows, drained of even more color. 'Why the hatred, Kelly?'

'The De Gamas, for one thing. The boy's mother, his uncle. Maybe the boy himself.'

'I had nothing to do with that.'

'Your dropped stone made the ripples, damn you.' Suddenly from the building came a muffled sound of voices, a shout, footsteps of someone running on the far side. A bullet seared the air near Boyle's face to splat into an empty goat pen.

'Kelly, you and me facing them...' Major Ransom coughed and bled slightly at the lips. He started to crawl again. Boyle at a higher elevation noticed blood on the back of the major's coat.

Rex Uland's voice came sharply from the building across the alley. 'Al, I spotted the major. Behind that low wall yonderly.'

'Why didn't you shoot him good while you had the chance?' Quester demanded.

'Him an' Boyle both behind the wall. Our luck. We got the two of 'em like a coupla hogs in a box!'

'We better move quick or it'll be dark. An' I don't trust the damn' Mexicans.'

'They won't horn in. They've had enough of Anglos.' Uland raised his voice. 'Al, you an' Chick get in behind that wall. I'll cover you.'

'You an' your god-damn' orders!' Al Quester yelled.

'When the major's dead, I'm top dog! Better damn' well remember it, Al.'

Quester mumbled something Boyle failed to make out because at that moment wind gusted to send a *shushing* of sand along the wall. Then Quester was shouting: 'Come on, Chick! An' watch out for that god-damn' Pete Lambourne.'

In the twilight came the sounds of two men running behind the building. Boyle lifted his head to eye level along the wall and saw Rex Uland with a rifle far to the right at a corner of the building. Uland saw him, flung up the rifle, and snapped off a shot. But Boyle was ducking as a few inches of wall erupted from Uland's screaming bullet.

Crouched behind the wall, Boyle studied his bloodied pants leg. A bullet had cut through the calf of the leg. As far as he could tell, it had missed bone. *'Gracias a la Madre de Dios,'* he muttered, the pain more intense now.

As the sounds of men running continued, he glanced at the major who lay on his side, lips slightly parted. No help from that quarter, obviously, even if he wanted it. Powder smoke stung eyes and nostrils. His leg throbbed.

Boyle turned toward the slowing sounds made by Quester and the Box R man, Chick, who were coming around the far end of the building. It was getting dark. Before he could get both legs under him and straighten up, something cold touched him on the back of the neck. Boyle, cursing, looked carefully around. He had carelessly exposed his back, and now Major Ransom pressed harder with the pistol evidently drawn from under the bloodied coat. In the fading light Boyle saw the fierce eyes, the smile on pale lips below the mustache.

The major's snarl, however, was weak. 'Now who's the son-of-a-bitch?'

'You haven't got enough strength in your finger to pull that trigger, old man,' Boyle taunted.

'*Old* man? I'll blow off your head.'

Boyle tensed. Cold sweat ran down his neck to the steel eye of the pistol held to his flesh.

Hurrying footsteps sounded far to the left. Then Al Quester shouted from a distance. 'Chick, come in the other side of that burned-out house. I'll come in from this side.'

Suddenly Boyle shoved the major aside. A sob broke from the man as his gun fell into the shadows. 'God, to end it like this, Kelly. On my knees. On my *knees!*' The major stared up into the purpling sky, a pitiful hulk of a man, despised by a daughter who was married to the man who had shot him in the back.

Boyle tensed, wondering if he could trust his full weight on the left leg. Then he glimpsed Al Quester suddenly loom up beyond the empty goat pen. Quester spotted him at the same instant, and a red eye of muzzle flash winked in the lengthening shadows, but the bullet missed. Boyle was moving aside, the left leg holding, thank God. And he fired the old Remington as Al Quester charged. A hole appeared in Quester's throat, the heavy slug blowing apart the Adam's apple to exit out the back of the neck.

Chick, a lean shadow, lifted a rifle at a corner of the ruined house. Boyle's snap shot caused the lean shadow to collapse among charred roofing timbers.

Whirling, Boyle skirted the major, now lying on his side. At a limping run he reached the break in the wall. His intention was to finish Uland before his luck ran out. It ran out swiftly. At each step his left leg weakened, the boot squishing. He reached a corner of the building he had riddled with bullets only minutes before – it seemed like an hour. Uland appeared with leveled rifle. Boyle knew if he started to bring up the pair of increasingly heavy pistols the rifle would blow him in two. He came up on his toes, waiting.

'My lucky night.' Uland's teeth were white in the shadows. 'First the major and now you. Right into my bear trap you run.'

'If you had the guts, you'd drop the rifle and go for your pistol. I'll holster one of mine and drop the other.'

'You'd like that. You remember any greaser prayers? I want to hear it. Make it a short one. That's all you got time for.'

Roone appeared suddenly from midway down the building, bleeding from the head, reeling, no weapon in sight.

Boyle took a chance. 'Pete, get in behind Uland!'

It caused Uland to jerk his head around. Instead of Pete Lambourne, he saw his own man. Boyle fired the Remington, but Uland was moving swiftly. Uland spun, firing the rifle, a dry click instead of a roar. The rifle was empty. He hurled it. Boyle had to throw himself flat in order to keep the butt plate from crashing into his face. Uland drew a pistol, fired it into the ground near Boyle's head. The ground shook.

As Boyle leaped up, Pete Lambourne ran from a screen of pepper trees. The old man appearing so suddenly, he failed to see Uland crouched in a pool of shadow by the building wall. The big redhead spun with cat quickness, got behind the older man, and caught him at the belt with one hand. Impact jarred the double-barreled shotgun from Lambourne's grasp. It fell harmlessly to the ground.

'Throw down your guns, Boyle,' came Uland's order. 'Both of 'em. Or I blow this old man's backbone right into your face.'

In Boyle's mind there was no doubt but

that he and a startled Pete Lambourne were as good as dead. But the old man's whine and trembling body were meant to deceive. Something flashed in Lambourne's eyes, in the shadowed face. A signal meant for Boyle. Lambourne suddenly flung himself face down before Uland could free the hand locked at the belt. It pulled Uland off balance.

Boyle aimed the Remington, wanting to even things up for the dead Maldonado, but the weapon malfunctioned. Before Boyle could thumb his .44, a gunshot exploded from behind him. Uland got a sudden, foolish look on his face, swayed, then toppled onto Pete Lambourne who had flattened himself on the ground.

Boyle wheeled, his bad leg nearly giving way seeking the source of the shot that had brought Uland down.

Major Ransom on both feet, swaying, had somehow staggered to the alley, a pistol gripped in both hands. 'I was aiming for you, Kelly. And instead I hit my own son-in-law.' A burst of wild laughter seemed to take the last of his strength, but he managed to say: 'That's the damnedest lie a man ever told.' He started to shift the gun and aim it at Boyle with Boyle a breath away from dropping his gun hammer.

A sudden weary smile twisted the bloodied lips as the major slowly collapsed.

This time he did not get up, and with him went Bluewater's dream of railroads and greatness, to remain always just a cow town.

Into the 20th Century the great Box R spread, that became Diamond Deuce, was known by old-timers as *el rancho de las viudas* – ranch of the widows – Mrs. Rex Uland living out her days in Italy, Florence Ransom remarried and residing in San Francisco. Neither woman ever returned to Texas, leaving the running of the vast ranch to their partner Kelly Boyle, his wife Samantha, and their eldest son, Guillermo De Gama Boyle.

The publishers hope that this book has given you enjoyable reading. Large Print Books are especially designed to be as easy to see and hold as possible. If you wish a complete list of our books please ask at your local library or write directly to:

The Golden West Large Print Books
Magna House, Long Preston,
Skipton, North Yorkshire.
BD23 4ND

This Large Print Book, for people
who cannot read normal print,
is published under the auspices of

THE ULVERSCROFT FOUNDATION

... we hope you have enjoyed this book.
Please think for a moment about those
who have worse eyesight than you ...
and are unable to even read or enjoy
Large Print without great difficulty.

You can help them by sending a
donation, large or small, to:

**The Ulverscroft Foundation,
1, The Green, Bradgate Road,
Anstey, Leicestershire, LE7 7FU,
England.**
or request a copy of our brochure for
more details.

The Foundation will use all donations
to assist those people who are visually
impaired and need special attention
with medical research, diagnosis
and treatment.

Thank you very much for your help.